Returning with his guitar, he sat next to Katy on the couch.

"I usually can't write with others around, but you've inspired me." He tuned a few chords while strumming. "I'm calling this 'Katy's Song.' "

"Oh…goodness." Her eyes misted, and she touched his sleeve. "I'm speechless."

"Don't get too excited. It's still rough." He side-smiled and looked down at the strings. "But I like where it's going."

As he tapped his foot to the beat, she watched his dancing fingers. The musky scent of his guitar was as intoxicating as barrel-aged bourbon. She couldn't believe her close proximity to the musician and his creation. Mesmerized, Katy remained perfectly still, willing him to play forever.

Katy's Song

by

A Reese

Alison Reese

Katy's Song

Cover Art by *Kristian Norris*

The Wild Rose Press, Inc.
PO Box 708
Adams Basin, NY 14410-0708
Visit us at www.thewildrosepress.com

Publishing History
First Champagne Rose Edition, 2019
Print ISBN 978-1-5092-2756-3
Digital ISBN 978-1-5092-2757-0

Published in the United States of America

Dedication

To my dear husband, John.
In my eyes, you are a true rock star.

Chapter 1

Thousands of screaming fans bolted from their seats as Noe Burke strolled onstage holding his guitar. Lights blinded and blazed, and the odor of beer and weed mingled with dust. It could be Anytown, USA from his viewpoint, but the audience paid good money to see him, and Noe wanted them to feel appreciated.

"Hello, Miami," he roared into the microphone, pointing to devotees in the front row and beyond. Thunder from the crowd climbed to deafening levels and the chanting began. "Noe. Noe. Noe." To his ears, the words sounded like "snowy, snowy, snowy," disconnecting him from the name he'd chosen so many years ago.

"It's an honor to be in a city founded by a woman." He paused, searching his memory for her name, so he could pay tribute to her spirit. "This one's for Julia Tuttle."

Despite the display of adulation, or perhaps because of it, Noe felt trapped inside a continuous loop. Gone were the days of adrenaline rushes, crazy energy, and the urgency for his songs to be heard. Every milestone he'd imagined as a teenager had been met and surpassed—an embarrassment of riches that left him feeling strangely dissatisfied.

After adjusting his in-ear monitors, Noe strummed his first chord. Soon, he and his band created a protective circle for themselves inside the music through the kind of telepathy that emerged when good friends worked well together. They played for two hours and offered three encores. By the end, Noe was drenched in sweat.

Backstage, he leaned against a jamb and guzzled electrolytes. Wiping his mouth on his sleeve, he asked his drummer, "Want to hear somethin' else about Miami?"

"No, man," Beau said, inspecting his sticks. "Not my turn to care."

"Aw, come on," Noe said, grinning. "It's really cool."

"None of your trivia's *cool*," Beau said. "Hasn't anyone ever told you that?"

"Let him talk," keyboardist Abby chimed as she plopped in the chair next to Beau.

"Thank you," Noe said, exaggerating his words and beading his eyes at Beau. "Spoken by my dearest friend."

"Otherwise," Abby said, "he'll bombard us with texts about this shit all night."

Ignited by their mockery, Noe rambled off facts. "Miami has a bunch of Art Deco architecture, and some ATMs are specifically designed for skateboarders."

"Make it stop," Beau said to Abby.

"There's this guy nicknamed Raven who's been running on the beach every day since 1975." Noe pinched a layer of fat recently formed around his middle. "We should add a treadmill to the tour bus."

"What'd ya mean *we*?" Beau said. "Got a mouse in your pocket?"

Abby fake-yawned and glanced at her watch,

avoiding the topic altogether.

Noe stretched, joints audibly popping.

"Ouch," Abby said.

"Yeah." Noe massaged his achy leg. "It's been giving me trouble lately."

"Rethink your knee-slide at the end," Beau said. "Maybe."

"But it's so damned fun." Noe tossed the empty Gatorade bottle into recycle. "See you two tomorrow."

Climbing the steps to the tour bus, he anticipated a cool shower. His girlfriend Phoebe greeted him with a kiss at the door.

"I'm so glad you're back. I've been waiting for hours."

Would it kill her to attend one of his concerts?

Already dressed in party garb, she followed him down the hall to the bathroom. "I heard about this fabulous club in South Beach. A couple of artists I know moved here six months ago, and they're meeting us there after midnight."

Flinging his clothes into the corner, he stepped into the shower. He stood with one leg forward, hands against the wall, and head under the spray. Watching water drip from his nose, he felt triumphant when ten drops in a row landed in the center hole of the drain—a new record. "Can we make it another time? I'm exhausted."

"You're always tired," she protested from outside. "Isn't there a pill for that?"

Phoebe was too social for him. He knew now. But he still held hope they'd find balance as a couple. Did he love her? Not yet. Could he love her? He wasn't sure he was capable of loving anyone again, but that wouldn't stop him from trying.

Cutting his shower short, he towel-dried and headed for the bedroom.

"My friends are gonna freak when they meet you," she said, slipping into high-heeled sandals. "They can't believe I'm dating *The* Noe Burke."

Feeling like a performing seal, he donned navy-blue boxer-briefs and a T-shirt. "I'm not going anywhere."

Phoebe seemed not to have heard him.

"My sister's so jealous," she said, head lolling to the side like a puppet without strings.

He remembered Phoebe's sister, Connie. While his band toured in and around New York, he stayed with friends in Brooklyn. One evening, he sat next to Connie at a dinner party. Eyes too shiny, she licked her lips as if he were dessert. And her smile seemed diabolical as she leaned into his personal space, brushing her breast against his arm in the guise of reaching for the chardonnay.

In comparison, Phoebe had enchanted him after dinner with anecdotes about bartending for charity events at MoMA. Her eyes were the color of summer, and her chestnut hair swayed as she spoke. When she entered her number into his phone, he felt the stirrings of anticipation. She seemed mature then, and down to earth. Someone he could see himself with long term.

Had she been acting? Or had he been delusional? Maybe he was being greedy to expect true love to strike twice. At times like these, he pushed aside thoughts about his late-wife, Charlotte. If she hadn't died two years ago, he wouldn't be searching for someone new. But if he dwelled too long on his sorrow, he'd be reaching for the whiskey again.

"Isn't your sister married?" he asked, recalling the enormous rock on Connie's left hand.

"Her husband gave her a free pass," Phoebe said. "You're a legend."

The idiom made him feel ancient and empty—his life in the rearview mirror with nothing left to accomplish.

"Too bad I wasn't included in the negotiations," he said, wondering which *legend* Connie's husband was entitled to harass.

"Hurry up and dress," Phoebe said, pouting. "I'm hungry."

"Eat the leftovers in the fridge."

"Chicken nuggets and pizza? No thanks."

"We could order Chinese?"

"Ugh," she groaned. "You want to stay in again, don't you?"

"I really need to, yes," he said. "Care to join me?"

"And do what? Cuddle?" She spat the word as if he'd suggested dumpster diving. "And what's the plan for tomorrow? Senior day at the early-bird café?"

He'd wanted Phoebe to stick around until Seattle, hoping to show her his hometown. Get to know each other in a normal setting. But that scenario became less probable by the minute.

"Tell ya what." He ignored her insult and flipped open his wallet. "Here's a card worth five-hundred bucks. Knock yourself out."

"Are you buying me off?" she said. "'Cause I'm not a hooker."

"Ah, jeez, Phoebe. You know I didn't mean it that way." Placing the card on the dresser, he stepped toward her for a hug, but she dodged him in annoyance.

"God, Noe," she said. "You're nothing like I expected."

He'd heard this before. Women attracted to him wanted non-stop action, no matter how forthright he was. The nights of his concerts, he needed major down time. And he wasn't into the bar scene. In fact, he'd rather catch a movie than a buzz. But these women didn't believe him—because of his profession. They wanted to hobnob with movie stars and dance all night at exclusive clubs. If he partied like a rock star, he'd be dead by forty. And that birthday was an oncoming train.

"I ran a marathon tonight," he said, feeling every one of his thirty-nine years. "What do you want from me?"

"Not a damn thing, old man," she said. "My sister can have you."

"Nope, sorry." He dropped onto the bed and opened a pristine collection of Calvin and Hobbes cartoons he'd found at a secondhand store. "That ticket's non-transferable."

Phoebe huffed and pinched the pre-paid card off the dresser. Her theatrical attempt to slam the door had little impact on the bus. He wished he could say the same about his ego.

Noe texted security to remove Phoebe's name from the list and to come get her things. By night's end, he'd book her an expensive hotel for a week in Miami, and he'd purchase airfare vouchers for wherever she wished to go next. Lastly, he'd email the information to her along with a goodbye note. Unfortunately, this process was becoming all too familiar.

Chapter 2

On a warm spring evening in Fort Worth, Katy
Moore stood at the butcher block in her kitchen,
chopping vegetables from her garden and tossing them
into a quinoa salad. Cornbread baked in the oven as
four-bean stew simmered on the stove, perfuming the
room with fresh garlic, roasted tomato, and onion. Of
all the vegan dishes she created, her boyfriend Greg
declared these to be his favorites. Although her lentil
puree was at the top of his list as well.

The kitchen was the only renovated room in Katy's
tiny 1960s farmhouse. Slate countertops in mottled
purple glistened with lemon oil. Stainless-steel
appliances, porcelain double sink, and ceramic tiles
shone with newness. Pots and pans hung from a rack,
utensils were bouqueted in a crock, and cookbooks
were shelved alphabetically. The rest of the home,
though tidy, languished in disrepair. Broken fixtures,
missing roof slats, and peeling daisy wallpaper were
noted but ignored.

Six months ago, Katy's luck had finally changed
for the better. She'd been given a VIP pass to bluesy-
rocker Noe Burke's charity event held at Botanic
Garden as a special thank-you for a last-minute
accounting job. And to Katy's surprise, the ticket
included a post-concert "meet-and-greet" with the
famous musician. But competition for his attention was

fierce, and when he finally turned in her direction and was close enough to touch, someone with an official-looking lanyard whisked him away. If anyone asked what she remembered most about Noe Burke, she'd say his shirt was damp with perspiration and he smelled strongly of coffee—never mentioning how weary he looked or his expression seemed tinged with sadness.

But as odd as that encounter had been, all was not lost, because later in the beer garden she'd met Greg. Smiling now, she thought about the series of yeses that led to breakfast in bed the following morning.

Tonight, Noe Burke's music played, and his rumbling, whiskey voice crooned a sensual tune. Hips swaying, Katy closed her eyes, imagining an ideal weekend with the man she adored. Saturday afternoon picnic at the creek behind the farmhouse. Midnight stroll in the woods. Sleeping late on Sunday, tangled in sheets.

In the dining room, Katy smoothed wrinkles from the linen tablecloth with her palms. Selecting blue Wedgwood dishes from the curio cabinet, inherited from her grandmother along with the farmhouse, she set two adjacent places at the table. After lighting tapered candles in a silver centerpiece, she dimmed the overhead lights.

Hearing Greg's motorcycle rip down the country road, she ran to the bathroom and checked her reflection. Not bad for thirty-seven. Her cheeks glowed pink and moist from kitchen heat, and her hazel eyes gleamed bright. She added a smudge of red gloss to her lips and fluffed her auburn hair.

The front door opened, and Greg's athletic body spanned the frame. Robust and tan from playing third base for the Rangers, he was a monument of youth at twenty-eight. Blond, blue-eyed, adorable. Katy's heart tripped at the sight of him. He made her feel like a teenager—reckless and invincible, her best years still ahead.

"Hello, beautiful," he said in his velvety Southern drawl, lifting her off the ground and spinning around. He smelled of freshly laundered shirts dried on the line. "I've been thinkin' 'bout this all damned day."

"You're not the only one." She giggled.

He kissed her lips, hard and hungrily, and nuzzled her collarbone. "You drive me crazy."

Katy's breath caught as his mouth moved downward.

"Don't you want dinner first?" she stammered.

"Hell, no." He hoisted her over his shoulder and carried her to the bedroom. "If I wait any longer, I'll burst."

****

Slivers of moonlight danced on worn hardwood floors as the ceiling fan spun lazily, infusing the room with woodsy cologne and lavender lotion. Katy luxuriated in cotton sheets, satiated and relaxed, feeling as if she were floating on a cloud. She spooned Greg's naked body and wove her legs over and through his muscular ones.

This, she decided, was how people made it through rough days and was what helped ease the myriad struggles of life. She wasn't even thinking about the sex, although that certainly was part of it. She was savoring the physical contact she'd taken so much for granted before her divorce.

Music drifted into the room, and Noe Burke's

hypnotic voice lulled Katy further into her dreamlike state.

"The lyrics are so lovely, don't you think?" she whispered to Greg.

"Hmm…" He sounded half asleep.

"The song? It's quite poetic."

"If you say so," he murmured. "I just listen to guitar riffs and shit."

"You don't care about the lyrics?"

"Nah." He snorted into the pillow. "Words are for chicks."

Typical guy, Katy thought, but considering how they'd met, she expected more sentimentality from him. "A man wrote it, you know."

"Probably a dork," Greg said. "Brilliant, though. Makes tons of money turning women on."

That much was true. Katy felt warm and tingly every time she heard Noe Burke sing. But she knew it had less to do with the musician and more to do with her feelings for Greg.

She kissed Greg's shoulder and ran a hand over his abs. "Speaking of money, did you look at my business plan for the farm?"

His stomach muscles flexed. "Not yet."

"It's just…" She twirled her fingers across his chest. "I think it would bring goodwill to your image."

"Maybe, but…why don't you create a non-profit?"

"You know how I am. I lack the social skills for fundraising," she said, trying not to sound pathetic. "Is there a reason you don't want to get involved?"

He didn't answer right away, and his breath quickened. "Listen, darlin'…"

Why had she even brought it up? This evening was

supposed to be about romance, not money. Now she felt cheap, as if she'd asked him to drop payment on the dresser before leaving. "Forget I said anything."

"It's just that, well, my…"

"Yes?"

"My financial advisor looks at everything first."

"Oh." Katy couldn't keep disappointment from creeping into her voice. "I can live with that."

"You don't know her," he said. "She's tough."

"I'd like to at least try."

"Okay, but don't say I didn't warn you." In one fluid motion, he disentangled and sat up, planting his large feet on the floor. "What time is it?"

"Still early," she said, shifting onto one elbow and resting her chin in her palm. "Are you hungry?"

"Starving," he said. "I'll stop by Sonic on the way home."

Fast food? She'd spent hours preparing a delicious meal and he'd rather eat junk? And had he forgotten this was their sixth-month anniversary? She tried another tactic. "I made your favorites."

"Aw, that's nice of you darlin', but I can't stay." His voice dripped, subtle and sweet like tupelo honey. He glanced over his shoulder, and a wisp of curly blond hair fell into his baby blues. "Four games against the Yankees and a road trip to Boston on Monday. I'm supposed to be in bed by nine."

God help her, he was cute. Knowing his schedule as well as he did, she gave him her most seductive smile and patted the bed. "That can be arranged."

He slapped her thigh and rose. "Tempting, but rules are rules."

Katy laughed to keep it light. "What about the 'no

sex' one?"

"A suggestion," he said, pulling on jeans and snatching his tee off the floor. "Besides, you know how much I need you."

Need? Love? Not exactly the same thing, but she'd accept it for now.

Slipping into new lingerie and a matching negligee, Katy followed Greg to the foyer as if tethered to him. Leaning against the jamb, she struck a casual pose.

"Want me to pack some food for you?" she said. "Won't take but a minute."

"Nah," he said. "I don't want to impose."

Before she could say it'd be no trouble at all, he spoke again.

"I almost forgot." He dug into the front pocket of his jeans and pulled out a package wrapped in white tissue. "This is for you."

Katy's hand went to her mouth and then to her breast. She reached for the object and nested it in her palm. It was small and almost weightless. Her fingers shook as she peeled away the layers. Earrings? Bracelet? Necklace? No. At the center, she found a bronze pin in the shape of a frolicking horse. Delicate. Perfect.

"I feel bad, you know, about your business thing taking so long and all," he said. "I hope you like it."

"Oh my, yes." She turned the pin back and forth.

"My sister makes them," he said, beaming with pride. "When I saw this one, I thought of you and Bandit."

Even if the present had nothing to do with their sixth-month anniversary, which she was sure it didn't, he *had* remembered how fond she was of the horse at the therapy center where she volunteered every Saturday. The same horse she dreamed of owning one day.

"Thanks," she said, holding back tears.

"Glad you like it." He flung open the front door and stepped into the warm spring night. "See you in a few."

Leaning forward, she plucked a honeysuckle flower from an overgrown vine and sipped its juice. "If I'm around." She smiled, feeling feather-light from his gift.

He stopped mid-step and turned back, looking injured. "Don't even joke about it, darlin'."

She laughed and nodded toward the Harley parked by the barn. "I bet you're not supposed to be riding that either."

He grinned like a schoolboy with a lizard in his pocket.

"Say," he said, smile fading. "I've been meaning to ask you something."

She straightened. "Anything."

"Why do you play that dork's music every time I'm here?"

"Noe Burke?" She frowned. "We met at his concert."

"We did?" he said. "I thought we met at John Mayer."

Her hand moved to her hip. "I've never seen him."

"Sure you have. After the show, we went for Japanese and drank sake."

"We ate Mexican and had margaritas."

"Really? 'Cause I could've sworn..." Greg dragged the toe of his boot across the dusty deck, creating a tiny dirt devil. "I always get those two mixed up."

"The musicians, the food, the drinks, or the…"

Katy stopped herself from saying anything more. Had she understood correctly? Was the bastard sleeping with another woman? She could feel her cheeks flash with anger.

Greg returned and touched her waist. "I really do have to go. Can we talk about this later?"

"When?" Katy averted her eyes, hating how childish she sounded and how needy she felt.

"Come to Boston," he said. "I'll find some time."

Wouldn't that be a shocker if she actually showed up at an away game? She met his gaze. "One of these times, I'm going to take you up on your invitation."

"Awesome. So we're good?"

"Of course." She flicked her hand in dismissal, unprepared to declare an ultimatum or to face a breakup. "Go on with your sweet self."

His eyes sparkled with relief, and he pivoted on his heel and sauntered away.

She couldn't stand watching him leave and slammed the door behind her. Storming into the dining room, Katy removed the Noe Burke CD mid-song and examined the photo on its front. He was undeniably appealing with his five o'clock shadow and smoky-gray eyes. But his mouth held a hint of a smile as if mocking her with the truth. "Don't you judge me."

She bashed the disk against the table's edge. Nothing happened, so she brought it down a second time, harder. Third time the same, so she frisbeed the CD against the wall. It ricocheted off a chair and slid under the table.

Having no intention of ever listening to Noe Burke's music again, she left the CD where it landed. She'd be switching to country music—women singers only—effective immediately. Blowing out the candles, she strode into the kitchen and dumped the stew into the garbage. She was sick of that pot anyway.

Katy slumped against the counter and studied the bronze horse pin, listening to the trailing whine of Greg's motorcycle. She recalled the last time she and Greg were in public as a couple. It was a BBQ at his buddy's house, where two of the ballplayers' wives, both beautiful and in their mid-twenties, looked at Katy and joked in Spanish that Greg had brought his aunt, how sweet. The women had no idea Katy was born in Mexico and spoke their language, because she resembled her Irish father. So it came as a shock when she asked in flawless Spanish where to place the fresh guacamole and handmade tortilla chips she'd brought for the potluck. Wide-eyed and silent, both gestured toward the outdoor patio.

"*Gracias,*" Katy said.

What she'd wanted to add was something about karma or the inevitability of aging, but for the life of her, nothing biting came to mind. She fumed the rest of the day but never told Greg about the incident.

Chapter 3

After Phoebe's tantrum and departure, Noe couldn't sleep. Not because he'd miss her, but because he knew he wouldn't. Most times, valerian root tea eased his insomnia, but on this night his mind refused to stay quiet.

At two in the morning, he found himself staring at the ceiling. At three, he paced the tiny bedroom of the tour bus, cursing when he stubbed his toe on the nightstand. At four, he stepped outside with his sketchbook and glared at the bothersome moon that hung like a ping-pong ball over Miami.

Mild and pleasant with a slight breeze, the spring weather reminded him of Seattle summers. And, as most port towns tended to do, it smelled of swamp and brine. But there were other scents as well—some more agreeable than others. Olive oil, garlic, and cumin. Brewed coffee. Spent gasoline. Warm sand. Gardenias. Even at this late hour, he heard clinking glasses and laughter, which made him feel excluded and alone.

Winking his left eye, Noe spyglassed his hand and brought it to his right eye, scanning the horizon for imaginary merchant ships. As a kid, long before discovering his musical proclivity in eighth grade, he'd wanted to be a pirate when he grew up. He and Rebecca spent hours brandishing swords made of driftwood, scaling evergreens to their crow's nests, and helming bicycles into battle. Sometimes still, peril on the high seas seemed more appealing than life on the hard road. But knowing he'd been one of the fortunate few who succeeded in the music industry, he never complained aloud. But he was ready for this tour to be over, relieved to be coming to the last leg of the journey. One more concert in town, and then they'd make the turn toward Seattle, cutting diagonally across the country and stopping at several venues before arriving home.

Home. The word lost all meaning to him. It seemed more accurate to call it a house now—a structure where he stored his things. Absent of warmth and love and heart.

Noe sat on the top step and opened his sketchbook onto his knees. Using a technique his therapist had taught him—a form of self-hypnosis that eradicated distractions—he closed his eyes and cleared his thoughts. Then he summoned all his senses, allowing an image to take shape. His mind asked questions. Was it cold or warm? Were birds chirping or did he hear traffic noise? Was the air fresh, artificially perfumed, or stale? Who, if anyone, sat beside him? Were those raindrops on his tongue? Was moss under his bare feet? Counting down from ten, he opened his eyes and began to draw.

At first he doodled a squiggly line with his pencil. Nothing intentional. No object in mind. Then he followed each whim and allowed the drawing to become what it wanted to be. To force the image would cause ruin, requiring him to start again. Although he could see the page and was aware the hand belonged to him, he felt removed by a degree, and was always surprised by the outcome. In no way did Noe consider himself an artist, but he admitted some of his doodles were pretty damn good.

After fifteen minutes or so, Noe viewed the drawing. It was a rough sketch of his cabin on Bainbridge Island. The property appeared in disarray, which was quite possible considering he hadn't been back in two years, despite the quick ferry ride from downtown Seattle.

Was Noe meant to be at his cabin? By tending the property, could he somehow fix himself? Satisfied with the kernel of hope, he closed his sketchbook and stepped back inside the tour bus. Maybe blessed sleep would come to him after all.

****

Katy hadn't wanted to think about Greg after he'd left, but her brain refused to comply. Standing at the sink in sweats and an oversized T-shirt, she smeared vegan butter onto saltines and popped them into her mouth, one cracker after another. When the sleeve was empty, she climbed onto the counter and slipped a hand to the farthest corner of the deepest cabinet, removing a pack of Virginia Slims, a book of matches, and a bottle of tequila.

After pouring two fingers of Patrón into a highball glass, she trudged outside and collapsed like a wing-clipped sparrow onto a plastic lawn chaise by the frog pond. Lighting a cigarette, she held smoke in her lungs until they ached. In between drags, she sipped liquid fire. It buzzed on her lips, burning like nettle all the way to her belly. The pain was fitting and welcome.

Staring at the pond, Katy listened to the symphony of frogs and watched as their shadows leapt chaotically into the murky water underneath the lily pads. The smell of mossy peat and rotten leaves reminded her of simpler, happier times of dressing barn cats in baby clothes, collecting cicada shells in paper sacks, and imagining Christopher Robin and Pooh Bear living in the woods behind the farmhouse with Piglet, Kanga, and the rest.

Tears escaped down Katy's cheeks, and she swiped them away with the back of her hand. Now was not the time to be rash. She wasn't absolutely sure Greg was seeing anyone else. After all, she hadn't asked him the question outright. And just because he couldn't keep musicians straight didn't mean he'd been disloyal to her. Greg could be scattered at times, and he certainly hadn't made any promises, so he hadn't broken any.

Regardless, she had a few weeks to decide how to proceed. Was it time to broach the subject of becoming exclusive? Or could she shift her heart for a while and be blasé, not caring who he saw on the side? Strange she'd even ponder it. But considering her options, it wasn't as bad as it sounded.

Katy's opportunities were dwindling, because she was on the losing end of thirty—made painfully clear when her husband left her in the most cliché way possible. He'd fallen in love with a younger woman and was now anticipating his first child, something Katy was physically incapable of providing.

According to online articles, time had come for Katy to compromise. To lower her standards and expectations. To settle. And if she disregarded the advice, they cautioned, she'd be alone the rest of her life. Truth be told, she was an expert at being alone. But just because a person was good at something, didn't mean they wanted it to continue.

Did she even possess the strength to dive back into

the dating pool, already knowing what awaited her? She'd been on several match-up sites after her divorce, and, at first, the choices seemed plentiful. But none were as desirable in person.

There was the narcissist who couldn't walk past a mirror without checking his reflection. And the lothario who ghosted her for expecting more than the implicit one-nighter when she'd suggested swing-dance lessons. And the pilot who invited her to his home. When she'd arrived with a nice bottle of Pinot Gris and mushroom risotto, magazines were stacked to the rafters and his kitchen reeked of Raid and dirty socks. The rest of her matchups were on the mediocre scale, and they seemed to feel the same about her.

Why was it so difficult to find a compatible sexual partner who was open to experiencing new things outside of the bedroom? Especially one who didn't treat women like cheap cuisine at an all-you-can-eat buffet?

This night had taken a terrible turn, and Katy needed a sunrise to bring promise of a better day. She drowned the cigarette in tequila and rolled into the fetal position, squeezing her eyes tight against the optimism and light of the cream-colored moon.

Chapter 4

In Seattle, Noe waited as Rebecca selected a bottle of Dom Perignon from her wine fridge and popped its cork. Always stunning, she wore a spring-green gown that plunged to her navel and complemented the color of the champagne. Her wavy blonde hair swept upward, accentuating her heart-shaped face.

Rebecca's beauty had minimal effect on Noe. They'd known each other all their lives. Their moms had become best friends during natural birth classes at UW Medical Center, so Noe and Rebecca were raised as siblings. They'd shared teething rings, training-wheels, and zit creams.

After tonight's gala at the Paramount, Noe had planned to go straight home and pack for his trip to the cabin, hoping to catch the ferry to Bainbridge by mid-morning. But Rebecca cajoled him into a nightcap, promising one quick drink.

"Why are these charity events always so formal?" he asked, wriggling out of his jacket and throwing it over a kitchen chair. He loosened the knot on his black bowtie and unhooked the top button of the over-starched shirt. Detaching the cufflinks, he plunked them into his front pant's pocket before accepting the outstretched bubbly. "I feel like I'm back in Sunday school."

"I love playing dress-up, and you look fabulous in

your tux," Rebecca said, clinking her glass with his. "Beats your faded jeans, T-shirt, and ball cap."

"You *do* look pretty amazing," he said, dropping onto the comfy sofa in front of the fireplace and staring into the crackling flames. He drank half the contents of his glass in one gulp. "That doctor sure thought so."

"Oh, please," she said, waving her hand as if swatting a fly. She sat down beside him and crossed her long, tanned legs. "He's a gynecologist."

"So?"

"Can you imagine the number of women he's seen naked?" Rebecca said and snorted.

"As a medical professional," Noe said. "It's not the same."

"You're right. It's even worse. I'd feel like I'm on the examination table."

"Yeah. I can see your point," he said. "Poor guy. Probably doesn't have much of a love life."

"Speaking of which," she said. "How's yours?"

"Nonexistent. After Phoebe left, I gave up trying," he said. "I've decided to become celibate."

"What?" She choked on her drink. "Why?"

"Health reasons."

"Are you…" She placed a hand on his knee and became overly dramatic as was her habit. "Are you dying?"

"It's nothing like that," he said, patting her hand. "I'm too young to feel this old."

"Nonsense." She rose, taking their empty flutes with her. "This tour's been brutal. You'll be fine after a month. You always are."

"It's more than that," he said, following her into the kitchen. "I need to be a normal guy."

"As opposed to what?" She laughed, lifting the bottle. "An abnormal one?"

"You know what I mean, Becks," he said, looking straight into her gold-flecked eyes. "I want to be Jon Abbott again."

Rebecca set the bottle down next to the glasses and raised her eyes to study his face, as if searching for evidence of the boy inside the man. Was she remembering the kindergartner who dreamed of flying to Mars on the back of a shooting star? Or the scrawny kid who carried his guitar like a shield in eighth grade? Or the pimply teenager who fainted when the tattoo needle pricked his bony shoulder?

"I see," she said. "'Noe Burke's' persona not sitting well?"

"Not lately." He grabbed the champagne bottle and pressed it to his lips for a swig. He offered the bottle to Rebecca, but she shook her head. He shrugged, took another drink, and returned it to the counter. "I'm taking a hiatus from touring."

"I figured as much," she said. "For how long?"

"A year," he said.

"What about the band and crew?" she said. "Abby's buying a house, and Beau and Jennifer are expecting twins. They're counting on a steady income."

"I've set aside funds for salaries, and the medical insurance will continue," he said, scratching a spot on his chin where his beard refused to grow. "Everyone can use the free time as they wish."

"That's very generous," she said, quiet for a moment as she processed the news. "You've been planning this a while."

"I guess I have." He chuckled, relieved it was

finally off his chest.

"I haven't heard that laugh in ages. I miss it." She smiled. "What will you do with your time?"

"I don't know," he said. "Doodle? Write songs? Heal?"

"Oh, sweetheart…" Rebecca brushed his cheek with her thumb and cupped his chin.

"They've been gone two years," he said, shoulders slumping from the tremendous weight of losing Charlotte and Emily. "Will the pain ever go away?"

"Not entirely. But the ache will lessen," she said. "You'll remember them as they were and not the void they left behind."

She knew of what she spoke. When Rebecca was twelve, her father battled leukemia. She and her mother tended his every need, helplessly watching as he transformed from professional skier into shadow-man. In stark contrast, Jon's wife and child died swiftly, leaving no chance for final goodbyes.

Rebecca folded Jon into her arms and rubbed his back in small circles. Subtle notes of vanilla and gardenia attached to his clothes like pollen. He was considered tall at 6'2", but when she wore heels, her height was significant. Strangers mistook them as a couple, because they matched well physically. But he and Rebecca had never crossed the friendship threshold.

That changed when he felt her lips linger on his neck. Bewildered yet intrigued, he turned his head and met her gaze.

"Remember the pact we made at twenty-one?"

"That if we're both single and forty, we'd give it a go?"

"Yes," she said.

"But we're not yet forty."

"Just around the corner," she said. "Why wait?"

"What if it doesn't work out?"

"And we agree we're not couple-material?"

"Exactly."

"We go back to being friends."

"Just like that?"

"We're both adults." She laughed. "We know how to behave."

Jon hesitated for a moment. They weren't betraying anyone, and their curiosity could be satisfied once and for all. And what if he and Rebecca were meant for each other? He'd never considered it. And now that the opportunity presented itself, there was only one way to be sure.

Chapter 5

Saturday morning, Katy drove with the windows rolled down to Horse Haven Physical Therapy Center. Empty, straight highways begged for speed, but ol' Miss Peabody wasn't up for the challenge and puttered along at a steady pace. Music from the country station 99.5 The Wolf played, and Maren Morris sang "I Could Use a Love Song"—Katy's new favorite.

Tucked between winter's chill and summer's swelter, spring was Katy's favorite season. Bluebonnets flourished by the roadside, waves of clouds softened the daylight, and hints of jasmine floated on the wind, perfuming crisp, clean air.

One of the first to arrive at the center, Katy parked in her usual spot underneath a pecan tree. Once part of a great orchard, the remaining, randomly scattered trees provided housing for migrating orioles and other critters, and, in autumn, plenty of nuts for cookies and pies.

Her footfalls on gravel the only sound, Katy strolled past the shadowed arena and three barn-red buildings. She carried two canvas bags containing homemade goodies. One day not long ago, when she'd run short of time, she'd bought pastries on the way to the center. Based on the grumblings, you'd have thought the tray contained shoe leather and rubber tires. Today, she brought beer bread and spicy plum chutney, filling the break room with festive aromas.

When she stepped back outside, Bert, a yellow lab and the center's mascot, danced alongside her. She threw him a dog biscuit from her pocket. He caught it mid-air then peeled away in search of his next mark.

At the stables, the tang of sawdust mixed with hay and manure. Katy felt at peace here. Her day-to-day worries were replaced with fond memories of the farm before the livestock was sold to cover her grandmother's medical bills. And working with disadvantaged children gave her a sense of purpose—a greater understanding of a world outside her microscopic focus.

Katy opened Bandit's stall and stepped inside. The horse, a black-and-white paint that stood fourteen hands, had been donated to the center a few years back by a Dallas banker. The banker's daughter had refused to accept Bandit as her sixteenth birthday gift, demanding a gold Corvette to complement her hair. Bandit, never wanted, was shipped to the therapy center as a tax write-off. Katy wondered how such a beautiful and kindhearted creature could be so easily discarded, like an unfashionable scarf.

When Bandit became hers, something she hoped would happen sooner than later, she'd exercise him daily and treat him to carrots and greens.

"Let's get you ready for your lesson," she said, rubbing his silken muzzle.

He nickered and leaned into her like a big, goofy dog.

****

Katy held the reins as Bandit's first pupil, Luna, climbed a mounting block. The instructor, a gentle giant named Vic who was hairier than the horses, lifted the child the last little bit onto the saddle.

Luna was eight years old and eager to learn. Undersized for her age, her body moved like a marionette's. She was excitable and had an angelic smile and a quick wit. Bandit was the perfect horse for her, because he wasn't spooked by the child's constant movement.

Katy pressed Luna's feet into the stirrups and straightened her form. Their conversation was spoken primarily in Spanish at Luna's request.

"Are you comfortable?" Katy asked.

"*Sí*," Luna said, nodding with her whole body.

"Please remember not to bounce, okay? It's not good for Bandit."

"Why is he called that?" Luna asked. "Does he steal things?"

The question was a game they played at the start of each lesson. Katy responded with little hesitation, giving the impression she'd devised an advance reply, but that wasn't the case.

Only a blanket of stars to keep him warm.

Only a nightingale's song to lull him to sleep.

Only a pinch of sugar to sweeten his dreams.

Katy touched the tip of Luna's nose with her forefinger.

"Only an ocean of love to bring him peace."

"I like that one the best," Luna said, as she did every week.

Katy walked Bandit around the arena, allowing Luna to adjust to the motion and to wait for other students to mount. "Are you closing your eyes, Luna?" That was new.

"I feel like I'm flying."

"But you might run into something if you're not paying attention."

"Isn't that why you're here?" Luna popped one eye open to gauge Katy's reaction and then smiled widely.

Katy couldn't help but laugh.

"We're studying the Aztecs in school," Luna said. "I want to go to Mexico City to see the ruins of Tenochtitlan."

"Sounds like a fine idea."

"My parents say we can't afford the trip." Luna's shoulders drooped as did her smile.

"Maybe that'll change one day." Katy empathized with Luna, because she couldn't afford a lot of things either. "Remember to sit up straight for Bandit's sake, okay?"

"Okay," Luna said, doing as she was told and then brightening again. "We're starting."

Beginning the group lesson, Vic's voice carried across the arena. As was his custom, he called each student by name and asked what horse they were riding and who was walking beside them. When it came to Luna's turn, she answered proudly in English. "Katy's my horse and Bandit's walking beside me."

Vic played along. "And what does your horse like to eat?"

"Carrots and greens."

"It's true," Katy said. "For the horse and the walker."

The remainder of the lesson was routine—steering the horses through cones, standing up in the stirrups, bringing the horses to center—and Katy's shift was over too soon. Running a palm down Bandit's chest and jostling Luna's foot, she was reluctant to leave. In Spanish, she whispered to both child and steed as if conspiring to storm the castle. "Dreams are worth fighting for. If we work hard enough, maybe we'll all get what we want."

Katy helped Luna dismount and watched her run through the gate to her parents. The next walker took Bandit's reins, and Katy waved goodbye to Vic. She sauntered from the arena, squishing loam under her boots and sidestepping manure, not missing the days when dung removal was her responsibility.

"Katy, wait," a woman called from behind. Katy stopped and turned.

Lori jogged to her, brown ringlets bouncing on petite shoulders. Her eyes shimmered with mirth as she showed Katy what she was holding. "This bread's delicious," she said, talking with a full mouth. "I can't believe it's vegan."

"Everything I make is, I promise," Katy said. "But where's the chutney?"

"Completely gone. I found the bowl in the dishwasher. I think someone licked it."

Katy flashed a smile. "I'll make another batch especially for you."

"You're a good person to know, my friend," Lori said.

"What are you doing here?" Katy said. "Weren't you and Sara visiting her folks in Austin this weekend?"

"Postponed. One of her patients went into labor last night. Two weeks early. We're going next Saturday instead." Lori ate the last bit of bread and walked with Katy toward the parking lot. "My cousin Norman's in town. Want to hang with us tonight?"

"The mumbler?" Katy groaned. "I don't think I'm up for it."

"What else ya got goin'? Isn't Greg busy?"

"Well, yes." Katy wasn't ready to discuss the disappointing anniversary date, even with Lori. "But we had a nice evening earlier in the week."

"Of course you did," Lori said. "Aren't you a little old for that type of thing?"

"No." Katy laughed and bumped Lori's shoulder. "Are you?"

"I'm talking about your thing for ballplayers."

Katy stopped, and her hand moved to her hip. "You're one to talk. What about your firefighter phase?"

"That was long ago, and I grew out of it." Lori's eyes took on a faraway look, and then snapped back to the present. "Isn't it time for you to let go of your obsession?"

Fair question. The boys of summer were to Katy what firefighters were to Lori. Catnip. But Katy had never dated a ballplayer before Greg, and she'd been pleasantly surprised by his interest. At the concert, she knew who he was, because she'd admired his moves for an entire season. She nudged her way through the beer tent to stand next to him. While retrieving her phone to request a picture, someone bumped his cup, and his beer spilled onto her jeans. Apologizing profusely, he offered to buy her a drink. Then he suggested dinner. And at his place later that night? Well, he touched all the bases before sliding into home. Katy felt a blush cross her cheeks.

She hadn't expected to see him again after that

night, but he'd called within the week, and they'd spent their free time together, out and about, alone—until she'd met his friends at the BBQ. But after the comment about her advanced age, she'd felt conspicuous, like a wallflower standing under a spotlight in the middle of a room. She fell into old conversation habits of sputtering about the weather and hyping the numerous benefits of horse manure. Greg tried to ease her jitters by staying nearby and making inquires as to which dishes were vegan. But that only made her more uncomfortable, because the meat-eaters felt judged, even though her mind didn't work that way. One couple scampered away after admitting they were on the Atkins Diet. And one of the assistant coaches argued with her for fifteen minutes, claiming Jesus provided fish to his followers, so who was she to think herself more righteous. It wasn't as if she expected anyone to alter their lifestyles because she had. In fact, she couldn't understand when people indulged as much as they wanted, but once they decided to change, everyone else had to do so as well. If only she and Greg could go back to before the BBQ. She'd do better this time.

"No matter a person's age," Katy said, "when a wish is granted, who wouldn't want to take it as far as it can go?"

"You make a valid point," Lori said. "But Greg's, what, half your age?"

"Hardly. He's twenty-eight."

"Physically." Lori plucked a piece of straw from a bale by the gravel path and stuck it between her teeth. "Shucks, darlin'," she twanged, digging her thumbs into her armpits and rocking back and forth on her heels.

"Care for a ride in the hay?"

Katy laughed. "He doesn't sound like that."

"No?"

"His voice is sexier."

"And his eyes are to die for."

"They are, aren't they?"

"And, oh that body." Lori attempted a whistle that sounded more like a sizzle.

Katy scrutinized her friend's face. "What are you getting at?"

"It's just that…"

"What? Tell me."

"Okay, but hear me out."

"If I must," Katy said, only half serious.

"You were so wrecked after your divorce, and God knows Greg got you out of your funk," Lori said. "But that's all he was supposed to do—help you rebound."

Katy waved her hand back and forth like a flag and lied. "It's a fling. No big deal. Could end tomorrow for all I care."

Lori stared at Katy without blinking. "I'm not buyin' it."

Katy stared right back. "I'm not sellin' it." But she knew when Lori had a point to make, there was no stopping her. Katy braced herself for the inevitable lecture and sighed. "What do you suggest?"

"A break," Lori said.

Katy assumed Lori meant from Greg but asked anyway. "From?"

"Sex."

"Um, what?"

Lori spoke slowly, emphasizing every word. "You need to take a break from sex."

"Are you kidding? It's the best part of being an adult." Katy glanced around the grounds, making sure no one else was listening. A few riders were in the arena but none within earshot. "Are you channeling some medieval priest or something?"

"You promised to hear me out," Lori said.

"I didn't know you'd gone insane."

"You'll thank me later."

"Doubtful," Katy said. "But go on."

"You don't understand the concept of casual sex."

"Um…I'm not sure I agree."

"And," Lori said, "if you continue this pattern, by the time you're fifty, your heart will be broken more often than eggs at Denny's."

"Well…I guess I'm hoping—"

"I know exactly what you're hoping, and that's the problem. How can I put this?" Lori thought for a moment. "Casual sex is about sampling—like eating candy. It's tasty yet temporary."

"Don't you think I know that?"

"In theory, maybe. But in practice, not so much. You treat casual sex like an entire meal," Lori said, "and expect long-lasting nourishment."

Katy nipped her next quip and paused, thinking about her ex-husband. Once she'd slept with him, she'd pushed for a commitment before he was ready, and look how that ended. And Greg? Fun, boyish, never-had-a-significant-relationship man-child? Embarrassingly true, she'd visualized growing old together. And those relationships were only the most recent examples.

"My point is," Lori said, "just because casual sex is an option, doesn't mean it's the best one for everybody."

"Ah, well," Katy said. "What's a woman to do?"

"I can't speak for all women, but I know you," Lori said. "You're seeking a long-term relationship, so you can't keep falling for short-term guys."

Katy snapped her fingers. "Like that."

"I'm not saying it's going to be easy," Lori said.

"Yeah, but—"

"But nothin'," Lori said. "You commit to the wrong man, and the next thing you know, you're six months older and starting over again."

"That's depressing," Katy said, as the words found their target.

"You need to break the cycle," Lori said. "Think of it as a reboot."

"Reprogramming of sorts."

"Exactly." Lori grinned triumphantly. "I suggest you maintain a physical distance. Get to know the *real* guy and not some romanticized version of who you're hoping he'll be. And maybe you could date someone who's not attractive to so many others."

"Says the woman in love with a gorgeous doctor."

"I lucked out with Sara for sure," Lori said. "But we're talking about you right now."

"One of us is," Katy said, growing weary of the conversation. "Chemistry isn't a switch that can be turned on or off."

"Then try turning it off completely. For a little while, anyway," Lori said. "Promise me you'll think about it, okay?"

"We'll see," Katy said. "I can guess Greg's reaction if I tell him I want to date platonically."

"Better give him a dictionary," Lori said. "Or he won't know what you're talking about."

Katy ignored the comment.

They continued to the parking lot. Sunlight flickered through the pecan trees, so the metal bumpers twinkled like diamonds.

"Did I mention my cousin works in accounting now?" Lori said.

Katy was relieved the conversation had shifted back to banter. "My dream date."

"I mean you two have something in common."

"A tedious job shouldn't be the catalyst for any relationship." Katy unlocked her car and opened the door to let out some heat.

"When are you going to get rid of that clunker?" Lori said.

"Shush." Katy petted the oxidized green paint on Miss Peabody. "She'll hear you."

Lori laughed and gave Katy a quick hug. "You know I love you, right?"

"Back at ya, kiddo," Katy said. "Tell Sara hello for me."

"Will do." Lori started toward the arena. "Let me know if you change your mind about tonight," she said over her shoulder.

What else *did* Katy have planned? Opening a week's worth of mail? Scanning the vegan forum? Binge-watching reruns of *Texas Country Reporter*?

"Where?" she asked.

"Stockyards," Lori said, turning around and walking backward. "Love Shack."

"Apropos of nothing," Katy said. "Still, they make a tasty mushroom burger."

"Does that mean you'll come?"

Katy's tone matched her enthusiasm. "Sure. Why

not?"

"Great." Lori's voice tinkled in singsong. "Meet us at seven."

Spending time with Cousin Norman might not be so bad. He was a nice guy, but his obsession with protein was maddening. More than once, she'd caught him eyeballing her plate and mumbling about why she'd become sickly if she didn't eat meat. As he spoke, she'd catch the waiter's attention and order deep-fried pickles or something as heart-stopping. She dreaded the evening already.

Chapter 6

At his cabin on Bainbridge Island, Jon slept the entire first week of his hiatus, or so it seemed. Steady rain pitter-patted on the roof and dampened the light. The dreams he remembered were of childhood camping trips where trees were too tall to climb and fish too clever to catch.

When the sun broke through, he could sleep no more, so he called his parents. His mother answered after four rings.

"Jon, dear. So lovely to hear from you."

"Hi, Mom." Comforted by her voice, he grabbed a sketchbook, sat at the kitchen table, and flipped pages until he found room to draw. "How's the weather in Palm Desert?"

"Nice and warm. Not like Seattle at all." Her laugh was much like her singing voice, contralto, which meant she could easily handle Karen Carpenter songs. "Even your father's arthritis pain has lessened"

"That's great." The doodle took the shape of a palm tree. "Where is he now?"

"Playing golf."

"But…Dad hates golf."

"I know. Isn't it a kick?"

Most of the time, Jon had no idea what his parents were thinking, because they spoke in code and never gave him the key. As the story goes, they'd met at

Woodstock when they fell into the same mud puddle. His mother, Joanna, was a half-baked, halfhearted flowerchild who played the mandolin with a traveling troupe of actors. His father, Joseph, fresh out of dental school, was enjoying one last adventure. Within the week, they were married in a questionable ceremony. Then they moved to Seattle to become caretakers for Joseph's family estate and to build his dental practice. Years later, Jon was born in the bathtub—delivered by a midwife. Over time, the estate diminished, as adjacent lots were sold to keep tax collectors at bay. After retiring, Jon's parents moved to sunny California to recapture their halcyon days. Jon spent a fortune on renovations to prevent the main house and caretaker's cottage from morphing into Bouivier's Grey Gardens.

"How's Rebecca?" his mother asked. "Still seeing that actor?"

"She dumped him. Too insecure." He omitted the real reason, which was that the guy tore Rebecca's blouse in the heat of passion and laughed when she demanded he replace it.

"Well…Louisa and I always hoped you two might end up—"

"Please, Mom." He felt heat rush to his cheeks at the memory of seeing Rebecca naked. "We're practically brother and sister."

"Not technically, dear. I thought I raised you with an open mind."

"It's a cornucopia." He squirmed at the idea of discussing his sex life with his mother. Bad enough, she'd given him the middle name of Noe in remembrance of the San Francisco neighborhood where he'd been conceived. Had he known its origin in his teens, he never would've chosen it as his stage name. "Have you thought about visiting Seattle?"

"Oh, honey," she said. "We're going on that cruise soon."

The Caribbean trip he bought them wasn't for another six months, but there was no use reminding his mother. She'd become quite the homebody, and she was probably already packed to ease the stress of leaving her nest.

"I could come see you." He doodled a boat next to the palm tree.

"That's sweet of you, dear. But you have a life to live."

"But, Mom," he said. "I miss you and Dad."

"And we miss you too," she said. "But you don't want to be stuck playing pinochle with a couple of old-fogies."

"Well…maybe I do."

"Are you okay?" she said, sounding concerned. "You're not…you know? Like after the accident?"

"No, Mom," he said, sad he'd worried her then and now. "I'm fine. Feeling a bit nostalgic."

"When your father gets home," she said, "we'll do a little FaceTime. How does that sound?"

"I'd like that." He knew she'd probably forget. Days weren't marked by schedules and obligations for his parents anymore, so time held no meaning.

Jon dropped the sketchpad on the table and stepped outside, perusing the grounds and throwing pinecones at evergreen trees. Because of deferred maintenance, the walking path into the forest was overgrown with blackberry bushes. Pine needles layered the fire pit, and the side fence listed. But he finally had time to tackle the chores, and he was eager to get his hands dirty.

During the following weeks, Jon replaced the hinges on the medicine cabinet and tinkered with the drippy faucet in the kitchen. He power-washed the front porch and hung fuchsias in baskets along the rafters. He built a decorative gate from blueprints he'd found on the Internet and used the excess lumber for a park-like bench.

Then he bought a brand-new bicycle.

The kid at the shop steered him toward a state-of-the-art motorized version. "For when you get tired on the hills," he'd said. "Easier on the ol' knees."

Jon would have none of it! He wanted a bike you could ride up a mountain. It didn't matter that the last time he'd been on one he'd been too young to drive.

"Are you sure you don't want company?" Rebecca had asked the day he left Seattle. "I could visit you on the weekends."

"In a few months, maybe," he'd said. "I'll let you know."

He and Rebecca had only spent one night together, but it was enough to satisfy his curiosity of what sex would be like between them—awkward, and not worth jeopardizing their lifelong friendship. She alluded to it occasionally, as an inside joke of sorts. When that happened, he changed the subject to books or sports.

Jon named his new bike "Rocky." Not as a reference to the fictional boxer, but for items found in the woods. And it sounded better than "Twiggy" or "Mossy."

On the afternoon of Rocky's maiden ride, Jon was surprised at how giddy he felt—like that kid who finally got the "Red Ryder" air rifle in the holiday movie. He thought about attaching cards to the spokes but couldn't find clothes pins.

The weather was cool and dry, and as a skier, Jon knew to dress in layers. He refused to wear spandex, though, opting instead for cargo pants. He stuffed his backpack with supplies: water bottle, protein bar, banana, beef jerky, phone, wallet, sunglasses, hat, compass, map. He left the headphones in the cabin, because chirping birds and rustling leaves were the kinds of songs he needed to hear. The helmet felt cumbersome, but he wasn't leaving without it. Understanding when caution was an absolute necessity was one advantage of getting older.

"Let's go, Rocky." He patted the side of the bike as if it were a mustang.

Thirty minutes into the ride and halfway up a hill, Jon's right thigh cramped. He winced in agony. He hadn't even gone off-road yet. Stopping to hydrate and walk off the pain, he cursed under his breath. Perhaps two hours on the first day was a bit ambitious. After all, his exercise for the past two years had been mostly onstage. And he wasn't exactly eating right either. Too much brown food, and not enough green. One too many beers.

He decided to return to the cabin. No big deal. Now he realized he needed to build stamina incrementally, he'd tweak the timeframe. Slowly add distance and elevation. The revelation delayed but did not deter him.

As Jon swung Rocky around, he heard what sounded like a hissing snake. It startled him, and he tossed the bike from his body and jumped back. Rocky flew sideways and clattered upon impact with the cold hard ground. The back wheel slowed to its final heartbeat.

What had Jon been thinking? There were no poisonous snakes on the island. He rushed to Rocky's side. The bike's metallic gray paint was scuffed and the seat was torn. Upon further inspection, Jon discovered the hissing had come from the front tire. It was as flat as a B chord.

Jon pulled his phone from the backpack and called roadside assistance.

"Yeah, hi, my bike is—"

"Hello? Anybody there?"

"Um, yeah, I'm here. I need help. I'm—"

"Hello? Hello? Must be crank."

Click.

"Wait," Jon yelled. He looked at his phone to search for bars. None. He extended his arm and circled five feet in every direction. No luck. "Shit."

****

Jon walked his bike for what seemed like an eternity, but it'd only been twenty minutes. Not one single car drove past. Rough estimate, he figured he'd ridden about five miles before stopping. His phone was still without signal. He should've packed a beer.

A blue pickup stopped ahead of him and then backed up. The driver rolled down the window, offering a ride to the bike shop. At first, the man's face was indistinguishable, because the sun's glare created a corona that obscured his features.

Jon cupped his brow to see the driver more clearly. The man's physique was slender but not gaunt. Based on his salt and pepper hair, he might've been older than Jon, but not by much, considering his lack of wrinkles.

Jon quickly assessed the situation for anything that might make him uneasy, starting with bumper stickers. "My Dog is My Co-pilot." "Coexist." "Embrace Diversity." The rear window was free of shotgun and rack.

"Thanks, buddy," he said, placing Rocky on old blankets in the truck bed and jumping into the passenger seat.

"I'm Sam," the guy said, and shook Jon's hand. "And you're Noe Burke."

"Yes," Jon said. "I'd appreciate it if you didn't tell anyone."

"Hard secret to keep," Sam said, shifting into gear. "But they won't hear it from me."

After a few bumps on the road, Jon felt something poking into his backside. When he reached around, he found a cookbook. The burger on the cover looked delicious. "I could use one of those about now," he said, placing the book on the seat beside him.

Sam tapped the book without taking his eyes off the road. "You like vegan food?"

"Vegan?" Jon said. "Don't know much about it. Why?"

"Well, that's a vegan cookbook."

"You don't say." Jon picked up the book and flipped through it. Every recipe appeared more appealing than the last.

"I wish I'd started at your age," Sam said.

"I thought you *were* my age," Jon said, still looking at the photos.

"Nah," Sam said. "What are you? Forty? Forty-five?"

Jon's head jerked up. "I'm thirty-nine."

"Oh." Sam smiled. "Sorry."

"How old are you?" Jon said, feeling goaded into asking.

"Fifty-four."

Jon's next words caught in his throat and came out as a whisper. "No way."

Sam pulled his wallet from the console and chucked it into Jon's lap. It fell open to Sam's driver's license. Sure enough, his birthday was fifteen years prior to Jon's. For further proof, Sam removed a photo from the visor. "That's me three years ago."

"Holy shit," Jon said. "You're, you are…"

"Fat? Yeah, I know," Sam said. "My blood pressure and cholesterol were through the roof, and I had type 2 diabetes. I've lost eighty pounds since then."

"How'd you do it?" Jon asked, fascinated by his inability to match the sickly man in the photo to the healthy one sitting next to him. "Gastric bypass surgery?"

"Nope," Sam said. "I started walking, and my wife bought me a book."

"A book?" Jon said. "Was it one of those power-of-suggestion kinds?"

"Not exactly," Sam said. "The book was written by a doctor."

"Dr. Oz? Dr. Phil? Dr. Ruth?"

"Oh, ha, that's a good one," Sam said, catching Jon's joke about the famous sex expert. "Dr. Joel Fuhrman. He wrote *Eat to Live* and touts the benefits of plant-based dieting."

"Vegetarian?"

"Not really. He doesn't condemn meat altogether, and he cautions against cheese, which vegetarians are allowed to eat. Mostly, he rails against overly processed foods," Sam said. "But based on the studies he cites, my wife and I took it one step further and became vegan."

"Huge leap," Jon said, impressed.

"It's pretty damned hard, and I still struggle every day."

"Then why do it?" Jon said.

"Can't lie," Sam said and smiled. "My wife thinks I'm hot again."

Jon chuckled. "Great reason to stick with it."

"In my opinion, there are two kinds of women," Sam said. "The ones who make us want to live and the ones who make us want to die."

"Sometimes they're both," Jon said.

"Sounds like you know what I'm talking about," Sam said. "You married?"

"I was," Jon said. "My wife died two years ago."

"I'm sorry for your loss."

"Not sure what's left for me now," he said, surprised at his confession to a total stranger. "Anyway. I'm trying to get my life back on track. Make better choices. Eat healthier."

"Here," Sam said, reaching into his coat pocket and pulling out the dog-eared *Eat to Live*. "You need this more than I do."

"Are you sure?" Jon said. "Sounds like it's your sacred playbook."

"Yeah," Sam said. "But I've committed it to memory, and I have another copy at home."

"Thanks," Jon said, taking the paperback.

A few minutes later, Sam stopped in front of the bike shop. Refusing gas money, he waited for Jon to retrieve Rocky from the bed. Sam tapped the side of the truck and said one last thing. "People need your music, man. Take good care of yourself, okay?"

"I'll try," Jon said, shaking Sam's hand. "And thanks again for the ride and the book."

Before entering the bike shop, Jon thought about exchanging contact information, but when he turned back to talk to Sam, the truck was already out of sight. So much for asking follow-up questions.

Later that night, Jon read *Eat to Live* from cover to cover. Then he downloaded a vegan grocery list he'd found on the Internet. The next day, he spent a small fortune at the co-op. The day after that, he looked inside his stuffed fridge and cupboards and had no idea what to do with any of it.

Chapter 7

Katy glanced at the clock above the oak credenza in the dining room. Her meeting with Greg's financial advisor was in a week, and she'd spent the last few hours reviewing her business proposal—now safe inside a satchel that leaned against the table leg. She'd examined the plan several times to be sure every number was in place. She'd even practiced her speech in front of the mirror. It wouldn't be the last time.

With two hours remaining before bedtime, Katy needed something to distract her. Opening her laptop on the dining table, she logged onto the vegan forum with her username KatyPatata for her love of potatoes. Her avatar was a close-up of Bandit.

Someone new had posted a question. JonNA39, whose avatar was a duct-taped bicycle seat. It pleased her when newbies showed genuine interest in veganism, because she knew how great they'd feel if they stuck with it.

She could do without one of the regulars, though. BBQMonsterMan—a bully who'd written she was a "waste of space on earth" for disagreeing with him on the best way to sort lentils. She'd suggested he find a support group to deal with his anger issues involving legumes.

JonNA39: I'm new to veganism. I bought too many vegetables and they're starting to turn? What can I do?

Must be a slow night, because, unfortunately, only one poster had responded.

BBQMonsterMan: Get off this forum. It's for vegans not morons.

JonNA39: Jeez, buddy. What's your problem?

BBQMonsterMan: I ain't your buddy.

JonNA39: Fair enough. What's your problem, BM Man?

BBQMonsterMan: Very funny!

JonNA39: It's a gift.

BBQMonsterMan: You want to know what my problem is?

JonNA39: Not really, but feel free to vent if it'll get you closer to answering my question.

BBQMonsterMan: My problem is with idiots like you who don't do their homework before ruining a bunch of food. Veganism's a lifestyle, not a fad diet. Why don't you think about that for a minute?

JonNA39: Tick-tock. Tick-tock. Tick-tock. Ding! Minute's up. How about answering my question now?

BBQMonsterMan: Get a life!

JonNA39: I have a life. And a question. Is now a good time for you to answer it? How about now? Or now?

BBQMonsterMan: You're an ass.

JonNA39: Takes one to know one.

Katy laughed. JonNA39 was holding his own, but she didn't want him thinking BBQMonsterMan represented all vegans.

KatyPatata: Welcome, Jon! Once you get the hang of it, you're going to love being vegan! Even if it's only for dietary reasons.

About those veggies: wash them, chop them (peel

and all), toss them into a pot, throw in some salt and pepper (maybe some oregano), cover them with veggie stock (or water), and add a bay leaf. Bring them to a boil and then simmer for one hour (covered), stirring occasionally. Afterward, transfer contents into smaller containers, and be sure to note the date. It'll be good 2-3 months in the freezer.

JonNA39: Thanks, Katy! Do you mind another question?

KatyPatata: Ask away.

JonNA39: Why can't vegans eat honey?

BBQMonsterMan: Didn't you do ANY research on your own, Bee Barf Eater?

JonNA39: That's BB to you, BM.

BBQMonsterMan: Enough! I'm done!

JonNA39: Promise?

BBQMonsterMan: Hell, no! I got here first!

JonNA39: I got here as fast as I could.

Goodness. This guy was funny.

KatyPatata: Jon, vegans don't eat honey, because we're careful to avoid the exploitation of animals, which is the key component of veganism. There are some vegan products that come close to honey in taste and texture, though.

JonNA39: So much to know!

KatyPatata: Baby steps, Jon. I'm still learning after two years.

BBQMonsterMan: Quit feeding the troll, Katy!

KatyPatata: We all have to start somewhere, BBQ.

JonNA39: Katy, would you be willing to teach me on the side?

KatyPatata: I'm no expert. I suggest you find a mentor in your area if you're feeling overwhelmed.

JonNA39: I'd rather not.

Why was that? Was he agoraphobic? Living in a remote location? Did it matter?

KatyPatata: I'd only be giving you the basics.

JonNA39: I'm okay with that.

BBQMonsterMan: Do it for the rest of us, Katy. Please?!?

She'd never known BBQ to back down before. Must be a good sign. Mentoring would be a great way to refresh her knowledge. And, more importantly, it might be exactly what she needed to quiet her thoughts about Greg.

KatyPatata: What's your email address?

JonNA39: Phone calls might be better…

KatyPatata: Baby steps, Jon.

JonNA39: Fair enough. I'll set up a temporary one and post it here. Could we have a mini lesson after that?

KatyPatata: Sure, why not? I have a few minutes to spare.

****

Jon pushed his chair from the kitchen table and stood, stretching his back. He'd been crouched over his computer most of the day, researching. That's how he'd discovered the vegan forum. He chuckled. What an eye opener. He'd heard vegans could be contentious, but BBQMan took the cake. Jon had known what to expect from reading previous posts, but when he saw Katy's comment about anger management and legumes, beer spewed through his nose. He grabbed another Manny's from the fridge and sat back down.

Katy: Hello, Jon. Are you ready?

Jon: Hello, Katy. I have tons of questions, but for

now, I'll keep it to just one.

Katy: Fire away.

Jon: What made you decide to become vegan?

Katy: Yikes! That's a loaded question!

Jon: Should I ask something else?

Katy: No. It's a fair one. BBQMonsterMan was right about one thing. Veganism might start as a means to a healthier lifestyle, but it also involves more than food. This is going to sound like BS, but veganism is about connection—to earth, to animals, and to each other. It can change you in ways you never thought possible. At least that's what happened to me.

Jon shifted in his seat. That was a lot more information than "because I was fat."

Jon: Please go on.

Katy: I think it's important to be completely honest. Otherwise, we should end this conversation now. Do you agree?

Complete honesty? Of course. Up to a point.

Jon: Yes, but only if we reserve the right to pass on any question. In other words, if we choose to answer, it has to be the truth.

Katy: That's a fine idea.

Here's my story (short version): Two years ago, my life was spiraling downward. Out of the blue, my husband (now ex) served me divorce papers while I was caring for my dying grandmother. (Turns out his girlfriend threatened to leave if he didn't marry her.) I became desperate to find something I could control.

Jon: Wow. Your ex sucks! But that doesn't really answer my questions. Why veganism?

Katy: Oh, right. I was out to dinner with my best friend, Lori, railing about the injustice of it all and getting pretty wrapped up in my righteousness. How could someone love you one minute and then treat you so callously the next? She told me people do it all the time, because we want what we want when we want it and don't think about the consequences. Before I could protest I always thought things through, she swept her hand across our plates. Look at us now, she said. We claim to love animals and yet we're about to enjoy these two perfectly prepared steaks. I immediately lost my appetite, sent my food home with Lori, and decided to become vegan right then and there.

Jon: Love that story! Our lives are kind of parallel. I was messed up (understatement!!!) two years ago too—only I hit the bottle instead.

Should he mention the tabloid fodder, bar fights, and onstage antics? Probably not at this time.

Jon: I tried to keep it hidden, but my friends say I wasn't fooling anyone.

Katy: Believe me. That was happening too. Patrón is vegan.

Jon: I'm a Jameson man, myself. But I need to keep that bottle closed, so I hope it's not vegan.

Katy: That's completely up to you. But when it comes to alcohol, it depends on how it's processed. Research further if you feel like it. Look up refined sugar while you're at it. You might be surprised. I know I was.

Jon: Will do.

He appreciated Katy's words were non-judgmental. She spoke in terms of how alcohol fit into the vegan system, not the condemnation of its sinfulness.

Jon: Quick question. Are you okay now?

Katy: Mending but still a little wobbly. Thanks for

asking. You?

    Jon: Same. On the mend, but wobbly.

    Katy: I'm glad. I probably should go, though. I don't know what time it is there, but, here in Fort Worth, it's nearly bedtime.

    Jon: Ah. I'm in Seattle, so I'm two hours behind. Are you free again tomorrow?

    Katy: If we can start one hour earlier, you bet!

    Jon: Perfect!

    Katy: And, you're right. Phone calls would be easier.

    Jon: I'll send you my number and look forward to your call. Take care and thanks!

After corresponding with Katy, Jon felt at peace. A walk seemed like a nice idea. Maybe a movie. The fissure from old life to new was widening. What if he never wanted to go back?

Chapter 8

Dressed for an interview or a funeral—white shirt, neutral knee-length skirt, and pumps with two-inch heels—Katy entered the lobby of Greg's financial advisor fifteen minutes early. Her hair was tied at the nape, but because the air was so humid a few strands had escaped and were stuck to her face. Not exactly the composed businesswoman she was trying to convey.

"I'm Katy Moore," she said to the perky receptionist who sat at a modest, orderly desk. "I have an appointment with Claire Young."

While the receptionist typed something into her computer, Katy's gaze fell to a photo on the desk. Two towheaded boys were hugging an animal that looked like a fox.

"Cute picture," Katy said. "What kind of dog is that?"

The receptionist touched the photo. "Ginger's a Shiba Inu. My kids adore her."

"Lucky dog," Katy said.

Right then, a door opened, and a fifty-something woman appeared. She was meticulously coiffed and elegantly dressed. The woman scolded the receptionist for failing to bring in afternoon tea, never glancing in Katy's direction.

If the receptionist was bothered by the exchange, she hid it well. To Katy, she said, "Ms. Young will be with you in a minute. Please make yourself comfortable." She gestured toward a set of plush chairs by a window with an expansive view of Sundance Square.

The receptionist left the room and returned with a tray that held a teapot, teacup and Earl Grey tea packets. Taking a detour on the way to her boss's office, she passed Katy and whispered, "You have toilet paper on your shoe."

"Thanks," Katy said, removing the tissue. It must've hitched a ride while she scrutinized her reflection in the first-floor bathroom before the interview. "I owe you one."

While waiting, Katy stared at the streets below— ones she knew well. The lunchtime crowd had disappeared, and the area seemed deserted. Seeing Miss Peabody parked at the corner brought a thin smile. From this angle, it looked like the car she and her father had used for housing in Mexico. Maybe she should get a new paint job.

She spotted the Flying Saucer sign where she and Greg had met once in their early days of dating, when he wanted to show her to the world. She thought about her ex-husband and the cozy apartment in Sundance they once shared. Holding hands and window-shopping at Earth Bones and Retro Cowboy. Dropping into Cupcakery and gaining five pounds from breathing the powdery-sugared air. She turned her back to the window and against the onslaught of unwelcome memories.

Katy had been too nervous to eat before the meeting, and her stomach protested with gurgles and pings. She closed her eyes, willing the embarrassing noises to stop. She was startled when the receptionist called her name.

"Ms. Moore? Ms. Young will see you now."

Katy smoothed her skirt and clung to her satchel as if thieves were lurking nearby. The receptionist smiled sympathetically and mouthed, "Good luck."

Claire Young sat behind a massive, cherrywood desk that could've doubled as a tank. Her body language was forthright and rigid. Ignoring subtlety, Claire looked Katy up and down.

Katy stifled the urge to follow the gaze, mind searching. Was a button missing? Had she spilled something on her shirt? Was her skirt tucked into her stockings? Surely the receptionist would've been kind enough to tell her.

"Please sit down, Ms. Moore," Claire said, not bothering to stand. Nor did she offer a hand to shake. In fact, she folded them on the desk, as a school principal might while tolerating rote excuses from a habitually misbehaved student. "How may I help you today?"

A thin layer of sweat formed on Katy's upper lip. She took a seat across from Claire. "First of all, I'd like to thank you for seeing me on such short notice," she said, proud to have executed the line exactly as she'd rehearsed.

"How could I say no? Greg said you were a special friend."

Was the word "special" emphasized, or was that Katy's imagination?

"I'm here to talk about...I'd like to discuss...I've plans that need—"

"I'm a busy woman, Ms. Moore. Please make your point."

Katy's words came out in a whoosh. "I'm hoping you'll find value in funding my plans to build an animal sanctuary. I'll cover the costs with after-school programs and day camps that will teach children the importance of nature." She fumbled with the latch on her satchel, hearing the wall clock tick-tick-ticking, as if she were on a game show and about to run out of time. Partially rising, she handed the paperwork across the desk to Claire.

Claire donned a pair of reading glasses and scanned the prospectus. She held the charts and graphs up to the light. "Hmm."

"You'll notice the infrastructure is already in place, needing only minor repairs," Katy said. "And there's plenty of land for the animals."

Claire raised her index finger for silence and continued reading.

Greg hadn't been exaggerating. This woman was hard core.

Katy placed her hands in her lap to control her nervous energy, crossing and uncrossing her legs at uneven intervals. Her stockings were itchy.

"Well," Claire said, removing her glasses and flinging them onto the desk. "I have to say, you prepared more than the others." She swiveled her chair and dumped the business plan into the trash. *Thud.*

Katy's mouth opened, but no words came forth.

"Listen, Kate. May I call you Kate?" Claire didn't wait for approval. "You're not the first 'special' friend my son has sent to me."

Son? Son? "Greg didn't tell me he was your son."

"He's not allowed. The instant someone asks him for money, he's to send them to me." Claire removed a checkbook from the desk drawer, making a grand gesture of opening it. Her pen circled like a plane waiting to land. "How much?"

Lost in confusion, Katy had yet to close her mouth. Her mind filled with sand. "You're funding my project? But then why…" She gestured toward the trash can.

Claire sat back in her chair, springs squeaking. She stared at Katy and formed each word slowly, as if Katy were the village drunk. "No, dear. I am *not* funding your project."

Katy was having difficulty breathing. What was this woman talking about?

"Greg said you were different, and I can see why. Most of you are in your early twenties. One even claimed to be pregnant. You're not, are you? Pregnant?"

Katy's hand moved to her abdomen, smoothing her skirt where the scar existed, a nagging reminder of her inability to conceive. She spoke without thinking. "I can't have children."

"Well, that's good."

"Good? How is that…" Katy finally found meaning in Claire's words, and the dawning throbbed in her temples. "I didn't come here to extort money."

"Then why *did* you come, Kate?"

"Because…I told…I need funding to build an animal sanctuary."

"Pipe dream at best."

Katy's anger got the better of her, and she stood. "That's one person's opinion."

Claire's eyes went wide and her nostrils flared. "Excuse me?"

Katy strode to the trash can, plucked out her

business plan, and shook off a wet tea bag. She moved to the door, but before exiting, she turned back toward Claire. "One last thing," she said. "My mother named me Katy right before she died, and it's the only thing I have left of her. So, *no*, you may not call me Kate."

****

Katy rested her arms and head on the steering wheel, fighting tears. What a fool she'd been to have asked Greg for money. They barely knew each other outside of the bedroom. Obviously, she'd never met his mother.

Katy dialed Lori's number.

"How'd it go?" Lori asked without saying hello. Her voice was breathless and full of anticipation, as if she'd been waiting by the phone.

"It…it…it didn't," Katy spurted with no attempt to hide the pain.

"Oh, no. What happened?"

"Too much to say over the phone," Katy said. "Are you free for a late lunch? I cleared my schedule for this afternoon."

"You bet. Where?"

"I don't know. I'll call you when I get there."

Starting the car and checking mirrors before entering traffic, Katy was surprised to see the receptionist on the sidewalk, holding something in her hand. Katy stopped the engine, stepped out of the car, and shortened the gap between them.

"You forgot this, Ms. Moore," the receptionist said and gave Katy her satchel.

"Thank you. How'd you know where I was?"

"I watched from the office window as you left the building. You've been here a while."

"Ah. Well. Very kind of you to return this to me."

"Claire's furious," the receptionist blurted.

"Oh?"

"No one's ever walked out on her."

"I find that hard to believe, considering her attitude toward prospective clients."

"She's only that way with Greg's girlfriends. She treats her real clients very well."

"I see." Of course. Katy was only one of Greg's girlfriends in his mother's eyes. How many others, she wondered, have sat in those same chairs, sweating in their stockings? "Well, thanks again."

"No one's ever refused her offer either."

Katy hesitated. "Really? Because I thought that was the most demeaning part of all."

"Don't you see? The few who've come before were thrilled to leave with a check, because they didn't care at all about Greg. Claire would've given you as much as ten thousand dollars to dump Greg."

Holy crap. Katy could've put that money to good use—repair the barn and fences, buy Bandit outright, purchase feed. Tempting. Tempting. Tempting. But no amount of money was worth the damage to her soul. "Claire doesn't have to worry. I won't be seeing her son again anyway."

"Please don't blame my brother," the receptionist said. "He's a sweet guy but not too savvy. He gets taken advantage of a lot, especially by women."

Did she say *brother*?

"When Greg got his signing bonus to join the team, he'd never seen so much money in his life. He bought a motorcycle. Threw elaborate parties. Handed out hundreds like they were matchsticks. Almost lost it all."

"Sounds pretty typical."

"He was on the verge of bankruptcy when Claire stepped in. She paid his expenses directly and put him on an allowance."

"And he's okay with that?"

"He's naïve, but he's not stupid," she said. "I'm Julia, by the way."

"Nice to meet you," Katy said. "Are you the one who made the bronze horse pin?"

"That's me." Julia's eyes lit up.

"It's quite lovely."

"Thanks." She looked at her hands and then up again. "Only a hobby."

Katy could tell from Julia's reaction that making jewelry was more than only a hobby. Dreams weren't easily hidden. "So, you're Claire's daughter."

"Stepdaughter. Greg's half-sister. I'm five years older."

"I would've guessed younger."

"Aren't you sweet," Julia said in typical southern manner of acknowledging a compliment without actually agreeing with it. "My father, um, how shall I put this? He and Claire were attracted to each other when she interned at his company. He was married to my mother at the time."

"That's not right," Katy said. "No matter how you look at it."

"No. No, it is not."

"And your mother?" Katy asked, genuinely concerned. "How's she doing now?"

"Better off, really."

"Glad to hear it." Katy hesitated, because she didn't want to pry, but she was too curious to let it go.

"How'd you end up working for Claire?"

"Because of Greg," she said. "He's happiest when everyone gets along, even if it's for show."

The things women do for the men in their lives.

"His baseball career is everything right now," Katy said.

"As it should be. But…" Julia cracked a smile and thumbed toward the building. "What you did in there?"

"Yes?"

"Made my day."

Katy laughed and held up the satchel. "Thanks again."

"No problem. Hope to see you around."

Katy didn't think that was likely, but stranger things had happened in her life.

****

Standing at the sink in sweats and an oversized T-shirt, Katy smeared vegan butter onto saltines. An unlit cigarette and a bottle of Patrón were on the counter.

What was she going to do about money? Meet with banks? Search the Internet for investors?

And what was she going to do about Greg?

He'd called earlier to apologize, but Katy hadn't answered for fear of caving. She would've understood if he'd explained the circumstances earlier.

"Please, Katy," his message had said. "Can we at least talk about this?"

She could see his point, of course, but that didn't make her any less angry. As it happened, she'd felt ambushed. At least he hadn't turned her over to his mother when Katy first gave him the business plan. That was something. She wondered if Greg's father was still with Claire, or if he'd moved on to another intern.

What if the behavior ran in the family?

Katy began composing a text. *We need to take a break from each other. Please...* Please what? Please disregard this text and call me the minute you get it? Please tell me you love me and everything will be all right?

Please honor my wishes by giving me some time and space to think.

Send. Sent. Shit.

Her heart sank to her toes. Maybe a call to Jon would lift her spirits. They'd been talking for a week, and she was convinced his voice held healing powers. Its strange familiarity was comforting, like a warm blanket on a cold evening. Too bad it couldn't be mass produced and sold as medicine.

"Hi," she said when he answered after one ring. "Got a minute?"

"For you? Always." As if sensing her somber mood, he asked, "Is everything okay?"

"Bad patch of road," she said. "Nothing life threatening."

"Need cheering up?"

"A bit," she said. "If you don't mind."

"Not at all. Let's see," he said, hesitating for a moment. "Oh, I know."

"Yes?"

"I stared down an alpaca today."

"You did?" She felt her lip twitch with the beginnings of a smile. "When?"

"On my ride this afternoon. I got off my bike, postured like Superman, and said, 'Not today, Bub'."

"But..." she said, losing herself in his gifted storytelling. "But, why?"

"That damn beast's been mocking me for weeks," he said. "It grazes at the bottom of this killer hill. When I pass, it pops its head over the fence, bares its teeth, and bray/oinks, as if it knows I'll quit before reaching the top."

"Sounds like a real ass," she said.

"Yes," he said. "I can be."

She laughed. "I meant the alpaca."

"Him too," he said.

"Is the alpaca always right?"

"He was until today," Jon said, sounding triumphant.

"Then you made it. Good for you," she said. "That gives me hope."

"Great. I'm glad. But I've gotta go," he said. "Let's talk longer tomorrow, okay?"

"I'd like that," she said. "And thanks."

Leaving the cigarette and tequila untouched, Katy shuffled off to bed. That was the beauty of living alone. No need to apologize for tossing and turning and keeping someone else awake all night.

Chapter 9

On a sunny Saturday evening, Jon swung open the cabin door and strolled off his front porch while looking down at his phone. Like a battering ram, his head hit Rebecca in the sternum and knocked her backward onto her butt. Stunned, she sat in the soft moss for a moment. Then she glared at him and raised her hand for assistance.

"I'm so sorry," he said, helping her to her feet. "I didn't see you."

"Clearly," she said, brushing grass clippings and dirt off her light-colored silk pants. "Did I get it all?"

He walked in a circle around her, assessing the damage. "I'll pay for the dry cleaning."

"What?" She contorted and noticed the dark green stain on her upper thigh. "Dammit! Now I'll have to change."

"Change?" he said. "You brought extra clothes?"

"Of course I did," she said, walking to her car and grabbing an overnight bag and white paper sack from the passenger seat. "Did you think I'd come all this way and not stay the night."

"How should I know?" he said. "I'm surprised you're here in the first place."

"Oh, Jon," she said in exasperation. "I left you a message on your phone this morning."

"Oh…well…I… it didn't record properly," he said.

"Bunch of hogwash."

She eyed him sideways. "Since when do you use words like 'hogwash'?" she said. "Besides, you knew it was me, so why didn't you call me back? I could've been lying in a ditch somewhere."

Feeling as if he were being scolded by his mother for fibbing, he didn't want to admit Rebecca's call had slipped his mind. "You weren't, though, were you, Becks? Lying in a ditch?"

"Well, no. But that's not the point." Walking past him and up the stairs, she shook the paper sack. "I brought Dick's. Cheeseburgers, fries, chocolate shakes. Our favorites."

His phone rang. It was Katy.

"Hi," he whispered, turning his back to Rebecca. "Now's not a good time. Can we talk tomorrow?"

"Sure. I guess."

"Great," he said, disconnecting the call and holding the phone to his pounding chest.

"Who was that?" Rebecca asked.

"The food police," he mumbled, turning back around.

"What?" she said. "I didn't hear you."

"Nothing," Jon said. "It was nobody."

"Ah," she said. "Those robo calls are the easiest to hang up on."

He felt a strange betrayal for referring to Katy as "nobody" but allowed Rebecca's comment to stand without rebuttal. He walked into the cabin behind her.

"Want to go for a walk?" he asked. "Skip stones on the lake?"

"God, no," she balked. "In these shoes?"

"Didn't you bring your sneakers?"

67

"Of course not," she said, expression souring as if he'd asked about dog poop. She dropped her overnight bag on the couch and carried the paper sack to the dining table, setting it next to the salt and pepper shakers.

"We should probably be civilized and eat off real plates," she said.

"Why should today be any different?" he said, following her into the kitchen.

She stopped abruptly, and he barely caught himself before barreling into her a second time that night.

"What's all this?" Rebecca said, staring at the fruits and vegetable littered countertop. She ran her hand along his latest contraptions. Cuisinart food processor. Ninja blender. Breville juicer. Black+Decker chopper. "Did you get a pet rabbit or something?"

"What? No," he said. "It's for me."

"You?" she said, turning to look at him. "Why?"

He brushed past her and leaned against the counter, trying to block her view.

"I told you. I want to get healthy."

"Yes, but…" She swung open the fridge door. Then she opened the freezer and pulled out packages. "Meatless Meatballs? Veggie Patties? Vegan ice cream? Vegan cookie dough?"

He snatched them from her and threw them back into the freezer.

"Where's the fish?" she asked, gazing into the fridge as if searching for a secret panel. "Where's the steak?"

"I've given up meat," he said. "So I don't keep it in the cabin."

Brow crinkling, she searched further.

"I don't see any eggs. There's no butter or cheese," she said. "What am I supposed to eat for breakfast tomorrow?"

"The diner down the street makes the best omelets in town," he said.

She straightened and stared at him. "What's gotten into you, Jon?"

"Nothing's gotten *into* me, Rebecca," he said. "It's that…I'm trying to…I'm vegan now."

"Huh," she puffed. "First the celibacy thing and now this. Did you join a cult?"

"Don't be ridiculous," he said, taking her elbow and gently steering her out of the kitchen.

She plopped in a chair at the table in front of the Dick's Drive-in sack and sighed. "It's as if I don't know you anymore."

"I'm still the same guy," he said, taking a seat across from her. "I'm trying new things is all."

"But…" She opened the sack and removed the items, arranging them in front of her like beloved toys. "Who's going to eat Dick's with me?"

To appease her, Jon grabbed a cheeseburger, unwrapped it, and took a giant bite.

Her smile lit up her eyes, and she slowly pushed fries and a chocolate shake to his side of the table.

God help him, it all tasted so good.

Chapter 10

This morning, Katy had discovered one of Greg's T-shirts hanging on a hook in the closet. She dropped to her knees, curling like an armadillo and burying her nose in its woodsy scent. Despite her request for him not to call, he sometimes did. Last night, he texted, "I miss you." If she were to contact him, though, what could ultimately come of their relationship?

Katy's plans for the farm were as stalled as her love life. Several lenders agreed with Claire Young's assessment the business plan overstated profit. Katy needed another source of income to make the project work. Children's birthday parties? Weddings? Turning the barn into a bed-and-breakfast? Each endeavor sounded more complicated than the last. She was no closer to owning Bandit.

Thank goodness for Jon. He brought lightness to her dark. The first time she'd heard his sultry voice, her imagination went wild. Who was this man? But there was no flirting in his words, so she took the hint he was only looking for guidance and friendship. Which made things simpler, considering Jon lived two thousand miles away, and she wasn't ready to date again.

Her last conversation with him had been odd, though. Clipped as if he were annoyed she'd interrupted something more important. Why had he picked up in the first place?

Her cell rang and showed her father's name. Patrick Moore. She tap, tap, tapped the side of the phone with her thumb before answering. Was he calling for another loan? She hoped not, because he still owed her five hundred from the last one.

Stepping outside, she walked toward the woods.

"Hey, Dad."

"What's up, baby girl?" he said as he always did, as if neither was capable of aging.

It'd been a month since she'd seen him. His face was still youthful, even at fifty-four, but his goatee and long black hair were salted with gray. The look gave him an air of mystery, and, no doubt, tugged at the heartstrings of singletons at the private college in Atlanta where he taught Spanish.

"More questions about your quarterly taxes?" she asked.

"I sent them off this morning. Thanks for your help."

"Anytime."

Her father could charm the purr out of a wet cat, but he couldn't do math to save his life.

"How are your classes going?" she asked.

He hesitated. "I'm thinking of quitting."

Oh, no. They'd had these conversations before, most ending with long periods of not knowing where he was, because he'd leave the country and forget to take his cell phone.

"But it's your dream job. You love teaching Spanish."

"Not so much anymore," he said. "None of my students give a rat's ass about learning the language. Or the history. Or the beauty. They want easy A's."

"Maybe some will surprise you."

"Maybe." He didn't sound convinced. "You were my best student, you know."

"*Sí, yo sé.*"

How could she not have been? He spoke little else for the first six years of Katy's life, immersing them in the native language of Katy's mother Rosa, possibly to keep her memory alive. When they'd moved in with his mother in Fort Worth, Katy spent two years in remedial English, struggling to catch up with the rest of the students. English had been confusing to her, and she was still a slow reader compared to most.

"I was thinkin' 'bout your Gran today," he said, his accent turning to Ireland as he spoke of his mother. "She's been gone well past a year now. Can you believe it?"

"Not at all," Katy said, thinking her grandmother might call from the garden at any moment for help in gathering the latest crop. "Remember her *pico de gallo*?"

"I loved that stuff," he said. "Too bad she didn't leave the recipe in her will."

"I found it during the remodel," Katy said, having forgotten to tell him. "It was taped to the bottom of the junk drawer."

"You don't say. I would've thought she'd kept it at Fort Knox," he said. "Remember how she'd shoo us from the house when she made a batch? What gave it the kick?"

"She rolled the tomatoes in chili powder and smoked them over bourbon-soaked mesquite chips."

"And here I thought she had a drinking problem."

"Well, she did enjoy her occasional Irish coffee."

Katy missed her grandmother most when talking to her dad. No telling what would've happened had it not been for her. Katy's mother died shortly after childbirth in a hospital in Cancún, and Katy's father became a widower with a newborn at seventeen. By the time Katy turned four, they'd been evicted several times for nonpayment of rent. Living in their car, Katy and her father begged for food on the streets. Occasionally, he was offered cleaning jobs, and Katy worked alongside him, shining doorknobs and sweeping away cobwebs. Her father refused to talk about Mexico, so Katy could almost believe she'd imagined it. That is, until she felt the scar on her abdomen.

"Oh," he said, excited. "I almost forgot why I called."

She laughed at his childlike enthusiasm. "Well, don't keep me hangin', Dad."

"I've been seeing someone. A psychiatrist."

Katy was taken aback but also relieved. She'd been thinking of going to a therapist herself. Maybe, one day, she and her father could have a session together, and he'd finally open up about her mother. "That's wonderful, Dad. I think it's—"

"She's the mom of one of my students. We've been dating a month."

"Oh."

"What's wrong?"

"Nothing. I just—"

"I told her about my plans to write a travel guide, and she suggested we go to Bali. Her treat."

Of course he'd told her about his often-talked-about-yet-still-to-be-written travel guide. It was his surefire, fail-safe pickup line. The first time he'd used it was on a buxom car dealer who'd driven him across America in her Jaguar and proposed to him in Maine. He dumped her for a reedy waitress at the nearby lobster restaurant. Next came the flight attendant. Then the cruise director. Then the jetsetter, a merry widow. All wanted to possess him. None had succeeded.

"What about your classes?"

He coughed. "I've got 'em covered."

"Not Peggy? Come on, Dad. You take advantage of her."

"She enjoys helping. She said so herself."

"She's hoping for so much more, and you're stringing her along."

"I've been honest," he said. "I can't help if she doesn't believe me."

"Because you keep going back to her. Can't you leave her alone?"

"Hard to do when we work at the same college."

This "Peggy" wasn't the first. He had a long line of "Peggys" willing to care for him. Cook for him. Clean for him. Cover for him. Something snagged at the back of Katy's mind.

"When do you leave for Bali?" she asked.

"Tomorrow," he said. "Gotta go pack."

"Well, then, have a safe and uneventful flight, and please take your cell phone."

"Thanks. I will. Love you, baby girl."

"Love you too, Dad."

Her phone rang again, and this time it was Jon. She thought about sending it directly to voicemail. She wouldn't be able to hide her irritation at his brush off from last night. But it was better he know how it made her feel.

"Hi, Jon," she said. "Is *now* a good time to talk?"

"Oh, ha, yeah," he said. "Sorry about that."

"Why'd you answer if you couldn't talk?"

"I don't know," he said. "Habit?"

"Habit?" she said. "Pretty lame excuse."

"Okay," he said. "I wanted to hear your voice, but I had an unexpected visitor."

"Nothing serious, I hope," she said, realizing she knew so little about his life.

"Not serious," he said. "A meddlesome person who also happens to be my best friend."

"I have one of those," Katy said and laughed. "Her name is Lori."

"Mine is Rebecca," he said. "And she doesn't understand the vegan thing."

"How it works?"

"No," he said. "Why anyone in their right mind would consider it."

"Ah," she said. "A skeptic."

"That's putting it mildly."

"You sound…funny," she said. "Is everything okay?"

"It's…well…I…" he said. "I ate Dick's last night."

What the…? Such an abrupt way to declare his sexual preference.

"Um…are you saying you're gay?" she said. "Because it doesn't matter to—"

"What? Oh, God," he stammered. "You don't know about Dick's."

"I'm quite familiar with the male anatomy," she said, annoyed. "Maybe we should change the subject."

"I mean…Dick's Drive-In. Seattle's iconic burger joint," he said. "I ate a cheeseburger."

"Oh my. I see." She giggled. "Any physical reaction? Did it make you ill?"

"A little cramping," he said. "Probably because I hoovered it."

"Be careful," she said. "The longer you go without, the less you're able to tolerate cheese and meat."

"I feel guilty as hell," he said. "I betrayed you, and I'm truly sorry."

"Oh, Jon. I'm not your judge or punisher," she said. "This is about you and no one else."

"But I was feeling so good."

"And that *feeling* is a great motivator," she said. "But maybe you're not ready to be vegan yet."

"Is that what you think?" he said. "Are you giving up on me?"

"What? No. But you should find someone in your area for in-person help."

"Say," he said, extending the word to two-syllable length. "That's not a bad idea."

What had she done? If Jon found a local mentor, he wouldn't need her anymore.

"Wait a second," she said. "Let's think about this for a minute."

"You're absolutely right," he said. "I'm struggling at the cabin, and I'm isolated here with few temptations. It's going to be even harder when I'm back in Seattle and socializing again. Maybe I do need someone in town to help me."

"Yes," she said, resigned to losing her new friend. "That would be best for you."

"Someone to veganize my kitchen. Go shopping with me. Teach me to cook. Navigate restaurants."

"It's daunting for sure," Katy said. "I wish I could

be there for you."

"But, you can be," he said, sounding inspired. "You could fly to Seattle."

"Me?" she said. "Seattle?"

"Why not?" he said. "Didn't you tell me this was a slow time for you work-wise?"

"Yes, and that means I'm not making money," she said. "So I can't afford a vacation."

"I'd pay for the flight and all your meals. And you could stay in my guesthouse."

"You have a guesthouse?"

"A small cottage off the main," he said. "Two bedrooms with a kitchen and tiny bath."

It was the same description as the farmhouse, and she almost snorted. But she let him continue without interruption.

"The guesthouse was built for the caretaker's family years ago, but I've updated it," he said, going into sales-pitch mode. "It opens onto a nice garden overlooking the Sound, and there are some restaurants and shops within walking distance. You'd feel right at home, I think."

Not any home she'd ever lived in. How wealthy was this guy? Cabin on Bainbridge Island? Water view in pricey Seattle? Property that needed a caretaker? She hadn't thought to ask what he did for a living. Maybe he inherited and didn't need to work.

"I'd pay you for your time," he said.

"What?" she said. "Oh, that's not necessary."

"To make it official. I want to hire you for a week to be my vegan consultant. All expenses paid, plus an hourly rate. What do you say?"

"I'd say you're crazy," she said. "But let's make it

happen."

****

Jon's heart ping-ponged in his chest at the thought of meeting Katy. Her voice sounded like musical notes perfectly pitched. Even when she was annoyed, as was evident after his rude phone dismissal, her tone was never grating. And when she laughed? Oh, boy. Warmth surged through his body into his fingertips and toes.

Even though he'd acted on impulse when he invited her to Seattle, he was certain it was the perfect solution. He responded well to her teaching methods, and, based on their previous conversations, he believed her to be trustworthy.

"You're gonna love Seattle," he said.

"I'm sure I will," she said. "But if we're going to meet, we should exchange pictures."

Crap. It was a reasonable suggestion, and she'd find out soon enough who he was. But he didn't want her Googling him without context. Still. It was unrealistic to believe he could keep his secret until they met in person.

"I'll need a minute to find a good one," he said. "Can I call you back?"

"Sure," she said.

Jon sprinted to his bedroom and flung open the closet door. He grabbed a dusty shoebox off the top shelf and returned to the dining table. Flipping through favorite doodles, comic strip clippings, and baseball cards, he finally found a stack of old photographs held together with a rubber band. He placed a few on the tabletop and used his cell to create digital versions. He texted the first one to Katy, and his phone rang soon after.

"Ha. I see what you're up to," she said, laughing. "Cute baby picture. Is that a stuffed zebra in your crib?"

"It's supposed to be a dog, but my mother messed up the pattern, so its head is disproportionate to the rest of its body," he said. "Your turn."

"Give me a minute, will you?" she said. "I need to rethink my choice."

"I'll wait."

Two minutes later, he received Katy's picture.

"Awww," he said. "You're so little on that horse."

"She was my first. Her name was Miss Peabody," she said. "I was six."

"Brave girl," he said.

Jon sent a picture from a family campout at Beckler when he was eight. His too-short shorts exposed knobby knees, and his fishing hat obscured all but his toothless grin.

Katy countered with a photo from Halloween. Auburn pigtails, smattering of freckles, and a green plaid dress. She looked exactly like Pippi Longstocking from the Swedish books his mother loved as a child.

"Great costume," he said.

"It wasn't a costume." She laughed. "That was my school picture."

"Oh, no," he said, chuckling. "I need to step up my game."

Jon chose his prom photo, taken by his mother. He stood alone on the back deck in a powder-blue suit belonging to his father. Most of Jon's face was in shadow from the mid-May sun.

"Where's your date?" she asked.

"Rebecca was supposed to go, but she had mono."

"Awww," she said. "You had to go alone?"

"It's okay. I was working that night anyway."

"Afterward?"

"No," he said. "My band was the entertainment."

"Oh, wow," Katy said. "Any good?"

"We held our own."

The next photo Katy sent was on a catamaran. Although her sunglasses covered most of her face, her thirty-something body was lean and strong in boy shorts and tank. Lovely, he thought.

It was time to reveal his true self. He chose a picture from last year, showing him onstage at the Gorge Amphitheater—his favorite venue. He was looking down at his guitar with a concentrated expression as if lost in the music. There was no mistaking his identity.

"No way." She laughed. "I can't believe it."

"Listen," he said. "I'm sorry I didn't tell—"

"You had to pick him?"

"What?"

"I mean, you do kind of sound like him," she said. "But couldn't you choose someone like Dave Matthews? Or Tim McGraw? Or Adam Levine? Or that guy from Train?"

"I…uh…" he had absolutely no idea what to say. "What do you have against Noe Burke?"

"Well…um…" she said. "Does it really matter?"

"You heard about his breakdown," he said. "Is that it?"

"What breakdown?"

"Uh…never mind," he said. "You don't like him as a person?"

"I've only met him once, so I couldn't say."

Jon's heart skipped, and his voice cracked like a pubescent teen. "You've met him?"

"Well, yeah, kind of. But don't go fan-crazy about it. He wouldn't know me if he saw me," she said. "It was at a charity concert in Fort Worth. We didn't even speak."

Charity concert in Fort Worth? When was that? Six months ago? He'd met hundreds of strangers since.

"It's his music then," he said. "You hate his music?"

"It's not that, Jon," she said. "Why are you so upset? Is he a friend of yours?"

"Not exactly," he said, grasping to regain control. "I need to know what you think of him."

"Clearly you're a *huge* fan, as was I," she said, sounding strained. "Once."

"Once?"

"But his music brings sad memories of a newly failed relationship."

"Oh…well…I…"

"Happy now?"

Of course he wasn't happy. His whole musical career, he'd been unfairly credited for couplings and un-couplings. But this was different. This was someone he hoped to know on a personal level. He didn't want his presence, his very being, to be a nagging reminder of someone Katy once loved.

"I'm really sorry," she said. "I didn't mean to take my frustrations out on you."

"No. It's okay," he said. "I know what heartbreak feels like."

"It's that, well, I'm still not over it. I even switched to country music to avoid the hurt," she said. "And that's why I'm so grateful for your friendship. No pressure for anything more."

And there it was. She only wanted friendship. Nothing more.

Time to change the subject.

"What do you think BBQMonsterMan is really like?" he asked.

"What? Oh, ha," she said. "What made you think of him?"

"It's how you and I met. I'm going with the obvious. Napoleon-sized. Drives a big truck. Shoots signs for fun."

Katy laughed. Thank goodness.

"I'm thinking small-town preacher," she said. "Fire and brimstone on and off the pulpit."

"I can see him at the church picnic," he said. "Brandishing tongs to punctuate a point and splattering the congregation with BBQ sauce."

"His wife in the background, spiking her punch with vodka and falling into the bushes."

"How soon can you come to Seattle?" he asked.

"Wow," she said. "Your subject changes are giving me whiplash."

"Sorry. I was thinking about your visit. Things I need to do," he said. "Button-up the cabin. Air out the guesthouse. Stuff like that."

"How long will it take?"

"A couple of days?"

"That fast?" she said. "I'll need a week."

"You got it," he said. "What do you want to do for fun while you're here?"

"Oh, I don't know," she said. "It's your hometown. You decide."

"Pike Place Market. Pioneer Square. The Space Needle. Snoqualmie Falls."

"Sno-what-y-what?"

"Oh, ah," he said. "Lots of places have Native American names."

"Good to know," she said. "I pulled up the forecast. Looks a little wet."

"There's no bad weather, just bad clothing."

"Says the man wearing a duck suit."

"Now that's an image." He chuckled. "You might want to check a bag. Plan for the worst and hope for the best."

"Or," she said, "I could run to Target if I need anything."

"Yeah," he said. "We have one of those."

"Well, I should hope so," she said. "It's not like you live in Siberia."

While talking with Katy, Jon opened a website listing weekly events. There were concerts at the Tractor Tavern and new movies at the Majestic Bay. He looked up the Mariner schedule.

"Huh," he said. "Talk about coincidence."

"What?"

"The Mariners are playing the Rangers while you're in town. Do you like baseball?"

He heard something sounding like choking on the other end.

"Are you all right?" he said. "Katy?"

"Yes," she said, sputtering. "Wrong pipe. I'll be fine."

"Okay, good," he said. "I'll need your official name and birth date to book airfare. We'll play the rest by ear."

Chapter 11

The following night, Katy and Lori met on the deck of Bird Café in Sundance Square. The fire in the pit was lit and dancing, and the twinkling tree lights matched Katy's high mood.

"I'm flying to Seattle in a week," she said as casually as she could muster. "To see Jon."

Lori dropped her menu and stared at Katy. "You're going where when?"

"Seattle. In a week," Katy said. "Jon's hired me to be his 'vegan consultant.'"

"Is that even a thing?"

"If it wasn't, it is now," Katy said and laughed.

"But you'll take a hit on last minute airfare and lodging. How will you afford that?"

"I won't be spending a dime," Katy said. "He's covering all my expenses, plus a minimum of $2500. And he's paying me in advance."

"Seriously?" Lori said. "Who is this guy?"

"I guess I'll find out soon enough," Katy said.

"What does he expect of you?"

"To veganize his kitchen. Teach him how to follow recipes. Shop with him. Show him how to order at restaurants," Katy said. "Things like that."

"Sounds like a pretty good gig."

"I'll say. And I can use the money for Bandit."

"Oh, Katy," Lori said. "I know how important that

horse is to you, but are you sure this guy is on the up-and-up?"

"I texted my dad for some travel tips," Katy said.

"And he answered you?"

"Shocker, I know," Katy said. "His new girlfriend makes him carry his phone."

"Good for her. What'd he say?"

"Have Plans B, C, and D for places to stay. Keep my money separate from my credit cards. Leave Jon's phone number and address with at least two people."

"Me, for sure," Lori said.

"I looked up his address in public records. The house is owned by J.N. Abbott."

"That's promising. He was truthful about his name," Lori said. "What about Google Maps?"

"That only showed a wall of large trees."

"Let's hope there's a house behind all that," Lori said.

"I'd settle for a shack," Katy said. "It was nice of him to offer."

"I'm Googling *him*."

"Don't bother," Katy said. "I already tried. His name's too common."

"That's too bad." Lori put her phone away and looked at the menu again. "By the way, I'm coming with you to Seattle."

"But you'll be in Hawaii for your brother's wedding."

"He'll understand." Lori eyeballed Katy. "It doesn't feel right for you to go to a strange city alone."

"Don't be silly," Katy said. "I'm a grown woman."

"Yes," Lori said. "But you haven't traveled in years."

"Then it's about time," Katy said. "Funny thing."

"What?"

"The Rangers are playing the Mariners in Seattle while I'm there."

Katy looked down at her menu, but she could almost feel Lori's gaze boring a hole into her skull.

"Please don't tell me you're going to see Greg."

"Not officially," Katy said. "He won't know I'm there."

"That's called stalking."

"You say it as if he's filed a restraining order against me."

Katy understood Lori's concern, but nothing could stop her from going on this trip. The possibility of securing funds for her project was motivation enough, but seeing Greg might bring closure.

"You're playing with fire," Lori said. "You know that. Don't you?"

"It's only smoke," Katy said, a little too confidently. "What harm could it do?"

Chapter 12

Jon sat on the porch stoop at his Bainbridge cabin, sipping tepid coffee and staring into the forest. He'd spent the last week preparing for an extended absence.

He reviewed his list for Katy's arrival.

      (1) Buy roundtrip ticket (first class)
      (2) Hire cleaner for guesthouse
      (3) Schedule inspection for boat
      (4) Buy Mariners tickets

Everything was complete.

Checking the ferry schedule, he anticipated a three boat wait, as was typical this time of year. If necessary, he could drive around to Tacoma, but there was plenty of time for the ferry route if he left within the hour.

Ever since he woke, his heart had sporadically thumped. Why was he so nervous? Katy only wanted to be friends. But heartaches eventually healed, and friendships sometimes led to romance, and this could be the start of something greater.

Jon stepped inside, washed his cup, and placed it in the drying rack. He'd already unplugged the appliances, emptied the garbage, and turned off all the lights. After one last look around, he clicked the button on the knob and shut the front door behind him. He dug into his jeans pocket for the keys to secure the dead bolt, but they weren't there. He patted other pockets, anxiety rising. He cupped his hands and pressed his face against the side window. Spotting the keys dangling on the rack, he jiggled the doorknob, but it wouldn't budge.

"Shit."

Going around to the back, he tried the other door. No luck. He inspected the windows next, but he'd been thorough in buttoning-up the cabin, because none were open or unlocked. For years, he'd meant to hide a key but never got around to it.

"Shit."

He searched the ground for a sizable rock, broke a window, and unclasped the hinge. Swiping away the glass with a grass-stained rag and using a paint bucket for a leg up, he shimmied inside and fell to the ground, headfirst.

"Oomph."

Brushing himself off, he grabbed the keys. Before leaving, he covered the hole with cardboard and duct tape and left a voice message for the local handyman.

Behind the wheel, Jon pushed the button to start the car, but it didn't come to life.

"Please, please, please, please, please," he said, trying again and again and again to no avail. Shoulders low, he grabbed his phone from the passenger seat and searched for nearby mechanics.

"Yeah, hey, I'm in a real bind," he said to the person who answered the phone. "I'm supposed to pick up a friend at Sea-Tac, and my car won't start. Can someone look at it right away?"

"Sure thing, fella," said the guy on the other end. "Give me your address."

****

Four hours and six phone calls later, Jon and his car were at the shop. The part had been ordered, but no promises were made as to how quickly it would arrive. Another hour was needed to install it.

He'd given up hope of reaching the airport in time to meet Katy. Unable to think of any other options, he dialed Rebecca's number.

"Hey, it's me," he said. "Can you do me a favor?"

"I'm pretty busy right now," she said, sounding distracted. "What's up?"

"I need you to pick up a friend at the airport."

"Why can't you do it?"

"I'm stuck on Bainbridge," he said. "My car won't start."

"I didn't know you were expecting a visitor," she said.

Damnit. He didn't want to go into details. "She's—"

"She?"

"Her name is Katy," he said. "She's staying in my guesthouse."

"Oh, really? For how long?"

"About a week."

"My, my, my." Rebecca clucked her tongue. "And you're just now telling me this?"

"Well...I..." Scrunching his eyes and hoping she'd believe him, he said the first thing that came to mind. "I didn't think you'd be interested."

"Ha! You know me better than that," she said, calling him on his lie. "How did you meet this woman?"

"Online. She's been—"

"Online?"

"Yes. We were—"

"Dating site?"

"It's not like that," he said, frustration growing. "Would you please let me finish?"

"Go on," she said, and he imagined her arms crossing.

"I was…we've been…" How could he streamline the explanation to prevent a thousand more questions? "I've hired her to be my vegan consultant."

"What?" she said. "You're still on that stupid kick?"

"I'm still trying to make it work, if that's what you mean."

"Why is she flying here?" Rebecca asked. "Couldn't you find someone local?"

"She's the best," he said, twisting the truth to resemble something Rebecca would appreciate.

"Is she a guru?"

"Not exactly…" He smiled. "But she comes highly recommended."

"From where?"

"Texas."

"Yuck," she said. "All the stories I've heard are about backward and ignorant people, except for maybe Austin."

"Don't believe everything you hear," he said. "Katy's neither backward nor ignorant."

"How do you know if you're just now meeting her?"

"We've been talking on the phone."

"Well," Rebecca said. "I suppose you know what you're doing."

"Can you do this for me, please? Can you pick her up at the airport and take her to my house?"

"I guess," she said, sounding unmotivated.

"Thanks," he said before she changed her mind. "I'll text you her flight information and phone number."

"When does she arrive?"

"In about an hour."

"An hour? I can't get there by then. I'm in the middle of something."

"Do your best," he said. "Oh, and you'll need to write her name on a piece of paper."

"What on earth for?"

"So she'll know I sent you."

"Oh for God's sake."

"Just do it, okay?

"Okay."

"And one last thing."

"You're pushing it, sweetheart."

"Could you tone down your driving? Just a little bit?"

"What's wrong with my driving?" Rebecca asked.

"All I'm saying is…oh never mind…safe travels."

Next, he left a voice message on Katy's phone, relaying the change of plans. Right before he hung up, he thought of one last thing to say.

"And Katy? There's something else you should know. The last photo I sent you was of me on stage at the Gorge. I really am Noe Burke."

Katy was soaring above the earth at that moment, and he hoped the events of his day weren't indicative of how her visit would unfold.

Chapter 13

As Katy's plane touched down in Seattle, she exchanged e-mail addresses with Donna, an elderly woman who sat next to her on the flight from Dallas. Donna's deep Southern accent, hearty laugh, and hand gestures reminded Katy so much of her grandmother she'd been drawn to the woman like a bee to a bud.

Donna was traveling from New Orleans to Anchorage to reunite with a man she'd known from college. They'd been hopelessly in love, but her family hadn't approved because he was of another faith. He'd found Donna again through Facebook, and they'd been corresponding ever since. "Funny how the ones who said we couldn't be together are long ago gone," she said, shaking her head.

After disembarking, they hugged and then split in different directions.

The clickety-clack of Katy's suitcase rollers on tile seemed to be admonishing her. *Settle down, settle down, settle down.* It's a working vacation, opportunity to spend time with Jon, chance to reconcile with Greg. What? Her heart beat a little faster with each step. *Settle down, settle down, settle down.*

Katy searched baggage claim on tiptoes. No one held a sign with her name on it, as was the plan. She hauled her luggage from the conveyer belt and moved to a bank of chairs. While waiting, she watched travelers come and go—a kaleidoscope of activity. The same scene played over and over. Smiles of recognition, hugs of affection, questions about the flight. Children running in circles. The room emptied and refilled. Still no sign of Jon.

Where was he? Was he having second thoughts? Had he been in an accident? She pulled out her cell phone and realized it was still in airplane mode. Once she clicked over, the phone whistled, indicating new messages. One was from Lori, requesting a call as soon as Katy settled in Seattle. The second was from Jon.

Hi, Katy, it's me. Bad news. I was leaving Bainbridge to pick you up, but my car wouldn't start. I'm at the shop now, and I won't be back in Seattle until late tonight or early tomorrow. Rebecca...the friend I told you about...has a second set of keys. She's running a little late, so hang tight, and she'll take you to the house. Please make yourself at home. Call me if you feel like talking.

He said something else, but his voice cut out and his words were lost to the ether.

As Katy put away her phone, she noticed a statuesque woman near the escalators. The woman was dressed in a fitted DROP IN THE PARK Pearl Jam T-shirt. Her painted-on jeans were tucked into what looked to be army boots. Her blonde curls were wrangled into a ponytail threatening to break free at any moment. Held flat against her side was a piece of cardboard with Katy's name scrawled on it, misspelled with an "ie" at the end.

Katy felt shabby in brown chino shorts, flip-flops, and a simple white shirt. Grimy from the flight, she finger-combed her hair and waved to get the woman's attention.

"Katy?" The woman quickly approached. "Sorry I'm late. Traffic was a bitch." She offered her hand in greeting. "I'm Rebecca."

"Thanks for coming. Jon told me about you."

"Oh, he did, did he?" Rebecca's eyebrows shot up. "I only just heard about you."

"Well, I—"

"No matter," Rebecca said. "Any friend of Jon's is a friend of mine." She hefted Katy's large bag as if it were full of cotton candy and headed toward the sky-bridge doors.

"Um." Katy struggled with the rest of the luggage and followed. "What'd he tell you about me?"

"Not a damned thing until today. Got a last-minute call to come get you." She swung the bag to her other hand and pulled out a set of keys from her pocket. "Asking me to drop everything! As if *my* shit doesn't matter."

"I could've taken Lyft."

"And then what?" Rebecca said. "Break a window to get inside the house?"

"Well, no," Katy said. "But I hate putting you out."

"Pshaw. I'm here, so all's well."

Katy had to run to keep up with Rebecca and her impressively long legs. By the time they reached the car, Katy was sweating.

"It looks like you packed for a month," Rebecca said. "I thought you were only staying a week."

"I got carried away."

"Done that myself." Rebecca opened the trunk to her cherry-red BMW, releasing a pleasant scent of vanilla and flowers. She hefted the luggage into the back and stuffed it between wine boxes and Nordstrom sacks.

They climbed into the front, and Rebecca lurched the car backward before Katy's seatbelt was fastened.

"First time in Seattle?" Rebecca said.

"Yes."

"Jon says you're from Texas. Which part?"

"Dallas/Fort Worth area."

"I've been to Austin. It's awesome."

"It is, but Austin's different from the rest of the state."

"Pity."

Katy didn't agree. Austin was fun during her college years, but all that partying was one of the reasons she'd taken so long to graduate. Now she enjoyed the quieter lifestyle of Fort Worth.

"So," Katy said, "you and Jon. Known each other a while?"

"Since birth."

"That's sweet."

"I don't think so, asshole," Rebecca screamed, startling Katy.

As Rebecca swerved into another lane and accelerated, the seatbelt locked and cut into Katy's neck. The front bumper of the BMW almost kissed the back bumper of the Mercedes Rebecca had pulled behind. She shadowed the other car until it moved to the right, allowing Rebecca to pass. The driver flipped Katy off. Was that fair?

Katy's seatbelt loosened, and she rubbed the sore spot on her neck. Were all Seattle drivers as aggressive as this woman? She was tired from the four-hour flight and disappointed Jon hadn't come to the airport himself.

"Is Katy short for something?" Rebecca asked as if nothing unusual had taken place. "Katherine or Kathleen?"

"No. My namesake's the katydid."

"The what?"

"An insect related to the cricket and grasshopper," she said, having answered the question often enough. "They look like leaves and are known more for their sound than anything."

"Huh. How'd you get the name?"

"My mother saw one soon after she got pregnant. She believed it was a sign of good luck."

"Wonder what she'd call you if she'd seen a cockroach."

Boy, as if Katy hadn't heard that one before.

Rebecca flipped the visor to block the glare from the sun. She checked her appearance in the rearview mirror and flicked something off her face, taking her eyes from the road too long for comfort. "Jon says you come highly recommended?"

"I do?" Katy said, utterly confused. "For what?"

"Vegan consultant."

"Oh, ha, yeah," Katy said, wondering why Jon would embellish her credentials. "I'm pretty selective with regards to clients."

"I'll say," Rebecca said. "But I can't imagine anyone turning Jon down."

"Why is that?"

"Well…" Rebecca glanced at Katy and then back at the road. Then she smiled. "Ah. You're kidding."

Katy didn't want to come across as ignorant, so she let the comment go. The landscape changed, and she straightened in her seat. She could see faded orange and blue boat cranes and multicolored cargo containers stacked next to railroad tracks. The Starbucks green mermaid peeked over a white clock in a brick building. Two side-by-side stadiums loomed large.

"Which one is for baseball?" she asked.

"Who cares?" Rebecca answered. "I know I don't."

That settled that on which subject to definitely avoid.

The road wound around and took a slight rise. Tall, short, wide, narrow, glassed and brick buildings dominated the right. Steps led somewhere hidden, and a large metal sculpture of a hammering man moved mechanically. On the left, a huge body of water commanded the view. It felt as if they were in a life-sized pop-up book.

This was the Seattle Katy had imagined. A step into a master's painting with a devastating beauty almost hurting her eyes—luminous blues and greens, rolling hills blanketed with trees, snowcapped mountains layered in the distance. Everywhere she looked, there was something to see. She almost felt claustrophobic.

"Whad'ya think?" Rebecca said, as if she'd created the whole thing herself and already knew the answer.

"It's certainly different from where I live," Katy said. "Some say it's so flat you can watch your dog run away for three days."

A Ferris wheel perched precariously at the end of a pier.

"Ever been on that?" Katy asked.

"It's for tourists," Rebecca said, crinkling her nose. "People like you."

"Looks fun," Katy said, ignoring the obvious jab. "Hey, there's the top of the Space Needle. It looks like a giant daisy."

"It's supposed to be a spaceship, but okay…"

Katy opened the passenger window and inhaled. "I smell food."

"That's coming from the waterfront. Pike Place Market and Pioneer Square are nearby too. You should check them all out while you're in town."

"I'm not sure what Jon has planned. He's deciding where to take me."

"Aren't you here to *work*?" Rebecca glanced over at Katy.

"Yes, but he offered to show me around on my off time." But he'd also told her he'd be at the airport.

"We're about to cross the Aurora Bridge," Rebecca said. "Lots of suicides. I looked it up. Over two hundred. That's why the fence was built. To stop people from jumping."

How had the subject turned morbid so quickly? "Is that what the city advertises in its brochures?" Katy asked, hoping to lighten the conversation.

"I wouldn't doubt it." Rebecca laughed, sizing Katy up and down. "You never know what someone might be looking for in this town."

Rebecca drove west through neighborhoods, turning left without yielding, ignoring pedestrians at marked crosswalks, and navigating hills like a rollercoaster off its rails.

In fear of losing the contents of her stomach, Katy dug through her purse, locating the plastic bag from the airport shop where she'd purchased magazines. She clung to it like a lifeline, hoping the ride would be over soon. Her pride wouldn't allow her to ask Rebecca to take it easy. For some reason, she felt as if she was being tested, and she wanted desperately to pass.

Finally, Rebecca turned into a narrow driveway flanked by green. Katy caught a glimpse of the house, but immense trees hid most of the structure. The driveway veered to the right and stopped at a wrought iron gate. Rebecca pushed a tiny remote on her key ring, and the gate swung open.

As the BMW approached the house, crushed rock on the path ground into the tires. Katy scooted to the front of her seat, as if watching a suspenseful movie.

Floor-to-ceiling windows in the front and back allowed a view of Puget Sound from the driveway. Katy could even see boats on the water. The guesthouse stood to the side and looked like a dollhouse in comparison. It was bigger than her farmhouse.

"Breathtaking," Katy said.

Rebecca parked and hopped out with an easy swing. Grabbing the luggage from the back, she strode to the guesthouse door and dumped the bags on the porch. "Jon's great-grandfather admired Frank Lloyd Wright's concept of incorporating nature into design. The main house was built with those principles in mind."

"I read a novel about Frank Lloyd Wright. It was written in the voice of his mistress."

"Hmm. Well. Anyway," Rebecca said, indicating lack of interest in discussing it further. "This is where you'll sleep. I'm guessing you'll be working in the main house, so why don't you freshen up and meet me there? I'll give you the tour."

Before leaving, Rebecca handed her a pouch.

Inside were keys to the guesthouse and main house, and a small remote for the gate.

Katy dragged her luggage inside and took a moment to explore. The pastel yellow and blue décor, simple and inviting, reminded her of the beach. Crown molding clung to the ceilings, and hardwood covered the floors. The ocean breeze blew through open windows, billowing curtains like ghosts in every room.

French doors led to a garden with a water view. Rhododendrons and azaleas dotted the yard, and chubby bumblebees flew low and slow on their promiscuous flight from flower to flower. Lights were strung up the trunk of a pear tree, and an evergreen's branches spread across a squat and solid Japanese maple. A teak bistro set, Adirondack chairs, and a fireplace completed the scene. Katy was enchanted.

Worried she'd dawdled too long, she quickly unpacked. After placing her clothes in a dresser across from the bed, she stored the empty bags in the bedroom closet. In the en suite bathroom, she set her toiletries in a small cabinet next to a pedestal sink. She washed her hands and face, brushed her teeth, changed her blouse, and reapplied her mascara and lip gloss.

Walking to the main house, she rapped on the front door, but no one answered. Opening the door cautiously, Katy said, "Hello?" and moved toward the living area.

Artwork, mostly impressionist, hung from sage walls, adding accents of reds and butters bringing the space together. Two oversized chairs covered in raw silk bookended a massive fireplace. A matching sofa faced the water, and a wooden coffee table pockmarked with age was strewn with an eclectic assortment of books. Katy didn't see a television.

The mantel held dozens of framed photographs, and she was drawn to a few. Several pictures, faded sepia and gray, were from long ago. In one, a thin girl wore a flapper dress, bangles, and a bob. In another, a tall man holding an ax stood by a giant evergreen. In the next, a woman with a baby leaned against a man in sailor whites, cigarette dangling from his mouth. Other photos, vibrant in color, were from more recent holidays, birthdays, and special occasions.

Katy reached over and picked up one of the frames. There were two women and a man in the picture. All stared into the camera with wide toothy grins. Katy didn't recognize one of the women, but Rebecca stood to her left. Katy couldn't place the man but was sure she'd seen him somewhere before. How could that be?

Rebecca spoke so close to her ear Katy jumped. "Now *that* was a perfect day. We were skiing at Stevens Pass. It was spring. The snow was fantastic. The sun was shining. And we had the slopes to ourselves. It doesn't get much better."

"How do I know this man?" Katy pointed to the person on the right.

"That's Jon," Rebecca said, as if she'd answered the question completely. She sipped from a glass of lemon water. "Didn't you exchange photos?"

"Up to a point," Katy said. "But I never really saw his face."

"You're kidding, right?" Rebecca said, eyes aglow with mischief. "This is too rich."

"What's so funny?" Katy said, feeling the butt of a joke.

"You might've heard of him by a different name,"

she said. "He also goes by 'Noe Burke.'"

"Noe Burke?" It took a moment to register. "The musician?"

"Yep," Rebecca said, taking another sip. "*That's* what's so funny."

"Holy crap," Katy said, almost in a whisper.

"Hey," Rebecca admonished, tugging the photo from Katy's grip and setting it back on the mantel. "You're bending the frame."

"Oh, sorry," Katy said, pulling out her phone. "Could you please give me a minute? I need to call Jon."

"Sure thing," Rebecca said, still grinning. "Tell him hello for me."

****

Jon sat at a coffee shop, waiting for an update on his car. The mechanic said Mini Coopers were temperamental, but the car was three years old and hadn't had any problems until now. His phone rang, and he answered, looking forward to Katy's friendly voice.

"Good to hear from you," he said. "Did you make it to the house okay?"

"Why didn't you tell me you were Noe Burke?" Katy's words dripped with venom. "I feel like a complete fool."

"What?" he said, straightening his slouch. "But I did."

"Ha," she said, not giving an inch. "You mean those pictures you sent? The ones from your childhood? The ones never showing your face?"

It didn't take genius to know how bad it would be to remind her he actually *had* sent a revealing photo.

"In my voicemail today," he said. "I told you then."

"No you didn't," she said. "You didn't mention it at all."

"At the end," he said. "I said it at the very end."

She was silent for a moment, and he began to wonder if she'd hung up on him.

"Oh," she said. "It was jumbled."

Damn phone. "I tried to show you earlier…with the photo…but…"

"Yeah, I know," she said, calmer now. "I didn't believe you. I'm sorry."

"No," he said. "I'm sorry."

"For what?"

"For not meeting you up at the airport," he said. "I should've found a way."

"Picked me up on your broken bicycle, perhaps?" she said, laughing.

Music to his ears.

"You want to go on a boat ride tomorrow?" he asked. "It's supposed to be a beautiful day."

"A boat ride?" she said. "Do we have time for that?"

"Sure we do. We can do the vegan stuff later," he said. "Does 10:00 sound good to you?"

"Sounds fine," she said. "But will you be back by 10:00?"

"You bet," he said. "Even if I have to swim all the way."

****

The moment Katy ended her call with Jon, adrenaline flooded her system. Had she really been talking to *The* Noe Burke? Feeling nauseated, she placed her palms on the mantel to avoid doubling over from the jolt of pain that stabbed her abdomen.

With a shaky hand, she picked up his photograph again and studied his face. There was something in his eyes drawing her attention. No wonder his image was displayed on the CD cover. He probably sold millions of copies to women who'd die to be standing in her shoes right now.

"Are you over your little tiff with Jon?" Rebecca said, rising from the couch and joining Katy at the mantel. "Do you still have a job?"

Katy ignored Rebecca's snide remark. She put the photograph down next to one of a small girl. The child couldn't have been older than four. She was dressed as a pixie in gossamer wings and a burnt sienna tutu. Alabaster skin, raven hair, and ice blue eyes gave her an ethereal glow matching her costume. She was a miniature version of the woman in the ski picture.

"What a sweetie pie," Katy said.

"That's Emily," Rebecca said softly, running a finger over the child's face. "Jon and Charlotte's daughter."

Jon hadn't mentioned either.

"Emily and Charlotte died in a car crash about two years ago," Rebecca said, without taking her eyes from the picture.

"Oh…" So that's what he'd alluded to when he mentioned his breakdown. It broke Katy's heart to think this little girl wasn't alive anymore. Death was hard enough with those who had lived long and fulfilling lives, but it was downright unimaginable to lose someone so young. "He must've been beside himself with grief."

"Way more than he could handle." Rebecca said. "He was fall-down drunk an entire year afterward."

Should Rebecca be airing Jon's secrets? Besides, it sounded like he had a legitimate reason.

"It was all over the media," Rebecca said. "Lock up your liquor cabinets, ladies and gentlemen. An open bottle was an empty bottle."

Rebecca sounded unkind, unsympathetic. Was she trying to discourage Katy from getting closer to Jon?

"Does he still drink?"

"Not whiskey," Rebecca said. "He'd be dead by now if he did. You wouldn't believe how many bottles of Jameson I found stashed around this house."

"Ah, well…" Katy said, searching for a way to change the subject. "Why does he spend so much time on Bainbridge?"

"He writes most of his songs in a small cabin there."

"Can't he write here?" Katy glanced out the window. "This would inspire me."

"Too many distractions," Rebecca said.

"Oh, that makes—"

"There's a new restaurant around the corner I want to check out," Rebecca said. "Meet back here in an hour? It'll give us a chance to get to know each other better."

Katy didn't feel like hanging out with this woman, but she couldn't think of a polite way to decline. "Sounds good."

Chapter 14

Jon dialed Rebecca's number. He'd finished reading the *Weekly* from cover to cover and refilled his coffee.

"Hello, sweetheart," she said with undeniable sarcasm. "To what do I owe this pleasure?"

"What'd you think of her?" he asked.

"Think of whom, dear?"

"You know 'whom'," he said. "What's Katy like?"

"Shouldn't you already know?" she said. "Considering she came so highly recommended."

"Well, uh…"

"Cut the crap," Rebecca said. "You two are practically strangers."

"I wouldn't say that," he said, squirming in his chair. He should've known better than to have called, but he couldn't stop himself. "Besides, I trust her. She's a professional."

"Professional what?" Rebecca said. "She doesn't even have a website."

"Okay," he said. "I admit it. I'm her first client."

"Boy, did she score big time with you."

"It wasn't her idea," he said. "Come on, please, tell me what she's like."

"She's country folk and a bad dresser," she said. "Plain."

"She's plain?"

"No," Rebecca said. "Her *clothes* are plain. *She's* homey."

"Homely?"

"What's wrong with your ears?" she said. "Homey. As in homebody-ish. One who enjoys drinking cocoa and sitting by a fireplace with an afghan thrown over their knees. Some people like that sort of thing."

"I like that sort of thing," he said.

"Oh, please," she said. "You're a stallion and she's…"

"What?"

"Commonplace," she said. "Like a tabby."

Could Jon rely on Rebecca for an accurate description? After all, she chose the same words to describe Anne Hathaway—an actress he thought was an absolute knockout.

"And she was telling me about some novel," Rebecca said. "Borrrrrrinnnng."

He chuckled. Woe be to the person who tried to engage Rebecca in book talk. It wasn't because she didn't enjoy reading. She'd even belonged to a book club once. But she thought rehashing stories was too much like homework. And she rarely agreed with what was worth her time. When the club decided to dedicate an entire year to romances set in the sixteen hundreds, she'd quit then and there. She said she didn't want to think about people having sex when bathing was a rarity.

"What's she doing now?" he asked.

"Good Lord, Jon" she said. "Do you want me to follow her around like paparazzi and record her every movement?"

"No," he said. "I guess not."

"Kidding. We're going to dinner tonight."

Jon felt a pit forming in his stomach. "Are you driving?"

"Not this time," she said. "We're walking to the Irish pub on 24th. The new one."

"Thanks for keeping her company," he said. "Put it on my expense account, okay?"

"You got it, chump," she said. "Oh, I need a favor."

Here we go, he thought. Whenever he asked for something, she was ready with her own request. Rebecca didn't like owing people and she didn't like being owed.

"There's this charity event in San Francisco. *Autism Speaks*? Anywho, the headliner dropped out last minute—something about back taxes."

"And you want me to fill in?"

"If you don't mind."

"I'm a little rusty," he said. "I haven't played much lately."

"They're aware of that," she said. "It's a great cause."

"I agree," he said. "Okay. You can count on me."

"Oh good," she said. "Because I already told them you'd do it."

"We've talked about this, Rebecca."

"Oh, come on," she said. "You love San Fran."

"When is it, anyway?" he said, sipping coffee. "I'll add it to my calendar."

"They need you tomorrow night to practice with the band. The event's the day after."

"What?" he said, hot coffee spilling down his front. He brushed it off with the newspaper. "What am I supposed to do about Katy?"

"Don't worry," she said. "I'll take care of her."

Chapter 15

"Hey, Lori," Katy said, clicking her phone to speaker. She stepped into the garden and sat in one of the Adirondack chairs, curling her legs underneath her body. The sea breeze carried a pungent odor of fish and salt. "How's paradise?"

"Exactly what I expected," Lori said. "They don't call Kauai the 'garden island' for no reason."

"Flowers everywhere?"

"Yep, and they smell so good and they're gorgeous. I'll send you pictures," Lori said. "How was your flight to Seattle?"

"Horrible," Katy said.

"What? I thought you flew first class."

"I did. Seats big enough for two. Free food and drink. Private bathroom."

"That *does* sound awful."

"Let me clarify," Katy said. "The flight itself was wonderful. Getting to the plane was the nightmare."

"What went wrong?"

"What didn't? I was running late. My bag was overweight. I was in the wrong line. I lost a shoe."

"Not the cute little sandals you bought for the trip! How?"

"Don't ask. I'm glad I had my flip-flops in my carry-on bag," Katy said. "Let's say by the time I dropped into my seat, I felt like a rag doll dragged across a picket fence. I'm already dreading the flight home."

"Don't think about it then," Lori said. "So, how's the guesthouse?"

"Oh, it's wonderful," Katy said. "It overlooks the water. There's even a cobblestone path and a lovely garden. I feel like I'm in a small town in England."

"And the main house?"

"It's huge. Has a panoramic view of the Puget Sound…" Katy startled and brought her hand to her cheek. "God."

"What?"

"I can't believe I haven't told you yet," Katy said. "Guess who Jon really is? You're not gonna frickin' believe it."

"Tell me!"

"Noe Burke."

There was a pause. "*The* Noe Burke? You're kidding. That must've freaked you out. What's he like in person?"

"Don't know. He's stuck on Bainbridge overnight."

"How'd you get to the house?"

"His friend Rebecca met me at the airport," Katy said. "She's beautiful."

"Well," Lori said. "So are you."

"Aren't you sweet," Katy said. "I'm really nervous about meeting Jon now knowing he's Noe Burke."

"You should tell him Greg thinks he's John Mayer."

"It's funny, isn't it?" Katy giggled. "They don't look or sound anything alike."

"That's Greg for you," Lori said. "Oh my

goodness."

"What's wrong?"

"Nothing. I Googled Noe Burke and there's tons of stuff."

"What's it say?"

"Blah, blah, blah," Lori said as she always did when she scrolled through text. "He's a multi-Grammy winner. Blah, blah, blah. He gives to lots of charities. Blah, blah, blah. Gosh."

"What'd you find?"

"Two years ago, Noe Burke's wife and child were on their way home from Leavenworth, Washington when the vehicle she was driving slammed into a tree. Both died at the scene. Test results showed no drugs or alcohol in her system. Officials ruled it accidental, speculating she fell asleep at the wheel or veered from the road to avoid an animal. Noe Burke was in Seattle at the time of the crash."

"I just heard about that myself," Katy said. "I can't even imagine…"

"It did a real number on him. He was trashed at concerts and couldn't remember his songs. Then he was involved in an altercation outside an LA nightclub— something to do with hecklers. He was arrested for public drunkenness and spent the rest of the night in jail. Hmmm," she said. "His mug shot's not that bad. He looks more tired than drunk."

"He alluded to the breakdown but didn't go into details," Katy said.

"Aren't you worried he'll relapse?"

"Maybe, but he's making great strides in improving his physical health," Katy said. "I need to see him in person to assess his emotional state."

"Umm…" Lori said. "You're not exactly the best judge of character."

"Oh, stop," Katy said. "I won't fall for him if that's what you're implying."

"Of course you won't," Lori said. "You're immune to men who are attractive and talented."

"Give me a little credit, will ya?" Katy said. "Besides. You assume he's interested in me."

"He's single. He invited you to his home. He paid for your trip."

"Yes, but that doesn't—"

"Then I've no doubt he's interested," Lori said. "And you'll seal the deal when you flash your 'look' at him."

"What look?"

"The one that instills hope in a man's heart and convinces him he's worthy of being loved."

****

Clouds rolled through and it started to drizzle. Katy insisted on walking even though Rebecca offered to drive. Rebecca acquiesced but only if Katy left her "hideous" polka-dotted umbrella at the house. Less than ten minutes later, they ducked into the Bending Bough, an Irish pub. The only other customers, a couple in a back booth, were silently staring at their devices.

According to Rebecca, Jon's neighborhood was called Sunset Hill and was part of the larger neighborhood of Ballard. Ballard had been annexed by Seattle in 1907, and some weren't pleased about the takeover. Which explained the "Free Ballard" bumper sticker on Rebecca's BMW.

"Sit where ya like," the bartender shouted from behind the bar. "I'll be with you in a sec."

They chose a table by the window holding a tiny vase with a single mum. Alongside the vase were a votive candle in a jelly jar and some Irish maps. Before sitting, Rebecca moved the items to a nearby table.

"Too crowded," she said.

Within minutes, the bartender brought their menus. "Can I get you something to drink?" he asked, most likely hired for his authentic Irish accent.

"Miller Lite, please," Katy said.

"I'll have your best cabernet," Rebecca ordered.

"We've only got one kind, but the customers seem to like it," he said. "How 'bout I bring you a sample?"

Rebecca nodded with her eyes closed, as if granting him a royal favor.

"Be right back," he said.

Katy perused the specials and let out a low whistle. "These happy hour prices are more than *regular* ones."

"What do you care?" Rebecca said. "Jon's paying for everything."

"I don't want to take advantage of his generosity."

"Suit yourself," Rebecca said. "I don't have any such qualms."

The bartender returned, placing Katy's beer on a coaster in front of her. He handed Rebecca her sample suspiciously similar to a full pour. As Rebecca sipped her cabernet to test for quality, his eyes never strayed from her face. "It'll do," she said, and he smiled like a love-struck poppet.

"Any questions about the menu?" he asked.

"I have one," Katy said, and he reluctantly pushed his gaze in her direction.

"Yes?"

"What's the easiest dish to convert to vegan?"

"Good Lord," Rebecca said and turned sympathetic eyes onto the bartender. "I forgot we had a picky eater on our hands."

"I get that question sometimes," he said to Rebecca as if they needed to solve the problem together. "Most Irish dishes are loaded with meat and dairy, but I can whip up a batch of colcannon using almond milk."

"What's colcannon?" Rebecca asked. "It's not on the menu."

"We ate it a lot as kids," he said. "Mashed potatoes with kale or cabbage."

"Potatoes of course," Rebecca said, smiling. "Being Irish and all."

"On Halloween," he said, warming to her interest in his home country, "we'd hide a thimble and ring and sometimes small coins in the dish as prizes."

"How wonderful," Rebecca said. "Sounds a bit dangerous."

"Sounds delicious," Katy said, annoyed they were talking around her. "I'll take it."

"And I'll have the shepherd's pie," Rebecca said.

"Excellent choice." He wrote her order on a hand-sized notepad. "Would you like dust with that?"

Rebecca eyed Katy for help.

Katy shrugged. "Dust?" she asked.

"Yes," he said, tucking the pencil in his pocket and glancing at Katy. "You know. Dust. Dust."

Katy shook her head still confused.

"I think he means 'toast,'" Rebecca said.

"Oh," Katy said. "Toast."

"That's what I said." He flashed an expression at Rebecca, showing sympathy for her plight of having to deal with Katy's foolishness. "Made with white bread."

"No toast for me," Rebecca said, brushing his hand as she gave him the menu. "But soda bread would be nice."

"You got it. I'm Elliott by the way," he blurted and then dashed away.

Katy took a sip of beer and glanced around the room. The restaurant was painted in terra cottas and rusts. A bookcase, loaded to capacity, stood along an entire wall. Lanterns appearing to've been salvaged from a shipyard hung the length of the bar. Comfy couches and chairs circled a large table in one corner. A small, black, ground-level stage was in another— complete with stools and standing mics for live music.

Outside the window, people strolled by despite the drizzle. Many of them had dogs. The Boston terrier was Katy's favorite because its black-and-white coat reminded her of Bandit.

"Are you enjoying the liquid sunshine?" Rebecca asked.

"Yes," Katy said, looking down at her beer. "It's refreshing."

"That's 'liquid courage'," Rebecca said. "I was referring to the rain."

"Oh." Katy giggled. "I've not heard that expression before."

"Looks like it's coming down harder," Rebecca said. "We should've brought the car."

"Or an umbrella," Katy said.

Rebecca snorted. "Only tourists carry umbrellas."

"It's true," Elliott added, returning with a basket of soda bread.

"But doesn't it rain here all the time?" Katy asked.

"Technically? No," Rebecca said. "It just seems

that way."

"But it does rain a lot," Elliott said. "We just don't *use* umbrellas here."

"Why not?"

"I've got my own theory." He tapped his temple. "Denial! We do everything in the rain, as if it's a dry, warm, sunny day—hiking, biking, camping."

Outside the window, as if on cue, a couple pushed a stroller on the sidewalk, and three joggers ran past. No umbrellas in sight.

"How do you know so much about Seattle?" Rebecca said. "You obviously weren't born here."

A hurt expression crossed his face but quickly faded. "Seattle is a sister city to Galway."

"Is that where you're from?" Katy said. "My grandmother was born there."

"Was she?" he said, looking at Katy as if for the first time. "We might be kin."

"Wouldn't that be something?" she said. "When did you move to Seattle?"

"About five years ago."

"That's perfect," Rebecca said, bringing the conversation back to herself. "We could use a tour guide if you're willing. I mean…I guess I could do it in a pinch, but, really, I don't know much about touristy things."

"What about Jon?" Katy said. "He promised to show me the sights."

"He's flying to San Francisco after the boat ride tomorrow," she said. "He won't be back until late the next night."

"That's news to me," Katy said and pulled out her phone to check messages. Sure enough, Jon had texted while they were walking to the pub. He claimed the trip couldn't be helped and he'd explain everything in the morning.

"Looks like I'm on my own for a few days," Katy said. "But I don't need to be entertained."

"Nonsense. I told Jon I'd take care of you," she said. "He's already bought tickets to the ballgame, so that covers tomorrow night for us."

"I'm not sure I really want—"

"And I'm betting Elliott here knows a bunch of touristy places to visit the next day."

"I do," he said, flopping his head like a puppy. "And I'm not working."

"Excellent," Rebecca said. "Why don't we meet you here around 9:00? Or is that too early?"

"It's downright perfect." Which is probably what he would've said even if Rebecca had suggested three in the morning.

If Elliott's behavior was any indication, Rebecca could sell rattles to a male sidewinder. So Katy wasn't up for seeing Greg in Rebecca's company. And she didn't want to spend all her free time with Rebecca either.

As far as Jon was concerned, there seemed to be no urgency for her official role as "vegan consultant," even though Katy was only in town a week. She was beginning to rethink her offer to help him.

Chapter 16

Jon paid the mechanic overtime to finish the repair, tripling the estimate. Well worth the price. He left Bainbridge at midnight.

When he arrived home, he immediately packed for San Francisco and scheduled a shuttle for the airport. His flight wasn't until 6:00, so that gave him most of the day to spend with Katy. He couldn't sleep from the excitement.

At 8:00, Jon pulled into the parking lot of Trader Joe's on 14th. He filled the cart with vegan snacks for the boat, mostly raw veggies and fruit and an assortment of rice crackers. On the way home, he stopped at Mighty-O on Market and bought organic vegan donuts. At 9:30, he texted Katy, inviting her to breakfast.

Shortly afterward, there was a knock on his door. He swung it open so strongly, it bounced off the stopper. Standing in front of him was Rebecca, dressed for a day on the water.

"You're not invited," he said, walking back into the kitchen.

"That's where you're wrong," she said. "Katy asked me last night."

"Well, then," he said, running a palm through his hair. "I'm *uninviting* you."

"Don't be like that, sweetheart," she said. "She's

apprehensive about being alone with you. The term 'loose cannon' came up."

"What?" Then it dawned on him. "She Googled me, didn't she?"

"'Fraid so."

"Shit," he said, pacing beside the counter like a caged panther. "Didn't you tell her I've changed?"

"Wouldn't have mattered."

"Why not?"

"How safe would you feel after reading that bio?" she said, reaching into the donut box. "Especially when you're about to be isolated far from land."

"You're right. Of course," he said. "You better come along."

****

It'd been years since Katy had stepped foot on a boat. Her ex-husband had owned a catamaran when they'd met. For the first six months of their relationship, they'd spent every Sunday tanning on the deck and frolicking in the pristine waters of Eagle Mountain Lake. And, every Sunday, his numerous friends tagged along with beer and tunes. At first, Katy enjoyed being part of a larger group. But over time, the parties became monotonous, and she held out hope she and her ex would go boating alone. Katy should've known then she'd be forever sharing him with others. Unfortunately, seven years into their marriage, that included his bed.

After showering, Katy donned her boating attire. She'd brought a tangerine-colored Speedo that concealed her scar. Over the swimsuit, she wore a white T-shirt and sun-yellow shorts. Keds without socks finished the outfit. Not knowing how long they'd be out, she added items to a tote—phone, sunglasses, sunscreen, mixed nuts, sunflower seeds, apples, water bottle, cash.

At 9:30, Katy received a text from Jon, inviting her to breakfast. Five minutes later, heart hopscotching, she ran-walked to the main house and knocked on the door. It swung open to a grinning Rebecca.

"Oh," Katy said. "I didn't expect to see you."

"Jon asked me to tag along," Rebecca said. "He was worried."

"About what?"

"Tabloids," Rebecca said, crinkling her delicate nose. "You understand."

"Well…" Katy said. "Not really."

Sticky glue. That's what Lori would call Rebecca. Was she going to hang around all week?

The door swung wider and there stood Jon—aka *The* Noe Burke.

He was dressed in a sapphire-blue T-shirt, faded jeans, and flip-flops exposing tanned toes with neatly clipped nails. His physique was sleek and strong. Seeing him in the doorway nearly wrecked her.

"Sorry about yesterday." He hugged her awkwardly, as if she were an acquaintance of his parents. "It's great to finally meet you in person."

"Nice—nice to meet you too," she squeaked.

"Rebecca's agreed to join us," he said. "So all's good."

Katy wasn't tracking the conversation, because she was trying to remember how to speak.

"Don't stand there, Katy," Rebecca said. "You're letting the flies in."

Somehow, Katy managed to put one foot in front

of the other as she followed Jon and Rebecca into the kitchen. Her hand shook as she removed the tote bag from her shoulder and dropped it next to theirs. She knew from experience her neck had turned a dangerous shade of red.

"Please sit down," Jon said, gesturing toward the barstools at the counter. "Would you like some coffee?"

She nodded but couldn't meet his eyes.

He poured a cup and set it in front of her. She concentrated on the rising steam, wrapping both hands around the mug for stability.

"Please excuse me, ladies," Jon said, leaving the room.

Katy's phone rang. It was Jon.

"Hello?" she said, almost in a whisper.

"Hi. It's me," he said. "Did you sleep well?"

"Yes, thank you" she said, shoulders relaxing at the sound of his familiar voice. "The guesthouse is ideal."

"I'm glad you think so," he said. "Ready for a boat ride?"

"I'm looking forward to it."

"Oh, good," he said. "But we should probably eat something first."

"I think that's best."

"I was wondering what kind of donut you prefer. They're all vegan."

"I like chocolate," she said, peeking into the box. "And sprinkles."

"You could have one of each or we could halve them and share."

"Sharing would be nice."

"Excellent," he said.

"I don't see any maple bars. I like those."

"I'm afraid I didn't buy any, but I'll remember for next time," he said, coming back into sight, still on his phone. He was standing in front of her now, his eyes gazing into hers. "Would you like a little almond milk for your coffee?"

"Yes, please," she said, hanging up her phone and smiling.

"You two are hilarious," Rebecca said. "We're burning daylight, so hurry up."

Sticky glue. Sticky glue. Sticky frickin' glue.

****

Katy was becoming familiar with the briny smell of the Sound. Cider-brown water lapped against the dock's sides as seagulls squawked for territory on the pier. Jon stopped at a thirty-foot power boat named *Emily's Gift.*

"Watch your step," he said, reaching for Katy's hand.

When they touched, a tiny shockwave shot through her body. His gaze was friendly and inviting. She found herself leaning into him.

"Not a cloud in the sky and already seventy-five," Rebecca said, unhooking the ropes keeping the vessel secured. She stepped aboard.

Katy wanted to toss her off the boat—goddess-golden eyes, long blonde waves, Barbie-doll legs, and all.

"Let's get this show on the road, shall we?" Jon said, clapping his hands and rubbing them together as if trying to start a fire. "Rebecca, you're in charge of mimosas. Katy, you sit back and relax."

Rebecca entered the galley kitchen and poured orange juice and champagne into three flutes. She handed one each to Katy and Jon.

"To being vegan," Jon toasted.

"To fulfilling dreams," Katy added.

"To a great day on the water," Rebecca finished.

The three clinked glasses and drank.

Jon set his glass down and started the boat. He backed out of the slip and navigated through the "No Wake" zone. As soon as was allowed, he sped up, distancing them from civilization.

Ocean spray spit across the bow as the boat hopped along the top of the water. *Jrrr, thwap, jrrr, thwap, jrrr, thwap, jrrr.* The revved motor made it difficult to talk, so Katy watched Jon as he commanded the wheel. His windblown hair and confident jaw reminded her of Hugh Jackman in the movie *Australia*. Jon was as sensual and seemed equally intense. When he turned and winked at her, she glanced away, embarrassed to be caught staring.

Soon, he slowed the boat and turned it off. The engine sputtered to a stop, and the vessel rocked on the gentle waves, creaking. He left the captain's chair and took another sip of his mimosa.

Rebecca set a platter of artisan bread with butter, charcuterie meats, and assorted cheeses onto the small table in front of Katy.

"Where'd this food come from?" Jon asked.

"I brought it," she said. "All your favorites."

"*Old* favorites," Jon said, examining the plate. "Katy and I can't eat any of it."

Rebecca shrugged. "More for me."

Jon sat next to Katy, and her breath caught. She forced herself to concentrate on something other than his thigh touching hers. She looked over at Rebecca, who was leaning against the galley door and snacking on cheese. Her face held an expression of puzzlement.

"Is something wrong?" Katy asked.

"No. Nothing. It's…nothing." Rebecca shook her head and took another bite of Gruyère.

"You were fortunate to have the weekday off," Katy said, hoping her voice didn't belie she wished Rebecca was anywhere but there.

"Not a problem," Rebecca said. "I work for Jon, so I have tons of free time."

"What do you do for him?"

"A little bit of everything," Rebecca said, moving her eyes to Jon. "I like changing positions. A lot."

Was she going for the double entendre? Katy wasn't sure.

"What about those Mariners?" Jon said.

"Why do you talk about sports so much lately?" Rebecca asked.

"I wish I could go to the game tonight," Jon said. "Perfect weather for it."

"Too bad you already bought the tickets," Katy said. "I could've waited."

"I hope you like the seats," he said.

"I'm sure they'll be great," Katy said.

Evidently, Rebecca didn't like being left out of the conversation, because she abruptly changed the subject. "I thought vegans were skinny."

"Rebecca!" Jon said.

"What?" she said. "I'm trying to understand."

"It's okay," Katy said. "It's a common myth."

"I mean," Rebecca said. "It's not that you're fat, but you don't look like you're malnourished either. Are you sneaking meat on the side?"

"No," Katy said and laughed. "There are lots of things vegans eat that offer a well-rounded diet. Fruits. Vegetables. Beans. Seeds. Nuts. Grains. Herbs and spices."

"But vegetarians are stricter," Rebecca said.

"Why would you think that?" Jon asked.

"Because they only eat fruits and vegetables."

Katy and Jon looked at each other and smiled.

"Vegetarians also eat egg and dairy and honey," he said. "Vegans don't."

"Oh," Rebecca said. "I thought…well…I know a few who…"

"And some vegans eat only raw food, but I'm not one of them," Katy said. "Smoked paprika alone can transform a dish."

"I'm looking forward to trying your recipes," Jon said. "We'll get started soon."

"Speaking of which," Katy said. "I'd like to veganize your kitchen while you're in San Francisco."

"You don't need to work while I'm gone. It wouldn't be fair," he said. "Say, why don't you come along to San Francisco and we'll—"

"You know how these things go, Jon," Rebecca said. "You'll be whisked here and there, and Katy will be left alone most of the time. Is that what you want?"

"No," he said. "That wouldn't be much fun."

"Besides, aren't you paying her?" Rebecca said. "She should do something for that money."

"Exactly my point," Katy said, turning to Rebecca even though it was none of her business. "I'll remove everything that doesn't comply and start a pile for the food bank."

"That's a great idea," Jon said. "Then you and I

can grocery shop when I get back."

"That's what I was thinking," Katy said. "Your kitchen will be ready for a whole new you."

****

As the day progressed, Jon's appetite increased, and he was tempted to snatch a few items off Rebecca's meat and cheese tray now in the mini fridge. Instead, he created a platter from the groceries he'd bought at Trader Joe's—grape clusters, pineapple chunks, orange slices, and dates. He poured Mediterranean olives into a small bowl and emptied a box of rice crackers into another, placing them on the table.

"Looks delicious," Katy said, removing a can of mixed nuts from her tote and setting it next to the platter. "These will go well with what you've brought."

Rebecca ignored their activity and stared at the ocean. Suddenly, she jumped to her feet and pointed toward the horizon. "Orcas."

"Where?" Katy joined Rebecca at the rail. "It all looks like waves to me."

"Near or far?" Jon cupped his palm over his eyes to soften the sun's glare.

"Quarter mile out, maybe," Rebecca said.

"There they are," Jon said, positioning Katy in front of him to show her the exact location. "At three o'clock. Can you see them?"

"Oh, gosh. Not yet," she said in anticipation. "I've never seen an orca before."

The wind picked up, churning the Sound and creating whitecaps. Jon understood why Katy might not see the whale spray. But he wanted this to be her first time to witness these amazing creatures and to associate him with the magical experience.

A moment later an orca breached in front of them. Glorious display of black-and-white majesty, its tail the last to disappear as it splashed down.

"Awww," Katy said and moved away from him to the stern, stepping onto the swim ledge for a closer look. "Do it again."

"Be careful," he said, enjoying her exuberance. "You'll scare them away."

Another boat must've been following the orcas, and it sped past like a race car, dangerously close. Drunken laughter followed. When its wake hit *Emily's Gift*, Katy lost her footing.

Jon's heart sank as he watched her fall into the water and disappear from sight.

****

Katy felt herself falling. At first she thought it was funny and corrected her form into a dive. No big deal. She knew how to swim. But when she hit the water, it was so frigid, her breath escaped and failed to return.

Katy's shoes took on water and dragged her downward. She toed them off and kicked her feet, and, thankfully, returned to the surface. The waves crashed over her head, choking her. She managed one deep breath but had trouble holding it and exhaled far too quickly. She'd never known water could be so cold. Panic crept up her spine, but she fought it, concentrating on keeping her head above water. Wait. She wasn't alone. Jon and Rebecca were there, right? Yes. Yes. Yes. She twirled her body, looking for the boat. Muffled yells gave Katy the sense of direction she needed. She thrashed against the waves toward the noise, adrenaline spiking.

Strong hands plucked Katy from the water and

brought her onboard.

"It's all right," Jon said, wiping hair from her face. "We got you out in time."

"What were you thinking?" Rebecca said to Katy and disappeared through the doorway.

"I was…I thought…" Katy's teeth chattered, making it difficult to complete a sentence.

"I need to remove your wet clothes, okay?" Jon said.

Katy nodded her reply. He stripped her of her outer garments, leaving only her swimsuit. He removed his shirt and brought her to his bare chest, wrapping her arms around his back.

Unable to stop shaking, her lips parted slightly. She looked up at Jon's face and glimpsed a series of quick emotions in his beautiful eyes—concern, confusion, desire. Without releasing his gaze from hers, he lifted her slightly as if to bring their mouths together but stopped within a paper-thin distance. Warmth flooded Katy's body. She gave herself over to his searing heat and relaxed into him.

"What the hell are you doing?" Rebecca hissed from behind.

"Preventing hypothermia," Jon said, his voice sounding throaty to Katy's ears.

"The threat's over," Rebecca said. "You can let her go now."

Jon whispered something to Katy before pulling away. The only word she heard was "mermaid."

Rebecca wrapped a blanket around Katy and led her to a nearby bench.

"Why so cold?" Katy managed to say.

"The Sound is fed with snow. Runoff from the

mountains. You should've worn a wetsuit if you wanted to swim."

"Accident," she stuttered. "I slipped."

"That's not what it looked like to me."

Rebecca's assessment and reprimand couldn't hold real estate in Katy's mind. Thoughts drifted back to the passion in Jon's eyes. He was warm as fever and solid as stone. Katy's lips tingled from the sensation of an imagined kiss. She brushed them with her fingers and smiled. When the marina came into sight, she realized how preoccupied she'd been with her musings.

They packed up the food, picked up the trash, and headed to the parking lot. Rebecca loaned Katy a pair of canvas shoes two sizes too big. They slapped against the asphalt like flapjacks, making Katy feel like a circus clown.

Jon drove them back to the house. The airport shuttle followed his car through the gate.

After retrieving his overnight bag, Jon said to Katy, "I'll call you when I get a chance."

"Safe travels," Katy said.

"Don't do anything I wouldn't do," said Rebecca.

And then he was gone.

Chapter 17

Jon nursed his beer at the hotel bar in San Francisco. The lights were dimmed, and dark fabric covered the windows and cushions. The bar top, walls, and floor were made from old-growth pine. At Jon's request, the piano player sang Bill Withers' songs, and the only other person in the room was the bartender who kept his distance until needed.

Rehearsal had gone well, which didn't surprise Jon, because he knew the other musicians and respected their talents. Afterward, the charity offered to buy him dinner, but he wasn't in the mood. All he really wanted was to be back in Seattle with Katy.

He thought about how Katy's body felt against his on the boat. Her cool hands refreshed like cucumber on his overheated skin. Maybe it was best Rebecca was there to prevent him from taking the next step. And time apart was a good thing. It'd help calm his urges and allow him to woo Katy properly, and not like some hormonal teenager. He'd forgotten how exciting unknowing could be.

The sound of heels on hardwood signaled someone else had entered the room. The clicking was replaced by scraping of a barstool against the floor. Of all the empty chairs, the newcomer chose to sit right next to him. He contemplated paying his tab and leaving, but his fries hadn't arrived. They were the only item on the menu not requiring a major overhaul to make vegan, and he was hungry.

"A little bird told me you were in town, Noe," a sultry voice said close to his ear. "Still into Bill Withers, I see."

Jon turned his head and eyed the woman on the barstool. Cleopatra in the flesh—at least Hollywood's version of her. Gold-clad and gorgeous with straight black hair and luminous skin. He'd been twenty-five the first time they'd met, and her beauty had intensified over the years. He was instantly aroused.

"Veronica," he said, as nonchalantly as he could muster. "I thought you moved to Brazil."

"Too hot," she said. "Buy me a drink?"

"Sure. Why not?" he said, thinking of a dozen reasons why he shouldn't. "The usual?"

"If you don't mind."

Jon caught the bartender's attention.

"For the lady," he said. "Grey Goose martini with a twist of lemon."

"And for you, sir?"

"I'll have another beer, thanks."

"You're in a better space than last time I saw you," she said after the bartender brought their drinks. "Things must be looking up."

"One foot in front of the other." He took a swig of Manny's. "And you?"

"Can't complain." With red lips resting on the tulip-shaped glass, she sipped delicately and then wiped the rim with her finger to remove the lipstick mark. "My last divorce netted me ten million."

"That's a tidy sum," he said, noting it was double the amount of the divorce before. "Are you dating again?"

"I'm off the market," she said, crossing her legs and exposing well-toned thighs as her dress inched upward. "But I'm willing to make an exception."

The bartender brought Jon's fries and placed them on the bar top. Veronica plucked one without asking and slipped it into her mouth, barely touching her pearly whites. Neither Jon nor the bartender could take their eyes off her lips as she chewed.

"Is this all you ordered?" she asked. "It's not exactly filling."

"Well...I..." he said.

"Could you please bring two tenderloins? Medium rare," she said to the bartender. "And some asparagus tips sautéed in butter?"

"Sure thing, miss," he said, willing to do her every bidding.

"A girl's gotta eat," she said to Jon. "You know how much I love meat."

He chuckled. They'd had an on-again-off-again casual sexual relationship for years. She elevated femininity to an art form, and he appreciated her efforts.

"It's been a while," he said, smiling.

"We can remedy that." She placed an elegant hand on his knee.

The plates arrived and Jon's jaw ached from the aroma of melted butter and perfectly prepared steak.

"I'm afraid I can't stay," he said, jumping off his barstool as if it had combusted.

"Noe?" Veronica called from behind, her chair squeaking as she swirled. "Where are you going?"

To take a cold shower, he thought. But she

deserved an explanation, so he returned to her.

"Listen, Vron," he said, reaching for her hand. "I'm not sure what the 'little bird' Rebecca told you, but I don't need cheering up."

"Oh?" she said.

"In fact," he said, "I've met someone, and I'd really like to see where it goes."

Her eyes softened. She patted his hand and kissed his cheek. "That makes me happier than you know."

"I hate to leave you like this, but I think it's for the best," he said. "Charge everything to my room, okay?"

"I'll never turn down a free meal." Grinning, she twirled back toward the bartender. "I don't suppose you'd care to join me, Hal."

Hal's eyes widened. "How'd you guess my—"

"Your nametag, silly," she said, pointing at his lapel.

The look on Hal's face led Jon to believe the bartender wouldn't be sleeping alone that night, and he envied him a bit. But Jon couldn't wait to text Katy and brag about staying vegan despite temptation. He wanted so much for her to be proud of him.

Chapter 18

Katy took Dramamine in anticipation of Rebecca's driving. The pills were part of a bulging first aid kit she'd tucked into her checked bag. Besides the typical items of antiseptic wipes, Band-Aids, and bug bite medicine, the pouch also included a pack of Virginia Slims, a book of matches, and three cordials of Patrón.

Promptly at 5:30, Rebecca honked, not bothering to get out of the car. Mellower behind the wheel, she only ran one stop sign and two red lights on her way to the baseball stadium. Katy held onto the grab-handle but couldn't help the few times her foot slammed into an imaginary brake.

After parking in the VIP section of the stadium garage, the two women walked five minutes to F.X. McRory's, the bar Rebecca claimed was quintessential to Seattle.

"It's on Jon," Rebecca said, as they settled at the bar.

"Yes," Katy said. "I know."

Rebecca ordered Dom Perignon and Katy asked for Miller Lite.

"That man," Rebecca said, shaking her head. "What are we to do?"

"What man?" Katy asked, thinking Rebecca was talking about the bartender.

"Jon."

"What about him?"

"He's like a kid in a toy shop," Rebecca said. "Distracted by something shiny. Plays with it. Tires of it. Then moves on."

"I'm not following."

"First the bicycle, then this vegan thing," Rebecca said. "What's next? Yoga?"

"Actually," Katy said, "all of those are positive steps."

"Quick fixes," Rebecca said. "Like groupies."

"Wow…um…" Katy was unsure how to continue.

"Take you for instance," Rebecca said as a revelation.

"Me?" Katy felt caught in the crosshairs. "I'm here to work."

"That might be how it started," Rebecca said. "But I saw how he looked at you on the boat."

"You did?" Katy brought a palm to her heating neck. "I wasn't sure if I'd read that—"

"It wouldn't take much for you to get the 'favored fan' treatment from him."

"Um…sorry," Katy said. "What did you say?"

"He chooses one every now and then, and he's monogamous," she said. "But it usually doesn't last past a week. Month tops."

"I…I…uh…"

"If you're worried about me, don't be," Rebecca said. "I'm used to it."

What the…? Was Rebecca Jon's pimp? Besides, Katy was already aware of how that would play out based on her relationship with Greg, except for the exclusivity part. She put her hands on the bar and leaned back on the stool, examining the painting that was the focal point of the room. Her focus was off, though, and the images blurred, making the painting as confusing as an unfamiliar language.

"I'd like to ask you a question. You can choose not to answer it," Katy said. "But if you do, I'd like the truth."

"Go ahead."

"Have you and Jon…um…ever slept together?"

The drinks arrived, and Rebecca clinked her champagne flute with Katy's beer glass, but didn't make a toast. Not out loud, anyway.

There was a long pause, and then Rebecca answered. "Jon and I are kindred spirits."

"So, is that a yes…or a—"

"He's butter to my bread. Pen to my paper. Blanket to my couch."

What was that supposed to mean? "Listen, if you'd rather not tell me, then—"

"We care deeply for each other, but our timing's always off," Rebecca said. "But that's changing."

Was she indicating their moment had finally arrived? Perhaps that's why he invited Rebecca on the boat. He couldn't bear being away from her too long. Maybe his love for Rebecca had inspired his health kick, and that's why he readily agreed to remain friends with Katy.

"So," Rebecca said, "if you're thinking of pursuing Jon for anything other than a fling, I wouldn't advise it."

"Thanks for the warning," Katy said. "But it ain't gonna happen."

Rebecca called the bartender over and ordered a dozen raw oysters, Kumamoto from Humboldt Bay,

California. The most expensive on the menu.

Of the foods Katy found disgusting, raw oysters were at the top of the list. Her ex-husband ate them with saltines and cocktail sauce, but that ruined the crackers as far as she was concerned.

Katy ordered a seafood salad without the seafood. She already knew they'd probably charge full price, but there was little else to choose, except for fries.

When the bartender returned, Rebecca added peel-and-eat prawns. She also asked for another glass of champagne. Katy was only halfway through her beer.

"How did Jon meet his wife?" Katy asked.

"Charlotte transferred to Seattle from New York near the end of our junior year. She looked like a porcelain doll. Well, you saw her picture."

"Yes," Katy said. "Quite lovely."

"Jon talked about her constantly." Rebecca's voice went high and she sashayed her head back and forth, reenacting the scene as if Jon had been a ninny. "'Charlotte waved at me at the game.' 'Charlotte touched my hand in the lunch linc.' 'Charlotte smiled at me in study hall.'"

Katy laughed at Rebecca's antics.

"Thing about it?" Rebecca said. "Charlotte didn't even know we existed, until our band won the talent contest."

"Were you jealous?" Katy said. "I mean, I would've been."

"Yeah, I was. Jon and I were a team, and she was messing with that," Rebecca said. "But Charlotte was so exotic, so worldly. I had a girl crush."

Katy knew what that was like. When she first met Lori in college, there was instant chemistry. Katy was so smitten she began questioning her sexual preference. One night, Lori was studying in Katy's dorm room, and Katy, drunk on wine coolers, tried to kiss her. Lori pushed her away and Katy passed out on the bed. The next morning, Lori shared her surefire hangover remedy—greasy burgers. While Katy choked down her burger and cried, Lori explained the difference between sexual attraction and the bonds of sisterly love. Thankfully, Lori hadn't allowed the misinterpretation to ruin their friendship, and they still laughed about it sometimes.

"What happened next?" Katy asked. "After the talent contest?"

"One day at lunch, Charlotte asked if she could sit with us. We were speechless, nodding in unison like bobble-head dolls. After that, she crashed our jam sessions." Rebecca kept her eyes forward, as if reliving instead of remembering the events. "We joked how she was our one and only groupie. We all got the same tattoo."

"Of what?"

Rebecca exposed her right shoulder. There was a tiny image of a naked baby with a black bow tied to a strand of hair sticking straight up on top of its head. The baby was crawling away and had a skull-and-crossbones on its bottom.

"Okay. Why?"

"The band's name was Brat's Asses," Rebecca said and grinned. "We thought that's what people were saying. You know? 'I don't give a brat's ass what you think.'"

"You're kidding." Katy laughed. "That's hysterical."

"Our parents didn't think so," she said.

"Wait a minute," Katy said. "When Jon took off his shirt on the boat, I didn't see any tattoos. Was his elsewhere on his body?"

"Um…well…I probably shouldn't tell you this…"

"You can't stop now," Katy said. "It wouldn't be fair."

"The day we got the tattoos, Jon went last," Rebecca said. "We could tell he was getting antsy. His face went pale, beads of sweat formed on his forehead, and he looked like he was going to vomit. The second the needle touched his arm, he passed out cold. His chin hit the table and split open. Blood everywhere."

Ultra-cool rock star suffers from fear of needles?

"So he didn't get the tattoo?" Katy said.

"Not technically. But his beard grows around the tiny scar. We refer to it as his 'Brat's Ass' tattoo."

"Awww, that's cute." Katy drank the rest of her beer and indicated to the bartender she'd like another.

"When Charlotte's parents found out, they yanked her from school and moved back to New York."

"Why?"

"To get away from our bad influence." Rebecca ordered a third champagne. "Jon was heartbroken."

"There's a logistics issues here," Katy said. "If Charlotte lived across the country, how'd she and Jon end up married?"

"I'm getting to that." Rebecca said. "Years later, Jon was playing with his band, the Volcanic Blasts, at the Tractor Tavern in Ballard. They were getting lots of press, especially Jon. By that time, the Volcanic Blasts had signed with a record label and were set to tour with Nickelback."

"Nickelback? Really? Because, I think—"

Rebecca misread Katy's awe and said, "Yeah, I know, they suck."

"But that's not—"

"It was the best paying gig the Volcanic Blasts ever had, though, and the exposure launched Jon's career." Rebecca's eyes squinted, and she pointed at Katy. "Don't let anyone ever tell you Noe Burke was an overnight sensation because that's not true."

"I won't," Katy said, as if it'd ever come up again.

Rebecca downed her third champagne and ordered another, but her words remained clear. "So, we're at the Tractor, and the Volcanic Blasts are playing the second set of the night, and Jon is in the middle of a song, when all of a sudden he sets down his guitar and walks off stage into the crowd."

"Was he drunk?" Katy said, thinking she might actually be asking the question about Rebecca.

"Nah. He didn't drink much back then. Beer, mostly, but never before a gig."

"Then what motivated him to—"

"Charlotte. Standing at the door. Without a raincoat. Soaking wet."

Feeling a bit tipsy and tired of waiting for Rebecca, Katy started in on her salad. "That must've been a shocker."

"You have no idea." Rebecca picked up an oyster shell and brought it to her lips, slurping the bivalve into her mouth.

Katy looked away, but the snotty image embedded in her brain, and she gagged.

Seeming not to notice, Rebecca continued. "Jon wasn't a boy anymore. He rarely slept alone if you know what I mean."

"I get the picture."

"But he had unresolved feelings for Charlotte," Rebecca said, "and he had no intention of letting her slip away a second time."

Katy was caught up in the story. "And?"

"Within the week, she and Jon returned from Vegas. She was officially *Mrs. Jonathan Noe Abbott*."

"That was fast," Katy said. "How'd you take the news?"

"I was angry," she said. "Tried to warn him."

"About?"

"That Charlotte wasn't right for him, and their union would bring him sorrow. Like it had before."

****

Katy followed Rebecca to the stadium seats, thanking those who stood to let them pass. The weather was clear, allowing an open roof. Thank goodness, because Katy thought baseball should always be played under a yawning sky.

The seats at the Mariners' stadium were amazing. Primo, in fact. Tenth row, middle, behind home plate. Katy donned sunglasses, uncomfortable being so close to the ballplayers. She'd brought binoculars, preparing to view Greg from a distance, but she wouldn't need them tonight.

"Nice seats," Katy said.

"Helps to have connections." Rebecca sat and handed Katy a program. "I've only been here a few times. Baseball's not my thing."

"I go to games all the time. America's pastime. Three up, three down. Hey, batter. Play ball."

"I have no idea what you're talking about,"

Rebecca said.

Katy hadn't seen Greg in a while. Anxious from anticipation, she hid her nervousness with small talk. "Beautiful night."

"Makes the boredom more bearable." Rebecca shifted in her seat. "Wake me if I start to snore."

Katy ignored the comment and listened to the announcements. Her heart skipped when Greg's face flashed onscreen in a live feed from the dugout. He looked better than he had in previous games. Less ruffled. More relaxed. He was engaged in an animated conversation with another player, and he laughed, perfect teeth gleaming. She could almost see the twinkle in his eye and smell his woodsy cologne. Greg turned his face toward the field, and Katy noticed his hair had been recently trimmed and was without its usual flip. She longed to touch him. Kiss his full lips. Run her fingernails down his muscular…

"He's a cutie," Rebecca said, bumping shoulders with Katy.

The Mariners took the field, and the Rangers lined up to bat. The first player hit a ground ball to second and was thrown out at first. The second did no better with a popup to the shortstop.

Greg was third at bat. He sauntered to the plate and went through his usual routine, touching the brim of his batting helmet and adjusting his cup. He took two practice swings and lifted his left heel. Ready.

The first ball went past without a swing. Smack into the catcher's mitt. Dust flying.

Strike one.

Come on Greg. You can do this.

The second ball tipped the bat and fouled into the

net behind home plate.

Katy flinched, even though she knew the ball couldn't hit her.

Strike two.

Katy clasped and unclasped her hands in her lap.

That's okay. You're still in it. All you need is one.

The third ball was hit solid, *crack*. It soared into center field. Back, back, back. Over the fence.

Home run!

Springing to her feet, Katy clapped wildly. Her heart pounded as Greg rounded the bases. When he crossed home plate his eyes looked upward into the stands. A bright smile lit up his face when he saw Katy. She pushed up her sunglasses and gave him a shy wave, until she realized he wasn't looking at her after all. Two rows down with her back to Katy sat a woman gesturing to Greg with her fist clasped overhead as if he'd won a prize fight.

"Oh, God." Katy dropped her hand and scrunched down into her seat, willing her body to shrink to the size of a pea and roll into a nearby corner.

Too late. Greg spotted her, and his smile turned to confusion. "Katy?" he mouthed.

"You know that guy?" Rebecca said, amazement evident in her tone.

Without looking in Greg's direction, Katy slinked from her seat toward the exit. Just then, Seattle's mascot, the Mariner Moose, appeared and blocked her way. He dodged right when she dodged right. He moved left when she moved left. Then, he acted as if they were dancing. A burst of collective laughter came from the stadium, and Katy was mortified to find his shenanigans and her humiliation displayed on the

Jumbotron. In exaggeration, he touched his cheek with his plush paw, indicating what he expected in payment for letting her pass. She pushed him aside and stumbled toward the concourse. Something happened next generating explosive boos, most likely directed at her.

Leaning her body and face against the cold, concrete wall, Katy started weeping. Chatter and laughter surrounded her, voices sounding like passing trains—deafening and distorted.

"I hate that damn moose," Rebecca said beside her. "I punched him in the nose. Are you okay?"

Katy shook her head no.

"Do you want to leave?"

Katy nodded and rolled off the wall.

Rebecca took her arm, gently, and led her from the stadium to the parking lot.

Composing herself, Katy straightened and breathed in the cool air. "Thanks," she said.

"Want to talk about it?"

On the ride back to the guesthouse, Katy told Rebecca about Greg. How they met. How they ended. How Jon appeared when she needed him most.

"You shouldn't rely on others to rescue you," Rebecca said. "I've never asked for anything in my life."

Katy wondered if maybe it was because Rebecca never *needed* to ask, but she kept the thought to herself.

****

Katy made a beeline to the first aid kit, digging deep to find cigarettes and a cordial of tequila. She went to the garden with her phone, blocking Greg's number so he wouldn't be able to contact her.

What had she expected? Could she really blame

him for moving on? He was a red-blooded boy with red-blooded needs, and she could only guess how many women threw themselves at him on a daily basis. Hell, she'd been one of them.

She took a drag from the cigarette and let it out slowly, watching the smoke wisp on the wind like a jet stream from a faraway plane. She lay on her back on the dewy grass, toe-tips and fingertips stretched in opposite directions. She brought her knees to her chest, hugging them to her.

The night sky was cloudless, but the stars were dimmed by lights from the marina. A train whistle blew, and she listened to the faint clickety-clack of metal on metal. She wondered where the train was headed, and what it would be like to ride the rails, leaving her heartache behind.

Katy and Rebecca were to meet Elliott at the Bending Bough tomorrow morning at 9:00, but the night was still young. Restless, Katy walked to the main house and began organizing Jon's kitchen. It'd be 2:00 a.m. before her head hit the pillow.

Chapter 19

The morning of Jon's charity concert, he sipped coffee and watched from his hotel window as the fog boiled across the Golden Gate Bridge.

He hadn't slept well, tossing and turning from frustration of being away from Katy. In a nightmare, he mistook a turkey leg for a sword and fended off Rebecca with it. She turned into a vampire bat and bit his neck. The dream seemed so real, when he woke, he checked for blood.

Jon pulled up the flight status on his phone. He was scheduled to leave at 6:00, but the airport was already canceling flights due to visibility issues. The fog was expected to worsen as the day progressed, and the closest airports were experiencing an influx of stranded passengers. Driving to Seattle would take thirteen hours straight, but if he rented a car to Reno, he might make it home by midnight.

There was a knock at the door, and he opened it to room service. It'd taken him thirty minutes to study the menu, searching for hidden ingredients that weren't vegan. There were many. Baked goods contained egg or butter or both. Oatmeal was mixed with honey. And bacon seemed to be added to everything, including donuts. He finally settled for cold cereal with almond milk and a fruit bowl without the yogurt dressing. That should keep him satisfied for about ten minutes.

His phone rang.

"Did I wake you?" Katy asked.

"No. I had to be up," he said. "Good morning."

"Good morning," she said. "How's San Francisco?"

"Foggy," he said. "How about Seattle?"

"Gorgeous. I wish you were here."

"Me too," he said, hating to be away from Seattle when the weather was nice, but especially now she was there. "What are your plans for today?"

"I'm meeting Rebecca at the Bending Bough at 9:00. We ate there the night you were stuck on Bainbridge. Not sure if you know the place."

"The new Irish restaurant on 24th?"

"Yes," she said. "That's the one."

"Good vegan food?"

"Not many options, but the bartender was kind enough to make a special dish for me," Katy said. "Rebecca talked him into being our tour guide. Poor guy."

"If I know Rebecca, he didn't see it that way."

"You're absolutely right." She laughed. "He lifted off the ground when she suggested it."

"Rebecca texted me you were going on a pub crawl with her friends tonight."

"Yes," she said. "Will you be home by then?"

"Not sure," he said. "The airport's socked-in, and they're grounding planes."

"That sucks."

"I'm looking for alternative routes," he said. "Maybe rent a car and drive to another airport."

"Oh, good," she said, sounding genuinely pleased. "You'll be happy to know your kitchen's vegan ready.

We'll go shopping tomorrow."

"It's a date. I mean…ah…" What was wrong with him? She wanted to be friends—at least at first. If he came on too strong, he was going to scare her away. "Let's plan for that."

"Perfect," she said. "But, maybe I'll see you at the pub crawl?"

"Save me a beer just in case."

Chapter 20

At 9:00, Katy arrived at the Bending Bough. Elliott was in the doorway wearing jeans and a navy-blue hoodie, arms held in front of him. As he hummed, he tapped his foot while staring at his shoes. Was he playing air guitar?

Katy tried not to laugh, but her amusement was hard to hide. "Am I interrupting?"

He looked up, startled. "Oh, ah, no. I'm a little punch-drunk from being up so early."

"We could've met later."

"Don't be ridiculous," he said, smiling. "Where's Rebecca?"

"I'm afraid she's not coming," Katy said. "I got a text from her fifteen minutes ago."

Elliott looked as if someone had punched him in the gut and stolen his candy. Rebecca's text referred to him as "that bartender." She was afraid he'd gotten the wrong impression, and she didn't want to encourage him further by spending the day with him. Katy was supposed to make up an excuse, but she didn't see the point.

"If you don't want to go," Katy said, "I'll understand."

"Um…" He thought long and hard. "No. It's okay. I don't have anything else planned."

"Good," she said. "Where to?"

"Mind if we take the Metro?" he asked. "I mean the bus?"

"Not at all." Katy needed to remember as a restaurant worker, he was probably on a tight budget like she was. For all she knew, he might not even own a car.

Truth be told, she didn't like the idea of public transportation. It reminded her too much of riding the bus to school—gum in hair, flying spitballs, sitting in throw-up. After much pleading on her part at fourteen, an old farmhand taught Katy how to drive the tractor. At sixteen, she passed her test in the 1975 Chevy Silverado used to haul manure and other compost around the farm. But her grandmother wouldn't let her drive the truck to school, and Katy couldn't afford to buy a car, even used, so she rode the bus until graduation.

The doors squeaked open on the city bus, and Elliott paid both fares. Choosing seats a few rows behind the driver, Katy slid to the window—her favorite spot.

Elliott's phone rang while he was still standing. "Oh, sorry, better take this. It's about an afternoon delivery." He moved to the back of the bus where no one was sitting.

Through the milky window, Katy watched cars scurrying past, each one looking like a colorful bug. She counted five Priuses in three minutes. Must be the preferred car for the environment-conscious Seattleite, she thought. She checked for messages on her phone. None. She texted Lori. *Sightseeing today. I'll call you later.*

Elliott rejoined her as the doors opened for a man

who was clothed in layered rags and whose face and hands were covered in filth. The stench of alcohol and body odor wafted around him. When he passed their seats, he asked for spare change.

Katy disapproved. Not because he needed money from strangers. She empathized with that part. It was because he didn't seem to want to do anything to get it. When she and her father lived out of their car in Mexico, they performed a type of vaudeville act for tips. He'd bought a harmonica at a secondhand store and learned to play. She wore a plastic top hat and danced to songs such as "Mr. Bojangles," "You Are My Sunshine," and "Camptown Races." On good days, they collected enough to stay at the youth hostel and take showers. On bad days, they were either soaked from rain or sweat, and relief was nowhere to be found.

Still, this man on the bus was clearly hurting, so Katy reached for her wallet. Elliott touched her arm before she could retrieve it. He dug into his backpack and pulled out a protein bar. The man accepted the offering and proceeded to the back of the bus. "I've got a stash just in case," Elliott said quietly.

What a great idea. She'd keep that in mind for later.

"Tell me about Ireland," Katy said.

"It's green like here, but not as many trees. Quite lovely," he said. "It was hard for me to leave."

"Why did you, then?"

"My uncle moved here five years ago, and my mother missed him somethin' awful. I needed a change, so I tagged along," he said. "Plus my ex-wife was pestering me to reconcile."

He didn't seem old enough to marry, let alone be

divorced already.

"We married at eighteen," he said, as if reading her mind. "Too young, but we were doing okay. I was bartending at a neighborhood pub, and she was waiting tables. We were living at her parents' house, saving money for a place of our own. But then she met a bloke named Andrew."

"Uh, oh."

"One minute we're talking about raising a half-dozen kids, the next she's telling me she's in love with a pharmacist," he said, anger rising. "And like that he dumps her, and I'm supposed to take her back like none of it happened?"

"Yeah. No," Katy said. "It doesn't work that way. Believe me, I know."

"What about you?" he said. "Tell me something about yourself."

"I'm divorced as well. Similar story to yours, but he had no interest in getting back together," she said. "Let's see. I met my best friend Lori freshman year of college, when I was studying in the library loft. My elbow knocked over a full can of Coke from the balcony, and it landed on the table next to where she was sitting."

"That must've cheesed her off," he said. "I mean, made her mad."

"You'd think, but she looked up and said, 'It *was* gettin' mighty dull in here.' Then she laughed. We've been friends ever since."

Elliott was mid-sentence in a tale about his dad, when Katy caught a snippet of conversation behind them. She ducked down and whispered, "Shush."

He mimicked her movement and whispered back,

"What?"

"The guys behind us are planning to steal someone's purse."

"Really? Whose?"

"The elderly woman across from us."

Elliott turned his head slightly to get a better view. "The one with the carpet bag as big as her torso?"

"That's the one."

"Bit ambitious, don't you think? You'd need a crane to lift it." Elliott pulled out his phone and set it on camera mode. Standing slightly, he whirled around and snapped their picture.

Katy peeked over the seat at the pair sitting behind. They were kids, no older than eleven or twelve.

"If anyone's purse goes missing today, or tomorrow," Elliott said, "I'm sending these photos to the Garda."

"You mean the police?" Katy said.

"Yeah." He laughed. "I mean the police."

The pair nodded slowly, wide-eyed, stunned. Neither was willing to look at the other. They dashed off the bus at the next stop.

"That was smart of you," Katy said to Elliott.

"Weren't nothin'. I did way worse at that age in Ireland. But the one time I got caught?"

"Yeah?"

"I was petrified. Changed my ways after that."

"I'd love to hear about it."

"Could take a while," he said. "You sure?"

She nodded and scooted to the back of her seat. "I'm not going anywhere."

"Well, it all began when my cousin's friend's mother sent him to the store for cigarettes, but he pissed the money away on a dice game in the alley behind the church. He started bawlin' and callin' us cheats. We swarmed him and were about to knock his manhood into next week, when my cousin came up with a brilliant idea..."

Katy grinned at her good luck of finding a new friend.

****

Around 10:00, the bus dropped them at Seattle Center. According to Elliott, if you could only do one touristy thing in Seattle, it should be the Experience Music Project, renamed the Museum of Pop Culture. MoPOP for short. But the Space Needle caught Katy's attention first.

"There's a revolving restaurant at the top," Elliott said. "I think it takes about an hour to spin around."

"We have one of those in Dallas," Katy said. "Reunion Tower."

"Sometimes people place a dollar on the side," he said. "When their table cycles back, something else will be in the dollar's spot."

"Like what?"

"A couple of crayons. Rubber ducky. Golf ball."

"Cool," she said, cranking her neck to take it all in. "Could we go up there?"

"It's kind of pricey to ride the elevator, and all you get is a view of the city," he said.

"How much?"

"Twenty bucks, I think. Maybe more."

"Too much," she said. She wasn't about to ask Jon for reimbursement. "Could you get a picture of me in front of it, though?"

"You bet," he said, taking her phone.

While they scouted the best spot, a passerby offered to take their picture together.

"Move in closer." The woman said, speaking with a slight German accent. "You make a cute couple."

"We're not a couple," they said in unison.

"Pretend, then," she said. "So I can get you both in with the Space Needle."

Katy and Elliott mashed their sides together and plastered on grins.

"Don't get any ideas, love," he said, making Katy giggle. "My heart belongs to ol' what's-her-name."

They thanked the woman and walked to MoPOP. Its exterior looked like a melting blob or one of those rubber hearts displayed in doctor's offices. Elevated monorail tracks seemed to be running through the building. Rising phoenix-like from the ground was a giant guitar. Katy wasn't sure what the rest of the mess was supposed to represent. Maybe it was explained inside. If not, she'd look it up later.

The price of the ticket to MoPOP was double what she'd expected. Elliott seemed to think the tour was worth the cost, so she sucked it up and handed over her credit card.

The interior was humongous—140,000 square feet, according to the brochure. The original idea, conceived by Microsoft co-founder Paul Allen, was to devote the entire space to Jimi Hendrix, but that quickly changed.

Katy was fascinated by the guitar sculpture cycloning to the ceiling. Invisible fingers plucked hundreds of strings, floating a lyrical tune into the atmosphere. Elliott had to tug on her elbow to bring her out of her trance.

"Check this out," he said, leading her away from

the sculpture.

They entered a room that exhibited memorabilia from local artists. She had heard of a few of them, but not many. When she and Elliott were halfway around the room, they found a Noe Burke display. His eighth-grade guitar was among the showcased items. The note beside it read *Noe Burke was encouraged by his band teacher, Mr. Hartt, to pursue a career in music. Up until then, Burke had been unfocused and struggling to find his place in the world. Burke will be forever grateful to Mr. Hartt for believing in his raw talent. He has dedicated several songs to Mr. Hartt, including "Turn Down the Day" and "Big Little Loves." They remained close until Mr. Hartt's death at the age of 92.*

"It's rumored Noe Burke lives in Ballard," Elliott said.

Katy debated whether to tell him about her connection but decided against it. She didn't know Elliott well enough, and she felt protective of Jon's privacy.

"Do you like Noe Burke's music?" she asked.

"Are you kidding," he said, eyes widening. "It's hatchet."

"Is that good or bad?"

"Oh," he said. "It's absolutely brilliant."

Lifting his arms as if he were holding a guitar, he stepped forward to an invisible microphone, and his face became serious as he strummed the air. Mimicking Noe Burke's mannerisms, Elliott sang a recent hit. His voice was slightly higher, and his Irish brogue was evident, but Katy was impressed with his sincere rendition.

Whiskey's blood runs through my soul, spilling in

the weed
> *Hearts surrender to the ghost, willing not to beat*
> *Time does heal, or so we're told, evidence unfound*
> *Burying pain of dying slow by diving underground*

The lyrics held more meaning now she knew about the accident and Jon's breakdown.

"Are you busy tonight?" she asked, thinking what a thrill it'd be for Elliott to meet Noe Burke at the pub crawl. "I'll be in Ballard with Rebecca and her friends. Would you like to come along?"

"Ballard with ol' what's-her-name?" Elliott dropped his hands and smiled shyly. "You don't think she'll mind?"

"Maybe. But if she does," Katy said, "you can hang with me."

"All right, but I can't make it until later," he said. "I promised my mum I'd help her move some furniture."

"Then I'll give you my number," she said. "You can text me when you're available, and I'll tell you where we are."

Katy was beginning to understand her father's fascination with chance encounters and the thrill of experiencing new things.

****

Minutes before 7:00, Katy heard a quick knock.

"Ready?" Rebecca chirped.

"Yep." Katy gathered her things and locked the door.

"You look like you're feeling better," Rebecca noted. "Did you enjoy your day with that bartender?"

"I did," Katy said. "So much so, I invited him to the pub crawl."

"What?" Rebecca said. "I didn't want to see him again."

"That's no secret," Katy said. "But he's my friend now."

"Aren't you the social butterfly," Rebecca said.

On the walk to downtown Ballard, they fell into a comfortable stride, more Katy's pace than Rebecca's. About five minutes in, a huge ruckus disturbed the evening sky. Dozens of crows from all directions descended and perched on the branches of a gigantic evergreen, looking like macabre ornaments. Their deafening caws sounded like hundreds of crying babies. Katy felt as if she'd inadvertently stepped onto the set of Hitchcock's movie *The Birds*.

"What's that about?" she asked.

"Crow funeral," Rebecca said. "Either that, or there's a vulnerable bird nearby."

"Wow." Katy said, placing an arm over her head. It reminded her of the grackles that terrorized downtown Fort Worth, destroying car paint and turning sidewalks into slip-and-slides. "Intense."

"Yeah," Rebecca said. "They're smart birds and are highly protective of each other."

Katy found their behavior touching yet unsettling.

As they walked, Katy studied the neighborhood. The majority of the houses were wood with brick accents, versus brick with wood accents. The ages ranged from brand new to a century old. Some were painted green, some yellow, and one was even a bright plum with peach trim. Whimsical, she thought. Positioned between freshly painted homes with manicured gardens were dilapidated houses with cluttered porches, mossy roofs, and yards choked with dandelions. Every house seemed to have a chimney, and some even had two.

"Does Seattle freeze in winter?" she asked.

"Not often," Rebecca said. "Too close to the water."

Katy noticed a large birdhouse-like structure on a post next to the sidewalk. She stopped to examine it further. The sign read, "Little Free Library." Inside, protected from the elements, were a variety of books. How-to's. Bodice rippers. Mystery cozies. But then she found a southern gothic in the back. *The Heart is a Lonely Hunter*. She showed the book to Rebecca.

"I've never read this," Katy said. "Have you?"

"Heavens, no," Rebecca said. "From the title it sounds positively depressing."

Katy tucked the book into her bag, making a mental note to return to this spot to replace it with one she'd finished.

Next door was a house for sale, and she read the flyer. "Charming Neighborhood" was the first thing listed, as if the house itself was secondary. To Katy, that was like complimenting the beauty of a blanket instead of the baby. The house needed major repairs, starting with roof and siding.

"My farm would cost a fortune if it were here," she said.

"The prices are outrageous," Rebecca said, urging Katy along by walking ahead. "Ballard used to be a sleepy town. Most people made a living in the shipyards, or in lumber, or by building planes. Hard work."

"What was it like?" Katy said. "Growing up here?"

"We spent a ton of time outdoors. Jon taught me

how to whistle. I taught him how to dive off the high board. Our favorite activity was swinging on an old tire. We found one in a vacant lot a few blocks away and rolled it down the street to my house. After hosing off dead bugs and dog pee, we tied it to a tree in the backyard. I could go higher than anyone."

"Sounds fun."

"I broke my arm jumping off, and my parents took it down before anyone else got hurt. God, we were wild. Feral really."

Katy smiled. How great would it have been to be part of a kid pack—wolves in children's clothing? Even now, it appealed to her sense of adventure and tapped into her longing to belong.

"Then Charlotte changed everything." Rebecca's tone held melancholia. "Jon blames himself for the accident."

"Why?" Katy said. "He wasn't even there."

"It was supposed to be a family trip," she said. "If he hadn't allowed work to get in the way, Charlotte wouldn't have driven home in the middle of the night and fallen asleep at the wheel."

They walked in silence for a while, navigating uneven sidewalks buckled by tree roots. Katy snapped a few stems from blooming lavender bushes and stuck them in her pocket.

The two arrived in downtown around 6:30. Katy followed Rebecca into the pub and was momentarily blinded by the darkness. They walked down a narrow hallway and into a vast space that reminded her of a grade-school lunchroom. The long tables encouraged communal eating. White pegboard lined the walls with child-like art for sale.

Rebecca waved to two women and two men sitting on benches at a picnic table in the back corner. The way they were paired—one of each on each side—Katy assumed they were coupled. They were around Rebecca's age, give or take a few years. The foursome rose, and Rebecca gave each man a kiss on the lips.

Katy lifted her eyebrows, as she turned to the two women to watch their reactions. Both were brunettes and close enough in looks to be sisters—shoulder-length hair, olive skin, upturned noses. But where the shorter one's eye coloring was chocolate brown, the taller one's eyes were greenish glass, almost completely devoid of pigment. Which one, Katy wondered impishly, was the evil doppelgänger?

"Rebecca kisses every man she knows," Brown Eyes said.

"You get used to it," said the other. "By the way, I'm Dawn, and this is Lisa."

"Nice to meet you. I'm Katy."

Lisa pointed to the two men who were accompanying Rebecca to the bar counter. "Tony's mine and Ryan's hers."

"Are you enjoying your visit so far?" Dawn asked.

"Oh, yes. I did touristy stuff today. The weather was perfect."

"Absolutely," Lisa said. "And the mountain was out."

"The mountain?" Katy had seen lots of mountains. Which one would be *the* mountain?

"Mount Rainier," Dawn said. "It was out."

Katy thought the remark comical. As if Mount Rainier came and went like Lewis Carroll's Cheshire Cat. Did it drop into the ground and rise again at will?

"Isn't it always out?" she said.

Dawn took no offense. "Well, yes. But it's not always visible. It was today. Big time. Like a sundae, ready for fudge and cherry."

"Oh, I missed it." Katy was disappointed. She hoped it would be *out* again before she left.

"Rebecca told us you were from Fort Worth," Dawn said. "I have a friend from Houston, but I've never been."

"I've never been there either," Lisa said. "But I don't know how anyone could live in that godforsaken state."

"Lisa!" Dawn admonished.

"What? It's so hot and there are, like, what? A bazillion bugs?"

For someone who'd never been there, Lisa had some pretty strong opinions about the enormous state.

"It has its charms," Katy said.

"Like what?" Lisa asked.

"Not all bugs are disgusting. For instance, fireflies are like tiny, twinkling stars," Katy said. "The people are genuinely friendly, and they'll literally give you the shirt off their back if they think you need it. Also, you can sit outside at midnight in shorts and a T-shirt and sip frozen margaritas without getting cold. And the Tex-Mex is delicious!"

"Okay," Lisa said. "What else?"

"The sweet smells and tastes of honeysuckle and jasmine, wide open spaces, warm-water beaches," Katy said. "Lightning storms."

"Lightning storms? Are you kidding?" Dawn said. "Who would think lightning storms were a good thing?"

"I'm not saying everyone likes them, but I do. I flip off all the lights, grab a cold beer, and curl up on the porch swing. It's like watching a laser light show with attitude. Sheet and bolt."

"Sheet and bolt?" Lisa said.

"Two kinds of lightning," Katy said. "Sheet lights up the entire sky as if it's midday and bolt can take down a tree with one zap."

"Oh," Dawn said, looking at Katy as if she'd been dropped as a child. "The warm-water beaches sound nice."

"How often do you do these pub crawls?" Katy asked.

"Twice a year," Lisa said. "It's a chance to let loose."

"Next time, we're going on the pedal-powered one," Dawn said. "You rent this contraption that holds about sixteen people, and each person has to do their part to keep it going."

"Sounds like a lot of work to me," Lisa said.

"It does," Katy agreed.

The two husbands and Rebecca returned to the table with a pitcher and six beer glasses.

"The first round was free," Rebecca boasted and scooted next to Katy. "Who're we missing?"

Lisa ticked her fingers as she rattled off names. "Dave and Ann. Jennie and Matt. Deb and Shawn."

"What about Carl and James?" Rebecca asked.

"Oh, they can't make it," Dawn said. "Babysitter problems."

"That's too bad," Rebecca said. "I was looking forward to catching up."

As the evening progressed, the group tangled into a

mess. Drinks flowed, and Katy became confused as to who was who and with whom. After calling several people by the wrong name, she clammed up and observed.

It was clear they'd all known each other for years. Someone was planning to visit England, seeking recommendations for cheap, yet clean, hotels. Two of them, coupled years before, took turns criticizing and praising each other's lives as their spouses spoke with others. Shenanigan-bragging melted and melded across the table like toffee on a hot sidewalk. No one bothered to include her in the conversation.

On her way back from the bathroom at the third bar, Katy found Elliott.

"Well, hello stranger," she said, leading him to the table. "It's about time you got here."

When they arrived, Rebecca slapped Elliott's chest with the back of her hand. "It's the bartender."

"Hello everyone," he said to the rest of the group. "I'm Elliott."

"Wait a minute," Tony said. "I've seen you before."

"Oh, yeah?" Elliott said.

"Aren't you the owner of the Irish pub on 24th? The Leaning Branch?"

"The Bending Bough," Elliott corrected.

"That's a rockin' place," Tony stood and shook Elliott's hand. "We were there about a month ago, sitting at the bar. There was a great band playing."

"I think I remember you," Elliot said, possibly out of politeness.

"Sit down," said Tony. "There's plenty left in the pitcher. Care for a pint?"

"Don't mind if I do." Elliott squeezed next to Katy and poured himself a beer. He flung an arm over the booth and around Katy's shoulders.

"Silly me," Rebecca said. "I thought you were the bartender."

"I *am* the bartender. And server. And cook."

"But you're so much more than that," Rebecca said, stroking his ego from across the table.

"Not really," he said, turning to Katy. "I had a great time today."

"Me too." She smiled.

Elliott stayed about an hour, and Katy stepped outside with him to say goodbye.

"What's up with Rebecca?" Elliott asked.

"What do you mean?"

"Is she a friend of yours?"

"No. She's best friends with the guy I came to see," she said. "His name's Jon."

"Well…" he hesitated. "She doesn't seem to like you very much."

"She's hard to read," Katy said. "One minute she's stand-offish and the next she's helpful. She's trying to decide if I'm good or bad for Jon."

"Why? Is he your boyfriend?"

"Heck, no," Katy said. "We're strictly business."

"In that case, come with me," he said. "I'm going to a midnight movie."

Her heart wanted to go with him. No one would miss her, she was sure. But what if Jon showed up and she wasn't there?

"I'd love to but I can't."

"Okay," he said. "But stop by the pub before heading home. I'd like to say goodbye."

They hugged and she went back inside.

The party made it to two more pubs before calling it quits. It was quarter past one. The knot exiting the last bar resembled something from an old slapstick film. Six at once tried to fit through the door, and everyone protested loudly.

"Shush. Shush." Lisa put her fingers to her lips and snickered. "The taxis will be here soon. We don't want them to think we're stinkin' drunks."

Rebecca began to sing, and Dawn started swinging her arms back and forth. Tony hopped from one foot to the other and ran back into the bar to use the bathroom. He bumped Katy on the way, and she stumbled backward, landing on a pile of garbage set against the side of the building. She gasped when the pile moved. What she thought was the stench of decomposing trash turned out to be a panhandler. Dirty clothing mixed with unwashed body and putrid breath. Disturbed from his slumber, he grunted. His arms encircled Katy, and he drew her closer like a lover awakened from a dream. Gripped with fear, the only sound Katy could produce was a whimper. She flailed her limbs in an attempt to break away but to no avail.

For the second time since she'd arrived in Seattle, a pair of strong hands lifted Katy from her plight and set her on her feet.

"Is this the way it's going to be, Katy?" Jon said and laughed. "Always in need of rescuing?"

Rebecca flung her arms around Jon's neck. "We thought you'd forgotten us, sweetheart."

"No one could forget you, Becks," Jon said, untangling himself from her vine-like grip.

"Awww," she said. "You're a doll."

"Speaking of dolls," he said. "I ran into Veronica in San Francisco."

"You did?" she said. "Small world."

"Not so small if *you* had something to do with her being there."

"How is ol' Vron?" she said.

"You tell me."

"Maybe we could discuss this over a nightcap."

"Let's save it for another time, shall we?" he said. "I'm almost out of coffee, and Lord knows Katy and I are going to need some in the morning."

Katy moved to the bar's entrance and leaned against the jamb. She was having trouble staying upright—a combination of early morning activities and lack of food. She wasn't drunk so much as tired, and she'd hit a wall.

Jon placed his arm around Katy's waist and led her to his car. She rested her head on his shoulder, breathing in his musky smell. The walk was short, but she stumbled a few times on the way. He helped her into the passenger side.

"We need to get you home and into bed," he said.

You can take me to bed anytime.

Katy wasn't sure if she said the words aloud.

She leaned her head against the window and fell into a deep sleep.

Chapter 21

After a quick stop at the 24-hour grocery store to buy coffee, Jon drove Katy to the house. She'd slept through the ride and snored softly in the passenger seat. He should've warned her not to match Rebecca drink for drink.

Parked in the driveway, he nudged Katy awake.

"Where are the keys?" he asked. "To the guesthouse."

"My bag," she said, falling back asleep.

Jon knew better than to dig through a woman's purse, but he couldn't remember where he put the extra set of keys. He opened the passenger door and brought Katy's feet around. Then he hoisted her over his shoulder like a sack of mulch and carried her to the front of the main house. Even with her dead-weight, he barely felt burdened.

He managed to unlock the front door and lug Katy down the hall to his bedroom. He cradled her head as if she were a baby and carefully laid her down on his king-sized bed. After removing her shoes, he tucked her inside the covers.

She was as lovely asleep as awake. He hadn't felt this drawn to a woman since meeting Charlotte, and it scared him. Longing to crawl into bed and feel Katy's warmth, he kissed her forehead instead and stole a whiff of her lavender-scented hair.

"Sweet dreams," he said, closing the curtains so she wouldn't be wakened by the early morning sunrise.

In the kitchen, Jon opened the fridge and pantry and admired Katy's handiwork. She'd been busy. Three full boxes were set aside for donation, containing things like tuna, chili, and unopened mayo. Another box was on the bottom shelf of his fridge and a bag was in the freezer. In the corner of the kitchen were three large containers: one for recycle, one for food scraps, and one for garbage.

The remaining items were neatly organized. Cans of kidney beans were in a line next to a row of chickpeas, and so on. Mixing bowls and spoons were strategically located with knives and cutting board. His toaster looked brand new from a thorough cleaning. And the oven and stove sparkled. He found a neatly written list on the counter, detailing kitchen items he needed to purchase: potato masher, hand-held garlic press, tofu press, colander, microplane (for zesting), mandoline (for slicing), grater, measuring cups and spoons, three sizes of soup pots, two non-stick skillets, cookie sheet, rolling pin, parchment paper, cheese cloth, immersion/stick blender, Bullet blender, and an air-pop popper. And in the margin she wrote, "No self-respecting vegan would be without an air-fryer."

Jon prepped the coffee maker for morning brew.

Exhausted, he removed a blanket and pillow from the hall closet and crashed on the couch after stripping to his boxer-briefs and T-shirt. The moon was high and full and appeared to be smiling. He fell asleep to gentle waves lapping against the beach and thoughts of Katy in his bed.

Chapter 22

Katy woke with a kink in her neck, and her breath tasted like swamp juice, but she didn't feel headachy or nauseated. Must've been all the water she drank in between beers. It also helped she'd slept until ten.

As she stood, her bladder expanded, and she ran to the en suite bathroom. Swinging open the door, she startled Jon who was standing at the sink wearing boxer-briefs and T-shirt. He held a razor in his hand.

"What the...?" she said, hopping from one foot to the other. "What're you doing here?"

"I live here," he said. "Do you need the bathroom?"

"Yes," she said, nodding vigorously. "Please."

"Let me know when it's safe," he said on his way through a side door.

When she was done, Katy washed her hands and face and finger-cleaned her teeth with Jon's toothpaste. Then she opened the side door and found him leaning against the wall.

"I thought this was the guesthouse," she said in way of an apology.

"I was afraid you might," he said, wandering back into the bathroom. "But you had the key, and I wasn't about to dig through your purse."

"I appreciate that," she said. "And the ride home."

"My pleasure," he said, slipping a chair from the

171

vanity and inviting her to sit. "Keep me company?"

Feeling shy, she sat with legs crossed at the ankle and arms dangling between her knees.

"My whiskers are going gray," he said, rubbing his jaw.

Katy noticed the tiny bare patch where his chin had hit the table at the tattoo parlor. She smiled from knowing to look for it.

He placed a hot, wet towel against his face for a minute. Then he slathered on foam. The smell of shaving cream drifted in the air, heady and rich. There was something special about watching a man shave. It was the equivalent of being asked to stay for breakfast. An indication you were still welcome in the morning.

"I Googled you," he said. "Did I ever tell you?"

"Really?" she said. "I did the same before I knew you were Noe Burke."

"Oh...uh..." he said, turning from the mirror. "About my Wikipedia page. I need to explain a few things."

"Not to me," she said. "Your actions were completely understandable."

"You think?" he said. "I thought maybe..."

"What?"

"Rebecca said you were afraid I was a 'loose cannon.'"

"She did?" Katy said. "I don't remember saying that."

"I must've misunderstood."

Katy wasn't so sure. Even in the brief time she'd known her, Katy suspected Rebecca massaged the truth to get what she wanted. Bless her heart.

The dilemma for Katy was separating fact from

fiction.

"What'd you find on me, anyway?" she asked.

"You might be surprised," he said, mirth dancing around his eyes.

Katy had never Googled herself, so she couldn't help being a bit worried. Maybe her prom picture was circulating. The one where her drunken dance partner had wandering hands. Or maybe there was a snapshot from when she'd lost her tank top at Eagle Mountain Lake. Or was it the perm gone wrong, where she'd left the chemicals on too long and half her hair fell out?

"And?" she prompted.

"Lots of images of Katy Perry."

"That's to be expected," Katy said, breathing a sigh of relief.

But then Jon asked her to retrieve his cell phone from the kitchen counter, and when she returned, he pushed a few buttons.

"I narrowed it down by adding 'Fort Worth' to the search," he said, handing her back the phone.

Not knowing what she'd find, Katy was shocked into silence. The woman in the picture was wearing a sombrero and held a gigantic frozen margarita aloft, hand-over-fist. Her face was leather-tanned and laugh-lined. Although it was impossible to determine her age, she had to be past seventy.

"Oh, dear," Katy said, gasping. "Did you really think this was me?"

"Maybe," he said, smiling.

"What about my phone voice? Do I sound that old?"

"Not really, but that doesn't mean anything," he said. "My aunt sounds like she's five."

"So you didn't mind I might've been this woman?"

"We were meeting as friends," he said, raising an eyebrow. "Has that changed?"

Was he offering her the "favored fan" treatment, as Rebecca had called it?

"No," she said. "We're just friends."

Frowning slightly, he dipped the razor underwater and whacked it against the sink.

She'd be more careful to hide her growing attraction. After all, he was a business client, and she knew how to be professional.

"Your name is spelled like the katydid," he said.

"You've heard of them?"

"Yes. The katydid makes clicking sounds—like a slow roulette wheel. There's a musical cadence I might incorporate into a song. Did you know their ears are located on their legs?"

"Um, what?"

"Oh, sorry," he said. "No one likes my trivia."

"I don't mind." She smiled, surprised he'd taken the time to research the katydid and hadn't cracked the typical joke about her being named after an insect.

"I enjoy learning new things," he said. "Reading about stuff and falling down rabbit holes."

"Me too," she said. "It's a great way to pass the time when I'm eating alone at a restaurant."

Jon's face had a kindness about it, especially around his mouth. Although handsome by most standards, he was the sort of man who'd be appealing at any age.

Finished with grooming, Jon brushed past her into his bedroom. Katy was about to leave for the guesthouse when he spoke over his shoulder. "There's something I want to show you."

"Do you want me to wait or follow?" she asked.

"Come in here, please," he said.

When he opened the curtains, she got a better look at the room where she'd spent the night. It had the same expansive view as the living room—Puget Sound and Olympic Mountains. On one end of the room, his unmade, king-sized bed was situated across from a fireplace. Her thoughts lingered for a moment, as she remembered his sensual, musky scent on the pillows. An antique dresser was scattered with books, and a side chair was stacked with more. The rest of the space was filled with a variety of musical instruments—guitars, keyboard, violin, drums, and a baby grand piano.

"It's a concert hall," she said. "When's your next performance?"

He laughed. "I had to blow out a wall to fit everything in."

"Do you play them all?"

"To varying degrees of success."

"Impressive." Katy had never been around anyone so talented, and she felt exhilarated and overwhelmed at the same time. "Is this what you wanted to show me?"

"No. I'll need a minute." He rifled through the pile of books next to the bed and then another on the dresser.

Katy waited patiently, enjoying the intimate scene. Eying the stack of books closest to her, she noticed several written by an author named Kevin O'Brien. Picking up one, she read the jacket.

"You like serial killer thrillers?"

"What?" he said, glancing up for a moment. "Oh. Nah. Rebecca knows that guy. He's local."

Katy examined the author's photo. "He kind of looks like a serial killer himself. Very dark expression."

"Actually, he's one of the funniest people I've ever met."

"Huh," Katy said. "Are his books any good?"

"Too good. I can't read 'em. They scare the shit out of me," Jon said, still searching. "Found it."

He picked up a sketch pad and handed it to her.

"You're an artist too?" she said.

"Not exactly," he said. "You'll see."

She flipped the cover open and found wondrous and colorful doodles inside. Every page was filled with drawings of intricate contraptions, anthropomorphic animals, and funny monsters.

"Is it okay for me to touch?" she asked.

"Sure," he said.

She rubbed her palm against her pant leg and wiped off natural oils. Running her fingers across the pages, she was fascinated by the texture of the pen marks.

"So cool," she said under her breath. "You did all these?"

"Yep," he said. "It's like self-hypnosis."

"Oh?"

"When a song surfaces but is slightly out of reach, doodling helps me relax," he said. "But sometimes I doodle for therapeutic reasons."

Maybe that's how he coped with the death of his wife and child after giving up whiskey.

Katy turned the pages, laughing at the images. One of her favorites was a gigantic duck wearing an orange raincoat with white polka-dots. The duck had Godzilla feet and was terrorizing a port town. The people looked like Lego figures and the buildings were constructed of JuJu Fruits candy.

He tapped the page and said, "You gave me the idea for that one."

"I did?"

"Remember? You commented about Seattle's weather and a man wearing a duck suit."

"Vaguely," she said.

"Want it?" he asked.

"Of course," she said, amazed by his easy generosity. "It's adorable."

He carefully tore the page from the sketch pad and gave it to her.

"It's the best possible souvenir," she said, holding it like a precious painting. "I guess I better get cleaned up, so we can go shopping."

"How long do you need?" he asked.

"I'll be ready in twenty."

****

Twenty minutes later with sack in hand, Jon knocked on the guesthouse door. When Katy answered, her luxurious auburn hair was loose around her shoulders. It took all of his resolve not to reach out and run his fingers through it.

"Hungry?" he asked, lifting the bag. "The corner market had vegan scones."

Her stomach growled.

"I'll take that as a yes." He chuckled.

"It's almost lunchtime," she said. "We slept until ten."

"That's typical for me," he said, thinking how it sounded as if they'd slept together. "Let's eat in the garden."

Katy gathered her hair into a ponytail and stepped outside with him. Breezing past, her lavender scent nourished his serenity.

He'd set the table to resemble a fancy restaurant in hopes she'd feel special. Carafe of coffee. Two porcelain cups. Sweetener and almond milk in matching containers. Vegan butter and a variety of fruit spreads. *The Seattle Times*.

"Oh, my goodness," she said. "It's beautiful."

"Thanks," he said. *So are you.*

Jon shook the scones onto a plate and waited while Katy examined them. Her hand hovered as she decided. He began whistling the theme from *Jeopardy!*

"Stop it." She laughed, plucking the blueberry one.

Choosing a cranberry one, he split it with his fingers and slathered both halves with vegan butter, as did she. They both reached for the almond milk at the same time, almost touching. He felt the heat of her.

"Please," he said. "You go first."

"Thanks," she said, pouring milk into her coffee. "I've made vegan scones before, but they always come out dry. Climate and temperature might be a factor."

"I never thought of that," he said. "What about these? Are they okay?"

"Delicious." She took another bite.

"Great." He reached for the newspaper.

"Could I have the funnies?"

"Certainly." He shook the section loose and handed it to her. "But I want them back after you're done."

"You read the comics?"

"All my life," he said, winking at her. "How else will I know what's going on in the world?"

Jon read the sports, while Katy smiled over *Red &*

Rover, *Pickles*, *Frazz*, and *Pearls Before Swine*. She showed him *Non Sequitur*, depicting a little girl in the woods with her talking horse.

"I can't wait for Bandit to come to the farm," she said. "I might teach riding lessons to cover his cost."

"I'm curious," he said. "How does using horses fit into the vegan lifestyle?"

"Because of the exploitation of animals?" she said.

"Yes."

"I grew up with horses, so I was curious myself," she said. "It's quite controversial."

"Most things that matter are," he said.

"I had to tweak my original plan."

"Was it difficult?" he asked, glad she followed her beliefs.

"Kind of," she said. "He'll need companionship, so I'll get him a goat."

"A goat?"

"Goats keep horses calm," she said.

"Huh," he said, "I'm a goat."

"Excuse me?"

"My sign is Capricorn."

"Oh, ha," she said. "Mine's Virgo."

"That makes us compatible."

"Oh?" she said. "Are you into astrology?"

"Not really," he said. "But I enjoy reading my daily horoscope."

"I do too."

"What else do you have planned?" he asked. "Besides getting a goat?"

"I'll teach the students how to care for Bandit before they ever get to mount him. There will also be a weight limit so his vertebrae aren't damaged."

"Your website will need to be specific," he said, appreciating her thoughtful consideration. "You might have fewer clients with those restrictions."

"That's only part of it," she said. "Saddles and reins can cause chafing and tissue damage, so I'll be teaching only bareback riding. And I'll never allow bits and whips."

"Where will you ride?"

"There's a path in the woods behind my farmhouse," she said. "Maybe I can instill an appreciation for nature while I'm at it."

He wished to see those woods one day, but he kept his desires to himself.

"You might not show any profit," he said.

"I've thought about that," she said. "I'll keep my accounting clients to augment my income."

"Or," he said. "You could start a vegan consulting company."

"Hmm," she said. "That's not a bad idea."

"I'll write a glowing review," he said. "You can use my name and image."

"Aren't you sweet," she said. "But let's not get ahead of ourselves. What if you decide you can't stay vegan, and *People* magazine runs a picture of you eating a Dick's burger?"

"I see your point," he said, smiling at her reference to his earlier indiscretion.

****

Katy and Jon continued reading the newspaper. How kind of him to listen to her dreams. She wondered if they'd keep in touch after she returned home.

What would it be like to be friends with a famous musician? To listen to his concerts from backstage and hang with him afterward? All the excitement of being a groupie but none of the heartache. But that was only true if she didn't sleep with him.

In the horoscope section, Katy was promised a nine out of ten, predicting romance for the next two days— as if she needed additional encouragement to tumble into Jon's bed. *The Fort Worth Star Telegram* didn't have a rating system, and she wondered how tempted she'd be to lock all the doors and pull covers over her head if she were given a one out of ten for the day.

"Want me to read your horoscope?" she asked.

"Sure."

"Let's see. Capricorn. Capricorn. Oh, here it is near the bottom," she said. "Today is an 8. Strengthen partnerships this month. Collaboration and negotiation will allow both sides to win."

"Well, there you go," he said. "What does yours say?"

"Nothing of note," she said. "It's pretty vague."

"That's the beauty of them," he said. "They're true no matter what."

Katy gave Jon the comics and picked up the front section. Politics as usual. But on page two, there were poignant articles about homelessness, police reform, and housing prices.

Both had noses in the newspaper, until Jon folded his and spoke.

"This is one of my favorite spots," he said, looking around the yard.

"I can see why," Katy said, folding her section as well and placing it on the table. "The landscaping's gorgeous, and there are hummingbirds."

A screeching sound pierced the quiet. *Chuck,*

chuck, chuck, waah, waah, waah. Chuck, chuck, chuck, waah, waah. It seemed to be coming from atop an evergreen branch.

What kind of bird is that?" she asked.

"It's not a bird," he said. "It's an angry squirrel. Probably scolding a cat or something."

"I've never heard that sound before," she said. "I'm surprised, because we have tons of squirrels."

"Maybe you hadn't noticed," he said. "You'll hear it from now on, though."

"That's so true," she said. "Isn't it?"

"Finagle's Law?"

"Whose law?" she said. "I thought it was Murphy's Law."

"Similar." He pointed to the Japanese maple. "My daughter used that as her fortress. She insisted we call her 'Princess Barefoot' for an entire summer."

Katy was surprised by the casualness of his voice, until she saw sorrow settle in his eyes. Without realizing what she was doing, she placed her hand on top of his. He turned his wrist, so they were palm to palm. His hands were warm and dry and he threaded his fingers through hers.

"Feel like going for a walk before we head to the store?" he asked, squeezing softly before letting go.

"Sure, but I've lost my pair of Keds," she said, glancing at her feet. "All I have are these flip-flops."

"What about those boat shoes Rebecca loaned you?" he said. "They might work."

Katy was about to explain why they wouldn't be the best choice considering their size, until she saw the gleam in Jon's eye.

"Ha," she said. "Very funny."

After returning the breakfast items to the main house, Katy and Jon walked to his Mini Cooper parked in the drive. Unlike the day of the boat ride, the top was down.

"So cute," Katy said as she ran her fingers across the yellow and orange striped surface. "It's like the sun."

"That's what Emily said when she chose the colors."

"What would you have picked?"

"Something boring like green."

Katy didn't mention her car, Miss Peabody, was that color. "What's the car's name?"

He looked startled. "Why would you think it has a name?"

"Boats have names. Why not cars?"

"It's just…" he stammered.

She watched him carefully. It was a simple question. Whimsical, really. If he wanted to tease her, so be it.

"I haven't…" He scratched his chin. "It's Tigger."

"From Winnie-the-Pooh?"

He nodded. "Emily was obsessed with the hundred-acre woods."

Katy's grandmother had read those same stories to her. That's how she'd learned English, poring over drawings of Pooh and his friends. Her grandmother's voice was the guiding light to a stable life.

"What a wonderful name for a car," she said.

"I think so too." He smiled. "Hop in."

She opened the passenger door. "Where are we going?"

"Green Lake," he said. "You're gonna love it."

Chapter 23

Jon parked Tigger in his favorite lot next to Green Lake Aqua Theater. As usual for this time of year, the area was abuzz with activity. Some people stretched against trees. Others spread picnics, sunbathed, and tossed balls. A few chased dogs or children or both. The air crackled with energy, conversation, and laughter.

"I spent lots of time here as a kid," Jon said, reminiscing about hours of summer light that allowed extended outside play. Oh, to feel like that child again with so few cares.

"It's right in the middle of the city," she said. "Looks like people are swimming."

"Yeah," he said. "But I wouldn't recommend it."

"Too cold?"

"No. Ducks and geese," he said. "If you don't immediately wash off after you swim, you'll get, ah, um…"

"What?"

"It's a disgusting term," he said.

"I grew up on a farm, remember?"

"We called it 'crotch rot'."

"Oh, no." She laughed. "That's hysterical."

"You wouldn't think so if you ever got it."

"I suppose you're right," she said, trying to hide her smile behind her hand, but her eyes gave it away.

"The path's about three miles around and mostly

flat," he said. "Think you can handle it?"

"If we don't go too fast," she said, examining her flip-flops.

"You set the pace."

Signs instructed walkers to stay in the lane closest to the water to allow wheels on the other, but many ignored the rules and spread across the entire cement path. That's why Jon didn't feel safe biking at Green Lake.

When there was a lull, Jon and Katy zippered like merging freeway cars.

At first, Katy seemed anxious to keep up with the masses. Jon saw her flip-flops curl and was afraid she might stub her toe, so he slowed way down to put her at ease. Soon they found a manageable pace.

"Aren't you afraid you'll be recognized?" she asked.

"Not really," he said. "When I wear sunglasses and ball cap, I look like every other guy."

"You're right," she said, glancing around. "I wouldn't think twice if you were to pass in front of me."

"Besides, most people don't react to celebrity in Seattle. Out of politeness, I think," he said. "I'm left alone, even when I'm recognized."

"That's unusual, isn't it?" she said.

He nodded, remembering a few unpleasant situations involving aggressive strangers. He wouldn't even call them fans, because most seemed hell-bent on belittling his music and declaring him overrated. Some guy even followed him into the bathroom once, griping about ticket prices as Jon tried to pee.

"Lots of people ignore boundaries," he said. "It's

as if they own me, or I owe them—something. I don't know. But it's the price of success, I suppose."

"How do you deal with it?" she asked. "The intrusion, I mean?"

"I avoid it when possible. Hang in dive bars. Places too dark to see my face."

"Don't you get lonely?"

"Sometimes," he said. "But I've got my regular spots, and they're protective of me. So I can't complain."

"I couldn't handle being a rock star."

"I wish people would stop calling me that," he snapped.

"Oh…um…I…I'm sorry."

"No, listen, I'm sorry," he said, contrite. "But it's such a ridiculous label, don't you think?"

"How so?"

"Star? Rock? As if I'm made of celestial dust. Like I'm not human."

"I hadn't thought of it that way," she said. "How awful."

"I even believed the hype for a while," he said. "I was a real ass to my band, and I dated women who would've never given me their number had I not been famous."

"Yes, well…" Katy said. "I don't know many guys who wouldn't do the same under those circumstances."

"I suppose you're right. One thing I'll never regret," he said, wanting Katy to understand he was capable of commitment, "I was faithful in my marriage."

"How were you not tempted with so many choices?"

"Is that a trick question? Aren't we all tempted by one thing or another on a daily basis?" He chuckled. "If we lose our desires, we're basically dead inside."

"That's a fair assessment," she said.

"How we act upon our temptations is what matters. Gauging impulses, weighing instant gratification against long-term satiation, and making split-second decisions that can make or break us," he said. "Some choices are easier than others."

"My ex-husband didn't think twice about cheating," she said. "And my last boyfriend wasn't faithful either."

"Is he the one you mentioned when I sent my photo?"

"Yes," she said. "I assumed we were exclusive, but he didn't even say he loved me. How stupid was I?"

"Did you love *him*?" Jon asked, hoping for a definite no.

"Of course," she said. "Otherwise it wouldn't still matter."

"I guess that's true," he said. "Do you keep in touch?"

"Once in a while he does," she said. "But probably not after seeing me at the ballgame the other night."

"The ballgame?" Jon said. "He's in Seattle?"

"I thought Rebecca might've told you," she said. "His name's Greg Daniels. He plays third base for the Rangers."

Jon veered from the path onto the grass and pulled out his phone. He opened Google and hit images, searching for Greg Daniels. It didn't bode well for Jon if this was Katy's type.

"Where'd you go?" Katy asked, walking back to

Jon after realizing he wasn't beside her. "I told a stranger 'my heart still hurts from our breakup.' You should've seen his wife's expression. At least I think it was his wife."

"I was looking up your ex-boyfriend," he said, raising his eyes to hers. "Kinda young, isn't he?"

"He's old enough," she said, feeling judged. "Besides, that wasn't the issue."

"What was?"

"Fame," she said. "Like you."

"What does this have to do with me?"

"Same situation," she said.

"He's a kid," Jon said. "It's an unfair comparison."

"Oh?" she said. "You're both in the spotlight. You both have fans. He couldn't keep away from his any more than you could. How is that different?"

"For one, I'm in control of my—"

"I was his good-luck charm. Not special enough to publicly declare our relationship," she said. "And if you and I have a fling, as I'm told is an option, I can be your 'favored fan,' which I'm assuming is the exact same thing."

"Favored what?"

"You know, 'groupie.' "

They were drawing unwanted attention.

"Let's move over there," Jon said, pointing to a copse of tall trees away from eavesdroppers. Once there, he said, "Who told you it was an option?"

"Rebecca," Katy said. "Was she wrong?"

"Well…no…I mean yes…I mean…" he said, struggling to redeem himself, but failing miserably.

"I can't keep falling for short-term guys, Jon—especially famous ones," she said. "Can you imagine what it's like to see your ex-lover's face in the media after they've dumped you?"

"Actually," he said. "I can."

"Well...I mean...of course you've been with—"

"Let me get this straight," he said, anger rising but still in check. "The sole reason you won't sleep with me is because I'm famous. And, by the way, I haven't said anything about wanting to sleep with you, so you don't even know if it's true."

His words stung. What if Rebecca had lied, and Jon wasn't remotely interested in sleeping with Katy?

"But, for the sake of argument," he said, "let's say I *am* attracted to you."

"Okay," she stuttered, heart pounding at the possibility of sharing his bed, even though she had no intention of doing so. "Let's."

"You'd turn me down because this playboy screwed you over?" he said, tapping Greg's photo on his phone. "And I'm guilty by association because I'm *a celebrity*?"

She grimaced and nodded.

"Huh." Jon stood silently for a long while, staring at the lake. "You don't think I might be looking for—"

"I can't do casual anymore," she blurted, taking advantage of her captive audience as if Jon represented every man she'd ever known. "I need to take a break from frivolous sex. Think about the long term. Not settle for less than what's best for me. You understand, don't you?"

"You think having sex with me would be meaningless."

"Well, yes," she said, relieved he comprehended. "There are hundreds, thousands of women for you to choose from, so it won't matter if…"

"Only one of my many fans turns me down?"

"Exactly. So you can see what I mean, right?" She spread her palms upward to emphasize her point. "You're looking for fun. A fling. No strings attached. Nothing wrong with that. And, a year ago, I would've jumped at the chance—especially with someone as amazing as *The* Noe Burke. But—"

"You can stop now," he said, voice low and dry. "I get the gist."

"Oh, I'm so glad."

"You're saying that it's not me, it's you," he said. "And I whole-heartedly agree."

Katy didn't quite register Jon's last statement. At that moment, she felt exhilarated. Her future was crystal clear. If she expected lifelong satisfaction, she had to stop reaching for the honey pot. Wasn't it Einstein who defined insanity as doing the same thing over and over, and expecting different results? She didn't want to be in love alone anymore.

"I'm sorry if I've hurt your feelings," she said, but he hadn't seemed to hear her. "Jon?"

"Don't worry about it," he said. "I'm a grown man. I've weathered worse things than being pigeonholed by someone who barely knows me."

"Of course," she said. "I didn't mean to imply—"

"Come on," he said, walking toward the path. "We've got a long way to go."

****

Back on the path, Jon's thoughts were twisting. If he doodled this, steam would be coming out of his ears and Rebecca would have a snake's tongue. Why had she told Katy he was only interested in a fling? His chances were slim to none if he couldn't convince Katy otherwise. And, worst of all, he might not ever see her again.

He hadn't realized how fast he'd been moving until he spun around and Katy was gone. He jogged in her direction and found her sitting on a bench.

"I'm sorry," he said. "That was rude of me."

"No," she said, looking up at him. "I'm the one who was rude."

"How so?" he said, sitting next to her.

"I replayed what I said to you in my mind, and it wasn't very nice."

"Neither was I," he said, reaching for her hand. Every nerve ending vibrated when they touched. "Rebecca had no right to say what she said."

"She must've figured it out."

"Figured what out?"

"That I'm attracted to you," Katy said, staring at their entwined fingers. "It's pretty obvious."

Not to him, it wasn't. He caught his breath at her revelation.

"So you think we could, maybe, move beyond friendship?" he asked.

"I'm entertaining the thought," she said, eyes twinkling mischievously. "But, I'll need a little more time."

"I understand," he said, whooping on the inside. "Say when."

"You'll know when I do," she said and then frowned.

"What's wrong?"

"I wish we had more than a week," she said. "Everything's moving so fast."

His phone rang. Rebecca. He sent it straight to voicemail.

"It doesn't have to end here," he said. "I could come visit you."

"Oh. That didn't cross my mind." She smiled. "I'd like that very much."

Absolutely and positively. So would he.

****

Back on the path, Katy noticed a group of people huddled close to the water's edge. They were staring through bushes at logs on the lake.

"What's that about?" she said, moving off the path to get a better view.

"Turtles," Jon said. "The sun brings them out."

"Oh, I see them," she said.

"There's a bird sometimes too," he said. "A blue heron or some kind of crane."

"No wonder you like it here so much," Katy said. "There's lots to see."

"I'm getting hungry," he said, as they returned to the path.

"How close are the nearest restaurants?"

"'Bout half a mile."

"Perfect," she said. "We can practice ordering vegan."

"Good," he said. "Because I've failed miserably at that."

"Been eating lots of French fries, have we?"

"How'd you guess?"

"It's usually the only item on the menu that doesn't need tweaking," she said. "Unless the restaurant uses the same oil to fry their meats. Then French fries are off limits."

"Oh, man," he said. "I didn't think to ask."

"Don't beat yourself up," she said. "The important thing is you're learning."

Movement from a tiny island on the lake caught Katy's eye. A bald eagle with an enormous wingspan circled above and then flew directly at her before lifting to perch at the top of an evergreen. "Wow. I thought it was going to hit me."

"That's a sign of good luck," Jon said.

"To be beaned by a bird?"

"Not exactly." He chuckled. "But according to Native American lore, eagles have magical powers. Maybe that one recognized your spirit and was drawn to you."

"I like that idea," Katy said.

On the way to the restaurants, the path curved, exposing a shallow pool crowded with kids and adults. Jon moved onto the grass and leaned against a tree, watching a mother putting blow-up fins on a little girl. Knowing he was remembering his wife and child, Katy slipped her hand into his. Soon, they crossed the street without saying a word.

Strolling along the sidewalk, Katy and Jon perused posted menus.

"This one's tough," she said. "Every single dish contains seafood."

"Probably because it's a seafood restaurant," Jon said, tugging her to the crosswalk and onto the next block.

She'd forgotten the simple pleasure of handholding and was amazed how quickly things had changed between them. Who would've thought an offer to help a stranger become vegan would lead her here?

Skirting the neighborhood for another half mile, they came to another cluster of restaurants. After several stops, they both agreed Shelter Lounge was the one to try, because the vegan dishes were clearly marked on the menu—including the house fries.

"Kind of expensive," she said.

"It's the location," he said. "But doesn't eating vegan cost more anyway?"

"Not really. It's all about buying only what you need," she said. "Do you know how much the average American household wastes on uneaten food?"

"No," he said. "How much?"

"Sixteen percent annually."

Before entering the restaurant, Jon removed his hat and sunglasses.

"Your hair's a little mussed," she said.

He brought both hands up and messed it up further. "Better?"

She laughed and reached over to smooth it with her fingers, sweeping his bangs into place and wanting to linger longer. He watched with amusement.

The restaurant had a ceiling, but the sides were opened to the air like a gazebo. He and Katy stepped to the hostess stand where a woman waited. She looked efficient and tidy in her white blouse and black slacks, but her purple-dyed hair was asymmetrical, indicating a creative side.

"Are there seats available overlooking the sidewalk?" Jon asked.

"I'll go check," she said.

The hostess walked away and returned seconds later. "There's a couple finishing up. It'll be about five minutes," she said. "Care to wait?"

Jon turned to Katy for the answer.

"Yes, please," Katy said, even though the hostess wasn't looking at her. Right then, Katy noticed an almost indiscernible reaction on the hostess' face—a slight widening of the eyes, one brow lifting. She must've recognized Jon.

"I'll be back in a few," the hostess said.

Katy watched her stroll to the bar. She leaned over the counter and whispered into the bartender's ear. He continued polishing a wineglass as if she'd said nothing of interest. About two minutes later, the bartender walked past Katy and Jon. His head pointed straight, but his eyes darted across Jon's face. He returned to the bar and nodded, ever so subtly, to the hostess. She smiled primly. There was no other indication they knew who Jon was. No fawning. No gushing. No special seating. If Jon hadn't told Katy how people treated him in Seattle, she would've thought he'd gone unnoticed. She also appreciated he didn't make demands to be treated better than other customers. That wasn't typical celebrity behavior. Not in her experience anyway.

The hostess returned, holding menus. "This way, please."

When they sat, Jon put his sunglasses back on but left his head hatless. Katy liked the old-fashioned gesture.

"Told you," he said. "The hostess and bartender?"

"You saw that?"

"It's one of the reasons I like living here."

"Amazing," Katy said, looking at the menu.

The waiter arrived to take their drink order, wearing the same black-and-white uniform as the hostess. His ginger eyebrows and mustache disappeared in the sunlight.

"I'll have iced tea, please," she said. "Unsweetened."

"That's the only kind we've got," the waiter said and turned to Jon.

"The same, please."

"Very good," the waiter said and left.

Katy glanced across the road to the lake. "Gorgeous."

"Yes," he said. "You are."

"Stop that," she said, tapping the top of his hand. "You're making me blush."

"Even better." He smiled, dropping his eyes to the menu. "What should we try?"

"We'll need to ask a few questions," she said. "I'm wondering if the veggie patty is vegan."

"Aren't they all?" he said.

"Some use egg as a binder," she said. "The vegan ones are usually made from beans or mushroom and sometimes beets."

"So if these are vegan, we could get the veggie sandwich without pepper jack and pesto mayo."

"Yes," she said.

"Won't that be a little dry?"

"Might be," she said. "Do you like mustard?"

"Yes," he said. "I do."

"Then we'll ask for some on the side," she said. "I also like dipping my fries in it."

"What if the veggie patty isn't vegan?" he asked. "What should we order?"

"You tell me."

He examined the menu for a moment, carefully reading the ingredients. She appreciated his sincere desire to make the right decision.

"We can rule out anything meat-centered, like the wings and seared ahi," he said. "The fried hominy is vegan, but it's only a snack."

The waiter brought their drinks, and Katy asked for another minute.

"What else?" she said to Jon.

"This is hard," he said. "I feel like one of those picky eaters, delaying everybody's order."

"You'll get the hang of it." Katy sipped her tea. "If you know the restaurant ahead of time, you can look up the menu online."

"Sounds smart."

"It works best with chain restaurants," she said. "And I noticed Seattle doesn't have many of those."

"Not enough cheap land," he said.

"Makes sense." She pointed to his menu. "Anything else catch your eye?"

"We can't have any of the large plates, because the cheese can't be separated from the dish," he said. "Maybe the mini wonton tofu tacos without chipotle crema?"

"I was thinking that too, but it brings up another issue," she said. "Tofu is a complete protein, which is great, but if it's deep fried, the calories double. It's like dumping dressing on a salad and calling it healthy."

"I see your point," he said. "The spinach salad without the gouda looks promising, but we'll need to ask what's in the vinaigrette."

"Now you're getting it," she said. "Lots of vinaigrettes are vegan, but some chefs add flavors to make theirs distinctive, like bacon or honey."

"Yeah," he said. "I noticed that."

"So if the vinaigrette isn't vegan, you can squeeze lemon wedges over the top of the salad and season with pepper and sea salt."

"Why don't we ask the waiter for a recommendation?"

"We could," she said. "But did you read the story about how often restaurants serve regular coffee when asked for decaf because it was more convenient?"

"No," he said. "That's terrible."

"You take your chances," she said. "Any other questions?"

"What if it's not enough food?" he asked.

"Then we order more," she said. "It's better to start with too little than too much."

****

After enjoying their lunch of spinach salad and tofu tacos, Katy and Jon walked the remaining mile around the lake. Soon, they were back at the parking lot. Before leaving, Katy spoke with an older gentleman who wore a smock advertising Spanish lessons.

"Beautiful day," she said in Spanish.

"Not as beautiful as the two of you together," he said, pointing at Katy and Jon. "You're both glowing."

"The sun's casting a mischievous light."

The man guffawed and clapped his hands. "You're a treasure, my dear," he said. "And he's a lucky man."

"That's what I keep telling him," she said. "Thanks for the delightful conversation."

"My pleasure." He turned from them, still smiling.

"I didn't know you spoke Spanish," Jon said. "What'd he say?"

"That it's a beautiful day."

"It is," he said. "But the conversation went longer."

"He also said we're both glowing."

Jon brought Katy's wrist to his lips and lightly kissed it.

"On that," he said, "we can all agree."

Katy wasn't sure how long she could resist Jon's charms or why she even bothered. He was the sexiest man she'd ever known. The relationship had short-term written all over it, because he hadn't promised more, and they lived miles apart. Why not enjoy one last binge, as if she were giving up other vices like smoking or drinking?

Late in life, which would Katy regret more? Turning down a magical night with an attractive and talented musician? Or losing her heart, which she knew she would, and learning from *People* magazine of the woman he eventually married?

Only time would tell.

Chapter 24

"That went better than I thought," Jon said, turning the ignition and lowering the ragtop. "I'm neither hungry nor full."

"That's one of the benefits of conscientious consumption," she said. "We start listening to our bodies when we stop stuffing our faces."

"Fast food is like a numbing drug," he said, thinking about the Dick's burgers he still craved. Mindful of distracted pedestrians, Jon backed out of the parking space. Three other cars jockeyed to snatch the coveted spot. "Where to now?"

"Grocery shopping," she said. "We need to restock your kitchen."

"Let's go to PCC," he said.

"PCC?"

"It's a co-op around the corner from here."

Jon likened shopping at PCC to wandering into a secret garden. All five senses engaged at once. The displays of reds and greens and yellows were arranged with an artist's eye, or so it seemed. Grinding machines whirled, and the scent of coffee lingered on the tongue. But when the doors opened, the first thing to assail was the deli and its plethora of meats and cheeses—something Jon hadn't noticed in the past.

Katy veered left toward the fresh produce section, and he followed with the cart.

"Smells good," she said, stopping in front of the fruit bins. "Like a spice shop."

"Rainier," he said when he noticed the cherries.

"Where?" she said, eyes turning toward the front windows.

"Oh, sorry," he said, holding up a bag. "I was talking about these."

"Ah." She giggled. "I still haven't seen that damn mountain."

"We'll remedy that before you leave," he said, smiling.

As Katy fondled the nectarines, testing for ripeness, Jon's body responded with a jolt. He wiped a bead of sweat from his temple and adjusted his shirt to hide a tightening crotch. When she rolled mushrooms in her hands and rubbed them with her thumb to remove dirt, his discomfort grew stronger. But as she reached for the English cucumbers, he added two to the cart before her fingers ever touched the phallic vegetable.

"Want to know what I find most difficult about being vegan?" she asked.

"Yes," he said, voice raspy. Collecting himself, he cleared his throat with a quick cough. "What's most difficult?"

"Being a guest at a sit-down dinner," she said, moving toward the bulk bins. "People work so hard to set a nice table, and I feel like I'm hurting their feelings by not sampling every dish."

"How do you get around that?"

"It's easier with potlucks, because I can bring a few dishes," she said. "But for sit-downs, I ask what's being served, and I make something similar, so my plate looks like everyone else's."

"Do they ever try to accommodate you?" he asked.

"Yes, but hosting is hard enough, and it's not like I have food allergies," she said.

"Good point."

"Lots of times, they don't understand how strict veganism is, and they'll forget to mention the dish has butter and eggs."

"The more I learn," he said, "the more impossible it seems to be vegan full time."

"Some people eat vegan at home but are vegetarians when out."

"I can see why," he said, picking up a box of crackers. After reading the ingredients, he set it back on the shelf. "Milk."

"I caved early on," she confessed.

"You did?" he said, feeling less guilty about his slip.

"About two months in, my grandmother fried some of her famous buttermilk chicken. It took me back to childhood, and I ate two pieces," she said. "But the longer I'm vegan, the more natural it becomes."

"Good to know," he said.

By the time they were finished, the cart was full. Most of the items were close to original form—raw fruits and vegetables, potatoes, fresh herbs, dried beans, raw nuts and seeds, and whole grains. A few were slightly modified, like tofu, almond butter, frozen fruit, pomegranate juice, canned beans, liquid aminos, red miso, hemp milk, and coconut oil. And some were vegan alternatives, such as cheeses made from cashews and breakfast patties made with soy.

On the way home, they stopped at Target for cooking items Katy noted while organizing Jon's kitchen. At the house, it took four trips to carry everything inside. While Katy unpacked the groceries and put them where they belonged, he unpackaged and washed the newly purchased utensils and cookware.

Jon enjoyed the ordinariness of this basic domestic ritual.

****

Lingering scents of nutmeg and cinnamon in Jon's kitchen transported Katy back to when she'd arrived at the farm. Every day, her grandmother offered new delights. Freshly baked apple pie, its golden top crust sprinkled with large grains of sugar. Gingerbread cookies cooling but still soft. Hot cocoa with tiny marshmallows that floated and bobbed and tasted like heaven. They were Katy's first flavors of a permanent home, and standing beside Jon in his kitchen, she felt an overwhelming sense of belonging.

"Ooo-eee, Big Billy," she said, washing her hands and wiping them on a towel.

"Um…what?"

"Oh, ha." She laughed. "It's from an old commercial for a car dealership in Dallas. My grandmother used to quote it randomly, because she thought it was funny."

"I do that too," he said. "I catch myself saying 'not my circus, not my monkeys' sometimes."

"Where'd you pick that up?"

"It's an old Polish proverb, but I don't remember where I first heard it," he said. "I think it means to ignore petty issues that don't concern me. At least that's how I use it."

"Good advice," she said. "Want a mocktail?"

"Sure," he said. "Can I help?"

"You bet," she said, handing him a lime. "Roll this to soften it. Then bring out some ice."

"You got it."

Katy pressed fresh rosemary with the back of a spoon in the bottom of two glasses then filled them one-fourth of the way with pomegranate juice. She dropped a few cubes of ice in each and then squeezed lime juice over the top. Pouring club soda in last, she stirred and added a rosemary sprig as garnish. "Done."

"Great," Jon said, leading her through French doors onto a large deck.

"It's like a living room," she said, glancing around for a place to sit.

"That was the intent." He pointed to two chairs covered in moss-colored duck canvas. "Here. It's the best view."

"Oh," Katy said, feeling the sea breeze on her skin and admiring the sight of the sun's reflection on the water. "It's lovely."

"Never gets old." He took the glass she offered. "What should we toast to?"

She couldn't think of anything.

"I've got it," he said. "To appreciating the good things in life while they're happening."

"I like that. I might borrow it sometime."

"It's yours." He smiled, his eyes sparkling in the light.

They clinked glasses and held each other's gaze for a moment before Katy pulled hers away, heart beating too fast.

"Tasty," Jon said, sipping his drink.

To Katy, the word sounded seductive. She dropped into one of the chairs, not trusting her shaky knees.

Why was she feeling this way now? They'd been together all day. At this rate, she'd lose all control and drag him to bed within the hour. She looked at the boats and tried to concentrate on something else.

"How 'bout some music?" he said, setting his glass down and disappearing inside.

The built-in speakers on the deck sparked to life, playing an instrumental tune—not Jon's own music. Not even his style. It was classical. Mozart, maybe.

When he returned, he sat next to her and reached for her hand, intertwining fingers. They fell into comfortable silence, both facing the Sound. The next song played, and Jon stood, swirling Katy into his arms for a dance. Instead of the usual prom sway, he put his palm on her waist and placed her hand on his shoulder for a waltz.

"You're pretty good," she said, matching his movements as they glided across the deck.

"You're not so bad yourself."

She felt his rumbling voice vibrate through his shirt.

"Sixth grade PE," she said. "Between square-dancing and aerobics."

"Group lessons in Greenwood," he said. "My mom hoped I'd meet a 'nice' girl."

"Did you?"

"Mostly old married couples and the recently engaged," he said. "I had a crush on the teacher, Ms. Franz."

"Did she know?"

"I'm sure she guessed. I acted like a remora and never left her side," he said. "Then I saw her at the zoo with her husband and three kids. My delusions were shattered."

By the time the song ended, Katy was entranced. Jon held her palm to his heart, and she was awestruck by the sight of his hand on hers and her hand on his chest. His warm breath, spiced with pomegranate and rosemary, brushed against her cheek, and his heartbeat accelerated under her fingertips. She glanced up and held his gaze.

Jon leaned into Katy and pressed his lips to hers. She did not pull away. Tender at first, the kiss intensified into molten lava. She felt consumed by him, and his skin scorched like desert sand as she slid her hands underneath the back of his shirt. He groaned with pleasure, and his growing erection pressed against her abdomen. She hungered to explore him from dimples to toes, and her body responded with the urgency to feel him inside. She pictured the two of them naked in his king-sized bed—together for the rest of their lives.

Then she heard the front door slam. Shoes against hardwood. Rebecca's voice.

"Yoo-hoo. Anyone home?"

"Shit," Jon said, separating from Katy as if embarrassed to be caught. He adjusted himself and stepped inside. Clearly he worried more about Rebecca's feelings than Katy's or he wouldn't have left so quickly.

Alone on the deck, Katy felt exposed. Hugging herself, she dropped into one of the chairs.

Only moments ago, the classical music seemed airy and bright. Now it sounded like a dirge. An enormous barge cut across the water, and a filmy haze dulled the sun.

****

Jon grabbed Rebecca by the elbow and steered her toward the kitchen, fighting the urge to toss her onto the front porch.

"Why are you here?" he said, keeping his voice low so Katy wouldn't be alarmed by his sudden anger.

"I was worried," Rebecca said. "You didn't return my phone calls."

"Because I'm *busy*. You need to leave," he said. "Now."

"You've changed, Jon." Rebecca wiggled from his grip and hopped onto a stool at the counter. "You're grumpy, because you're not getting enough to eat."

"We can remedy that," Katy said, smoothing her clothes as she entered the kitchen. "Time for cooking lessons. Care to join us, Rebecca?"

"What…" Jon stared at Katy as if she'd grown a second head. "I was hoping—"

"I'd love to," Rebecca said, grinning at Jon. "That way I can help when Katy leaves."

"Great," Katy said, all business and smiles as she donned her apron. "Give me a minute to set up."

Unable to speak, Jon sat next to Rebecca at the counter. Katy's demeanor had changed, and he couldn't fathom why. Was she regretting the kiss? Maybe it was best Rebecca arrived when she did. She could act as chaperone.

He'd never forgive himself if he pushed Katy away by being too aggressive. No more physical advances on his part. The next move would be hers.

Jon and Rebecca watched as Katy staged five separate stations on the countertop. Each section included a photo of the finished meal with a listing of ingredients and tools needed. If the dish required a can opener or knife or pot or spoon or colander, the item was placed next to the food. Once done, Katy set three bins on the floor—one for food scraps, one for recycling, and one for garbage.

"The best habit is to prepare all your ingredients ahead of time," Katy said. "Gather them, measure them, chop them, whatever, before turning on the oven or stove. That way, you won't panic when it's time to assemble. The French call it *mis en place*."

"Seems like a lot of work," Rebecca said.

Katy ignored the comment.

"First of all," she said, opening a rectangle container. "We'll need to prepare some extra-firm tofu for the air-fryer."

Jon had never seen tofu in its raw form. It looked like an underwater sea creature—pale and soggy, floating in a murky bath. Its texture reminded him of clammy palms and limp handshakes. He wondered if it smelled.

"That's disgusting," Rebecca said, bringing his thoughts to life. "You don't expect us to eat it, do you?"

"Not in this form," Katy said. "It's flavorless until we marinate it."

She squeezed the moisture from the tofu brick using the press Jon bought. Afterward, she cut the tofu into bite-sized pieces and tossed them into a zip-lock freezer bag. She added sesame oil, tamari, and grated ginger before placing the bag in the fridge.

"We'll need to turn it over once or twice for evenness."

"And then what?" Rebecca asked.

"We'll air-fry it and use it in a salad," Katy said. "You'll think it's chicken chunks."

Rebecca turned her skeptical eyes to Jon, but he looked away so Katy wouldn't think he doubted her word. Even though he did.

"Now for the appetizers," she said, pushing a cutting board, serrated knife, and baguette toward Jon. "See the picture? Cut the bread at an angle, one-half inch each."

After rinsing and draining a can of garbanzo beans, Katy dropped them into a shallow bowl. She gave the dish to Rebecca along with a potato masher. "Smash these until they're unrecognizable."

"Why do we have to do this?" Rebecca whispered to Jon while Katy's back was turned. "Isn't she the one getting paid?"

"Leave if you don't like it," Jon said, concentrating on his task.

While Jon and Rebecca were at work, Katy chopped, diced and minced—cherry tomatoes, red onion, fresh garlic, fresh basil, and vegan mozzarella. Throwing the ingredients into a glass container, she mixed in olive oil, sea salt, and black pepper.

"I'm finished," Jon said, presenting his near perfect slices.

"Great." Katy poured a small amount of olive oil into a bowl and seasoned it with pressed garlic and sea salt. "Lightly brush this on both sides, place them on the cookie sheet, and pop them into the oven. It's preheated to 375. Set the timer for three minutes, but it might take five. We want them toasty but not burnt."

"Am I done?" Rebecca asked.

"Not at all," Katy said, adding mustard to the mix. "Mash this for about a minute."

Katy returned to her chopping—celery, dill pickles,

green onion. She took the masher from Rebecca and replaced it with a large spoon. "Fold these in," she instructed.

The aroma of garlic toast scented the room. Jon hadn't known cooking could be so fun. He looked forward to tasting their collaborative dishes.

By the time the toast turned golden-brown and was cooling on the counter, Katy had shown them how to sauté raw pumpkin seeds for garnish or snacks and how to make brownies with walnuts and black beans. While the dessert baked, she washed three potatoes and chopped them, skin on. "That's where the nutrients are," she said. She dropped the potatoes in a pot of salted water and boiled them on the stove.

"I thought white potatoes were as bad as ice cream," Rebecca said.

"That's debatable, and as a vegan, I give up a lot of things already," Katy said, holding the paring knife like a tiny sword. "I dare anyone to try to take away my potatoes."

"Calm down," Rebecca said. "No one wants to touch your potatoes. Right, Jon?"

For sure he wanted to touch Katy's potatoes and every other part of her, but that wasn't any of Rebecca's business. "Can we try the appetizers now?" he asked.

"Feeling a bit peckish?" Katy said. She plopped the bruschetta mixture onto three pieces of toast and the "egg" salad onto three more, giving Jon and Rebecca one of each. "You don't want to make them all at once, because the toast gets soggy. And if you store everything separately, you can enjoy these for a few days."

Choosing the bright red bruschetta first, Jon bit into the crunchy concoction. The flavors burst in his mouth. "Oh my God," he said. "It's restaurant quality."

Rebecca stared at her plate. "There's an awful lot of garlic and onion in these."

"What's wrong?" Jon said, reaching for the "egg" salad on toast. "Hot date?"

"You never know," she said, biting delicately into the bruschetta.

"Jon?" Katy said. "I need you at the stove."

"Of course," he said, bounding off his chair. "What can I do?"

She simmered olive oil and garlic in a skillet and added broccoli florets. Her proximity made him flush, but if anyone noticed, he'd blame it on kitchen heat.

"I need you to stir these occasionally until they soften," she said. "Then pop them into the oven, pan and all, until their tips are slightly brown."

"I'm on it," he said, eager to oblige.

The rest of the menu was delicious, and he had plenty of sweet and savory leftovers. If Katy hadn't shared her dreams for the farm, Jon would've offered her a job as his private chef. He could imagine preparing mouth-watering dinners every night together, filling the house with new memories and bringing joy back into his life.

****

Katy put the ingredients away and scrubbed the counter as Jon walked Rebecca to the door. God forbid Rebecca would help clean up. But that was okay, because Katy was tired of dealing with her. There always seemed to be an underlying innuendo in her comments.

When Katy came in from the deck, she'd found Jon and Rebecca with heads together. And during the lesson, she heard them whispering, like besties passing notes behind the teacher's back. If Jon and Rebecca had an on-again off-again sexual relationship, then Katy wanted no part of being his "favored fan." In fact, he was losing all appeal and would need to do something spectacular to change her mind.

"Katy," Jon said, coming back into the kitchen. "You need to tell me what's wrong."

"Nothing's wrong," she said, scrubbing harder.

"I'm pretty sure that's not true." He took the sponge from her and set it out of reach. "Please look at me."

"I don't want to," she said, avoiding eye contact.

"Is this about the kiss?" he asked. "Are you regretting it?"

"No," she said. *God, no.* That moment would be a memory she'd bring out and polish for the rest of her life. "I don't regret the kiss."

"Then what?"

Her hand went to her hip and she brought her eyes to his. "You pulled away in an awful hurry. Embarrassed to be seen with me?"

"Of course not. It's that I—"

"Couldn't wait to be with her."

"Is that what you think? Come here." He gestured toward the living room. "There's something you need to know."

Katy followed him to the couch and sat at the opposite end, so there'd be no chance of touching. "Go on."

"Rebecca is worried about me," he said. "She

thinks I'm replacing whiskey with extreme deprivation."

Katy studied his face for sincerity. "You're kidding."

"She thinks I'm swapping one addiction for another, and you're an enabler."

"I've never heard anything more ridiculous."

"It does sound farfetched." He ran a palm through his hair. "But she has her reasons."

"Can you tell me what they are?"

"After the accident, I didn't want to live," he said. "And I was doing everything I could to end my life— short of outright suicide."

"The drinking and bar fights. That kind of thing?"

"Yes. And Rebecca witnessed it all."

"That must've been devastating for her." Katy's voice softened, and her tension eased. "Especially since it lasted a whole year."

"She went on tour, which she hates, and checked on me every day. She made sure I ate. She cleaned up my messes. And she constantly monitored my vitals."

"I see." Gaining new respect for Rebecca, Katy opened her mind to a truce of sorts. "She saved your life."

"She absolutely did, and for that I will be eternally grateful, but..." His gaze dropped to his fidgeting hands. When he finally spoke, he possessed resolve. "Listen. I know she lives like she drives, and she's kind of hard to take at times, but we've been though so much our lives will be forever woven together. Does that make sense?"

"It does." Katy hesitated, unsure if she could talk about her upbringing without disrespecting her dad.

Impossible, so she chose the simple truth. "I keep hoping my father will turn his life around and take responsibility for the poor choices he's made, but I've never doubted his love for me."

"You do get it." He sat back against the couch. "Rebecca is like family, and I believe she means well. But now she claims I'm slipping, because she thinks veganism is borderline cult."

"And she blames me for part of that."

"I'm not saying she's right."

"Thank goodness for that, or I'd be a worried about your motivations."

Jon laughed at Katy's joke, and she relaxed into the cushion.

"Her level of interference is escalating," he said. "And I don't want to give her any more ammo."

"And if she sees us kissing…"

"She'll think you're pulling me in further."

Katy placed herself in Rebecca's shoes for a moment. How would she feel if a stranger appeared in Lori's life? One who seemed influential in changing her core beliefs? "I can see why Rebecca might think that way."

"It's my fault, really."

"How so?"

"I should've told her about your visit."

His hands fidgeted again, as an ex-smoker's might. Was that why he doodled? To organize his thoughts?

"But honestly, I'm tired of her fussing over me."

"Without her fussing, you might not be here."

"It's a vicious cycle."

Knowing that Rebecca wouldn't be swayed until time passed and positive results were noted, Katy suggested the most obvious solution.

"I guess we should just be friends. That way she won't have to worry."

"Is that what you want?" His voice sounded small, like a child who discovered the truth about Santa.

Of course it wasn't what she wanted. She wanted to be in his arms. She wanted to kiss him again. She wanted to be in his bed. If the kiss was any indication, which kisses usually were, she knew he would be a fabulous lover, and she wanted that memory as well.

"It might be for the best," she said, regretting the loss of intimacy.

"Stay here." He drummed his fingers on the cushion between them and rose. "I won't be long."

Returning with his guitar, he sat next to Katy on the couch.

"I usually can't write with others around, but you've inspired me." He tuned a few chords while strumming. "I'm calling this 'Katy's Song'."

"Oh…goodness." Her eyes misted, and she touched his sleeve. "I'm speechless."

"Don't get too excited. It's still rough." He side-smiled and looked down at the strings. "But I like where it's going."

As he tapped his foot to the beat, she watched his dancing fingers. The musky scent of his guitar was as intoxicating as barrel-aged bourbon. She couldn't believe her close proximity to the musician and his creation. Mesmerized, Katy remained perfectly still, willing him to play forever.

"I'm thinking duet." At this, he lifted his head for a moment and winked at her. "With a country slant."

He started singing, and his rumbling, whiskey

voice penetrated Katy's body and vibrated inside her breast, changing the rhythm of her pulse.

Away, I fly, to feed my soul
Love and laughter bring me home
Buttoning my wings inside my jacket
I listen for your tune

Still strumming he said, "The chorus goes something like this."

Where are you, my dear
I search but I'm still alone
And so I eagerly wait
For you to find my heart

"For this next verse, imagine a woman's voice. Maybe a fiddle." His gaze dropped to the guitar and he began singing.

Worry not, my love
I feel and share your desire
I will call for you
And sing you into my arms

He played a few more chords and then dampened the strings.

"That's all I have so far." He leaned the guitar against the couch and raised his beautiful smoky-gray eyes to hers.

No one had ever written her a song—or even a bad poem. But here she was close enough to touch him, and one of the most talented musicians on the planet was singing directly to her. Never in her wildest dreams.

Holding his gaze, Katy reached for Jon's hand and kissed his callused fingers one by one. She imagined the countless melodies his expert hands had strummed. And the thought of these hands strumming her body thrilled her.

She stood and tugged him toward the bedroom, locking the door when they stepped inside the room.

Chapter 25

Jon spooned Katy's naked body, legs intertwined. He wanted to stay in bed with her forever, inhaling her lavender scent and running his palms along her velvety surfaces. His heart belonged to her now—too soon to declare aloud, or she'd think he wasn't earnest.

He was aroused for the third time and rolled Katy toward him onto her back. He kissed the scar on her abdomen, as she combed his hair with her fingers.

"How'd you get this?" he asked, following the scar with his tongue.

"It's a long story," she said, drowsily.

"I'm not going anywhere."

"You remember when I spoke Spanish in the park?"

"Yes," he said, resting his cheek against her belly. "Quite impressive."

"Did I tell you?" she said. "I was born in Mexico?"

"Not that I recall," he said. "Sounds exotic."

"Not so much," she said. "My father and I were homeless."

He lifted his head and looked into her hazel eyes. They held sadness. Moving upward, he folded her into a cuddle, stroking her back as the details spilled forth.

"My parents had me when they were seventeen, and my mother died soon after my birth," she said. "My father refused to leave Mexico, and he tried to make it work. But Dad wasn't the responsible one of the couple, and he couldn't hold down a steady job. Sometimes he cleaned houses, and after I learned to walk and talk, I became his helper."

"How long were you in Mexico?" he asked.

"Six years," she said.

"Were you homeless that whole time?"

"No," she said. "Only the last two."

"And the scar?"

"That happened right before we moved in with my grandmother in Fort Worth," she said. "Dad and I were cleaning the hacienda of a Mexican heiress. The caretaker's ten-year-old daughter challenged me to a game of hide-and-seek. I found the perfect hiding spot behind wooden pallets in the wine cellar and tried not to giggle at my good fortune. But the dungeon door slammed shut, locking me in total darkness for more than two hours. The cold stone walls absorbed my screams. Once I went quiet, every creak, every scamper, every moan was amplified in my ears. As time passed, my imagination grew more sinister. Zombies, trolls, goblins. When something rubbed against my foot, I panicked and knocked over one of the wine displays, bottles thundering as they broke. A large shard pierced my abdomen. The last thing I remembered was blinding white pain."

"My God," he said.

"The doctors repaired what they could, but…" she said. "I can't have children of my own."

Jon felt tears swelling, and he squeezed Katy tighter, knowing her anguish. "I can't have children either."

She positioned herself to see his face. "What about

Emily?"

"Emily was my daughter, but I wasn't her biological father."

"But, how…"

"Charlotte was pregnant when she came back to Seattle. She needed someone to take care of her and the baby, and I loved her so much, I would've done anything to keep her with me," he said. "We tried for another, and when we couldn't conceive, I got tested."

****

An aching chasm formed inside Katy's chest. Jon's tears fell unchecked, moistening his eyelashes. She held his face between her hands and kissed his cheeks. *Dear, sweet man.*

"As they were dying," he said, "I slept without a care to my name."

He was quiet for a moment, clearly tortured from the unimaginable and irreparable damage. His shoulders shuddered with an effort to keep the hurt inside, but the battle was already lost.

"My wife and child. The two I held most dear. My whole world," he said, wiping his tears with the back of his hand. "Gone in the blink of an eye."

Nothing Katy could say or do would relieve Jon's guilt. It was a burden he'd bear for the rest of his life. But talking about them might be what he needed right now.

"What was Emily like?"

"A whirlwind!" He sputtered. "It was all we could do to keep up with her. She loved dogs and tried to pet every single one at Green Lake. She gobbled strawberry ice cream by the gallons. She refused to wear shoes, and she could spend all day playing in the sand."

"My kind of kid."

"There was this one day…you know the kind? When you're convinced an ideal moment will last an eternity?"

"When colors are brighter and foods taste better and time seems to stand still?"

"Yes," he said. "It was Father's Day, and Emily couldn't wait, so she woke us at dawn."

"Oh, no," Katy said. "How long had you been asleep?"

"Two, maybe three hours? But Emily insisted we go to Shilshole, where her present for me was moored. I can see that day perfectly. She'd filled a picnic basket. Peanut butter and Skittle sandwiches, Cutie mandarin oranges, and Girl Scout cookies. The three of us floated on *Emily's Gift* through the afternoon and evening," he said. "That's how I picture them now. On the boat, peaceful and serene."

"What a wonderful way to be remembered," Katy said.

"I've never told anyone that before."

They silently held each other and must've drifted to sleep, because Katy awoke to the morning sun with Jon softly snoring beside her.

Chapter 26

Jon stirred and rolled toward Katy. Her back was to him, but he could tell she was awake, because she positioned her hand to block the morning sun.

He scooted closer and glided his palm along her hip.

Wriggling her bottom between his thighs, she said, "Again?"

"Yes, please," he said, nibbling her neck and shoulder.

After an hour of lovemaking, they showered and breakfasted.

"Where should we go today?" he said, sipping his coffee. *Back to bed?*

"Pike Place Market?" she said. "I'd like to see it before I go home."

Did she have to remind him? Maybe he could talk her into staying longer. Or he could go with her to Fort Worth.

"Could I ask you a favor?" she said.

"Anything." She could ask him to rob a bank, and he'd buy a mask and gun.

"You remember the Irish guy I told you about?" she said. "The one who owns the Bending Bough?"

"Yep."

"Well, he's been really kind to me, and he loves your music, and he doesn't know I know you, but…"

222

"You'd like to surprise him?"

"Only if you're comfortable doing it," she said. "I know how much you cherish your privacy."

"We'll go for lunch."

"Oh, thank you." She smiled and kissed him.

If a heart could burst out of a chest, his was near explosion.

"We better get going," he said. "We've got lots of things to see."

****

Katy's mind reeled. She'd fallen hard, as she knew she would. And she was sure Jon felt the same. But she also knew this was all in her head, because she couldn't trust her instincts. He never said he wanted a relationship. Only that he wanted them to be something more than friends. That did not equate to love. He'd tire of her within a week. But he was hers for now, and she planned to enjoy every precious minute with him. And not think about the massive devastation of when he moved on to his next "favored fan."

They climbed into Tigger with its top down, and Jon drove through the gate to the street.

"I want to take you across 520," he said. "Best view of the mountain."

She didn't care where they went as long as they were together.

As they drove south on I-5, Jon turned on the radio. Shortly afterward, one of his songs started playing. Katy reached for the controls at the same time as Jon.

"Are you turning it up?" Katy asked.

"I'm changing the station," Jon said. "I can't stand hearing myself sing."

Katy found that odd, but what did she know? She

wasn't a singer. Nor a songwriter. Nor could she play an instrument of any kind, unless she counted the plastic flute she mishandled in sixth grade.

"How 'bout some country?" he said.

She expected him to balk like everyone else at her poor taste in music, but he quickly tuned the radio to 100.7 The Wolf. She recognized Tim McGraw's song, "How I'll Always Be."

"I like this station. It's on 99.5 at home," she said, settling back into her seat. "You don't mind?"

"Not a bit. I listen to all kinds of music," he said. "I appreciate country, because it's a form of storytelling. The songs reveal joy or sorrow and sometimes both. Much like gospel."

"I never thought about country music that way," she said.

"And the cadence sets the mood."

"How so?"

"Take this song for instance. It feels like we're in motion. Moving forward. Clipping along. Like we're on a carefree, breezy car ride."

"We *are* on a carefree breezy car ride." She smiled. "But I see what you mean."

"Look," Jon said, pointing to the right. "The Space Needle."

"That's the best angle yet," she said. "What's that body of water?"

"Lake Union," he said. "Spectacular view, isn't it?"

"Stunning."

Exiting I-5, Jon zoomed onto 520, but traffic slowed to a crawl, and he slammed on the brakes. At that exact moment, he flung his right arm across Katy's torso to protect her from flying forward, even though she was wearing a seatbelt.

"Sorry 'bout that," he said, returning his hands to the wheel. "Must be an accident ahead."

"What're we going to do?"

"Nothing we can do. We've missed the last exit off this side of the bridge." He shrugged. "Good thing I filled the tank yesterday."

They inched along, but the day was so beautiful, Katy didn't care, and Jon didn't seem to mind either.

"What's that?" Katy asked, referring to a huge structure in the shape of an alligator's open jaw on the left side of the highway.

"Husky Stadium," he said. "UW."

"You dub?"

"Yeah. University of Washington," he said, not realizing she'd misunderstood. "Rebecca graduated from there."

Katy didn't feel like talking about Rebecca, so she returned the attention back to Jon. "Where'd you go?"

"Um, ah, nowhere." He laughed. "I barely graduated high school."

"It hasn't seemed to hurt you much."

"My parents were worried at first," he said.

"That you'd need another career to keep you going for a while?"

"That I'd live in the guesthouse forever, smoking pot and playing my music too loud."

"Oh, ha," she said. "Bet they're proud of you now, right?"

"I'm not completely sure," he said. "My dad *really* hoped I'd follow in his footsteps."

Katy laughed, because when Jon said the word

"really," his face scrunched.

"If you had, what would you be?" she asked.

"A dentist."

"Oh, no. That wouldn't be my first choice. But if you grew up with a dad who was one…" She sat back and stared at him. "I can kind of see—"

"Cut it out," he said. "I don't want you imagining me that way."

Katy was about to tease him further—maybe a comment about the sexy smocks dentists wear or about the elf, Hermey, in *Rudolph, the Red-Nosed Reindeer*—but her attention was drawn to the top of a lamppost. "Is that a bald eagle?"

"Where?" he said.

"Up there," she said, pointing.

"Good eye," he said.

Katy scanned the sky, surprised at how the birds thrived in the big city. First at Green Lake and now here.

"There's one flying too," he said. "See?"

"I don't…"

"Those crows are dive-bombing it."

"No!" she said. "Why?"

He laughed. "Are you feeling sorry for the eagle?"

"Maybe," she said.

"'Cause it's the crows you should be worried about. The eagle's probably found their nest."

"I don't like to think about nature's cruelty," she said. "And it has nothing to do with being vegan."

Mid-span, Mount Rainier loomed large across Lake Washington. The peak was the color of the sky and clouds. Katy was hesitant to glance away in case the illusion faded. Now she understood. *The mountain was out.*

Jon pointed toward a large clearing to the right of the bridge at the end of its span. "Bill and Melinda Gates live over there," he said. "I've been to their house for a charity event. It's amazing. Excessive, but amazing."

Good Lord. How did she keep forgetting about his "real" life? That he personally knew people in the news. People with influence, wealth, and celebrity. And he was actually one of them.

The traffic cleared, and with no stops, they were soon heading back to Seattle over the other floating bridge, I-90. Jon found a great parking spot only two streets from Pike Place Market, as another car was leaving.

"I don't mean to brag," he said, puffing his chest in comedic fashion, "but I'm a true rock star when it comes to parking."

The wooden structure housing the market was built in the late 1800s, Jon told her, and encompassed several blocks on a brick street. Despite sides open to the sun, the interior was moist and drippy and as dark as dusk.

Katy and Jon stopped frequently, examining items for sale. Baked goods, clothing, purses, cut flowers, jewelry, stationery, baskets, fruits, and vegetables. They tried on hats and sunglasses. She showed him a bracelet made from vintage typewriter keys. He had a conversation with a donkey sock puppet.

Katy sampled two spicy jellies, one infused with jalapenos and the other with ginger. And she couldn't resist a beautiful bouquet of seasonal flowers for the guesthouse. "Only five dollars," she mouthed to Jon with her back toward the vendor, as if they didn't know.

"What a bargain."

Katy watched street performers and listened to merchants hawking their wares. A seductive female voice offering *hot, sticky buns* made Katy think something other than food was being advertised. She glanced around and spotted a bakery but couldn't locate the temptress. When she turned back, she saw a napping opossum wrapped around the shoulders of a man. Others might find them revolting, but Katy had a soft spot for the unusual ghost-faced marsupials. So ugly, they were beautiful.

On the way back to the car, a group of children climbed on and off a large metal statue of a pig named Rachel. A barbershop quartet sang a tune. A dog wearing a clown outfit stood on tiptoes and balanced a rubber ball on its nose.

Jon drove south to the waterfront and found another great parking spot. For a while, they looked in store windows and watched other tourists. Katy saw a sign for Ye Olde Curiosity Shop and tugged Jon toward it. Besides tailpipe whistles, jumping beans, bullwhips and nesting dolls, on display in a glass box were the mummified remains of a human body. Katy couldn't help but stare. "Gross!" she said.

They stepped back outside, strolled to the edge of the sidewalk, and leaned against a wooden railing. Docked there was what looked to be an old pirate ship with ripped sails and discolored deck. For five dollars, they could go onboard the replica and have a look around. At the adjacent pier, a vendor was offering a three-hour boat tour.

Walking along the waterfront on a beautiful early afternoon with Jon was the closest thing to any waking dream Katy could imagine. Another perfect moment with him to add to her treasure trove of memories.

Chapter 27

"You go first," Jon instructed Katy as they formulated their plans outside the Bending Bough. "Get Elliott to turn his back to the door and then I'll come inside."

"I feel like we're plotting espionage," she said, kissing him.

Jon waited a few minutes, trying not to be obvious as he stared into the window. The place was empty, except for Katy and Elliott. She positioned him far enough from the door, so Jon entered without detection. He stood behind Elliott for a moment, eavesdropping on their conversation.

"I've added vegan items to the menu," Elliott said, as Katy sat down at the table. "Especially for you."

"That's so nice," she said. "Can't wait to try them."

"I'm glad you came back," he said. "I wanted to download the picture of us at the Space Needle."

"Oh, right," Katy said, pulling out her phone. "I forgot about that."

Jon widened his eyes and Katy got the message.

"But, first," she said, pointing to Jon. "There's someone I'd like you to meet."

Elliott turned slowly, and the look of dawning was priceless. His expression went from bewilderment to awe in five seconds, and his mouth fell open.

"Hello, Elliott," Jon said. "I'm told you like my

music."

No words came forth, as Elliott gasped air like a fish out of water. Jon thought about snapping his fingers to bring Elliott out of his trance. He noticed the small stage in the corner. "Do you play?" Jon asked.

"What?" Elliott said, following Jon's glance. "Oh, yeah, a bit."

"Do you have instruments here?"

"In the back," he said, flipping his thumb over his shoulder. "A guitar and fiddle."

"Why don't you go get them?"

As Elliott disappeared, Jon asked Katy, "Does this place get any business?"

"I think it's more popular at night."

Elliott loped from the back room, carrying a fiddle and guitar. He held them toward Jon as if they were for sale.

"Are they tuned?" Jon said.

"Yes, sir."

Jon side-smiled at Elliott's formality.

"Which one is yours?" he asked.

"The guitar."

Jon took the fiddle. "It's not my strength. But I'll try to keep up."

"You want to play?" Elliott said, voice cracking as if he were going through puberty. "With me?"

"Sure. Why not?" Jon said, turning to Katy. "Could you take a few pictures for Elliott?"

She nodded and gathered her things to move to a closer table.

"What's your favorite song?" Jon asked Elliott, following him to the stage.

"Well, if I had to choose, I guess I'd say my

favorite song of yours is—"

"Not mine," Jon said. "Pick an Irish tune."

"Do you know 'Galway Girl'?"

"Which version?" Jon asked. "Steve Earle or Ed Sheeran?"

"Steve Earle."

Jon leaned in so Katy couldn't hear. "Do me a favor then."

"Anything," Elliott said.

"Change the color of the hair and eyes to match Katy's."

****

If Katy hadn't already been in love with Jon, she would be now. She could only imagine how elated Elliott was feeling.

She was familiar with the song they were playing and knew the lyrics well. It was about a man who fell in love with an Irish girl. The girl had blue eyes and black hair. But when Elliott got to that part, he changed the eyes to green and hair to auburn, even though it threw off the rhythm and rhyme. If the grin on Jon's face hadn't given him away, his wink at her would've.

For someone who claimed fiddle wasn't his strength, Jon was expert. But despite his talent, he chose not to overshadow Elliott. If anyone had entered the Bending Bough during the song, Elliott would clearly be the star of the show.

Katy and Jon stayed for lunch, enjoying the vegan dishes Elliott had added to the menu.

When it was time to leave, Jon shook Elliott's hand.

"I'll drop by again if you don't blow my cover," he said. "And call me Jon."

"I'd be honored, Jon," Elliott said. "There will always be a table for you."

Katy and Jon walked back to the car, and she slid her hand in his.

"I'm so happy," she said.

"Me too."

They were silent on the short ride home.

"Let's take a walk on the beach," Jon said, bypassing his drive. "I need to tell you something."

Along the water's edge, they took off their shoes and chased the waves. Katy looked for seashells, as Jon collected sea glass. Neither seemed to notice the beach was teeming with people.

"What'd you want to tell me?" Katy asked.

"It's about Rebecca," Jon said. "I haven't been completely honest."

His head dropped and he started to pace as if looking for words in the sand. And like that, Katy's heart broke into a gazillion pieces in the nanosecond it took for him to form his next sentence. The wait was excruciating.

"Rebecca and I…we—son-of-a-bitch," he yelled, hopping to a nearby log.

Sitting, he lifted his right foot, and a rusty nail was halfway embedded in his heel. He yanked it out, and blood gushed onto the sand.

"I need your shirt," Katy said.

He pulled the tee over his head and gave it to her.

"This will stop the bleeding," she said, wrapping his foot. "I'll drive you home and clean it. Then we'll go to emergency for a tetanus shot."

Katy found a good walking-stick, and Jon used it to hobble to the car. At the house, she did her best to disinfect the wound and wrap it in gauze. Jon put on another shirt, and within ten minutes, they were in the car again. They found Rebecca at the end of the drive, and Jon rolled down his window.

"Where are you going?" Rebecca asked. "And why are you in the passenger seat?"

"I stepped on a rusty nail," he said. "Katy's driving me to Swedish."

Rebecca opened the back door. "Not without me."

Katy dropped Jon and Rebecca at the front and parked the car in a large lot behind the hospital. On the walk back, she decided not to assume what Jon was going to tell her. The longer she didn't know, the more time she could spend in her delusional bubble.

****

Jon limped to the admissions desk and filled out paperwork. The day was slow, so a room was available. Rebecca walked with him down the hall.

"A woman named Katy will be here shortly," he told the attendant. "Could you please send her back when she arrives?"

"Certainly," she said and left.

Jon sat on the paper-wrapped hospital bed, feet dangling.

"Remember when we got chicken pox in fourth grade?" he said. "We were sent to the nurse's office together?"

"And she thought we'd drawn the dots on ourselves and wouldn't let us go home?"

"Yes." He smiled.

"We'll always be together, Jon. You and me. That's for sure."

"I'm in love with Katy," he said, unintentionally

confessing.

"Are ya now?" she said.

"I need to tell her about us."

"Why?" Rebecca said. "It was before you even met her."

"She has a right to know," he said.

"What about me?" she said. "Have you ever thought I might have feelings for you?"

"Come on, Becks," he said, looking at his hands. "Don't joke."

"I'm not joking," she said, and from the look on her face he knew it to be true.

How had he been so careless? Not to have read the signs? If he'd known, he wouldn't have crossed the line with her. She meant more to him than that.

He patted the bed, and she sat down beside him. He put his arm around her, and she rested her head on his shoulder.

"It was only one night," he said. "Harmless experiment."

"It doesn't seem harmless to me."

"I love you, Rebecca. I really do."

"I know Jon," she said. "But that doesn't take the pain away."

"Can you ever forgive me?"

There was a commotion in the hallway, and five minutes later the nurse came in with a set of keys and a note from Katy.

Something's come up, and I won't be available for the remainder of your lessons. Be assured that I'll refund the days that are missed. It was nice working with you, and I wish you all the best. You'll find the rest of the keys in the guesthouse. Take care, Katy.

"Shit," he said, jumping off the bed and landing on his bad foot. "Shit."

"She must've overheard us talking," Rebecca said.

"I've got to go."

"You're not going anywhere," the nurse said. "The doctor is on his way."

"I'll take care of this," Rebecca said, grabbing the keys. "Catch a Lyft when you're done and meet me at the house."

****

Katy crammed clothes into her suitcase, as Jon's words burned into her brain.

It was only one night.

Harmless experiment.

I love you, Rebecca.

Can you ever forgive me?

When the suitcase wouldn't close, Katy removed random clothing and stuffed it into the garbage can.

She picked up the instruction booklet she'd created for Jon. It had everything he needed to help him stay vegan. She wanted to chuck it out the window, but then he'd know he hurt her. So she placed it on the kitchen counter instead. She kept the Bee Free Honee for herself, because he didn't deserve any more of her gifts.

Katy planned to Lyft to the Bending Bough. Elliott could help her find a reasonably priced hotel in a safe neighborhood. Then she'd call the airport and negotiate an earlier flight.

Her phone rang. She sent Jon's message straight to voicemail and blocked his number.

As she stepped from the guesthouse, she almost collided with Rebecca.

"What do you want?" Katy said, politeness be

236

damned.

"We need to talk about the thing at the hospital," Rebecca said, pushing past Katy into the guesthouse.

"I don't need an explanation," Katy said, dropping her bags on the porch and stepping back inside. "You told me yourself. You and Jon were meant for each other."

"Katy. Jon and I are—"

"Yes, I know," she said. "You're in love."

"What…?"

"And he and I are…what'd he call us…a harmless experiment."

"That's what you heard? You've got to listen to me, Katy," Rebecca said. "We love each other, yes, but—"

"Stop. Just stop," Katy said, extending her flattened hand like a crossing guard. "We both know you haven't liked me from the start. So, please, step aside, so I can get out of your life."

"But," Rebecca said, "I'm trying to tell you that—"

"I didn't ask to come here. It was Jon's idea," Katy said, shaking her head and moving her hand to her hip. "And I'm tired of being a pawn in your sickening relationship that's been cultivated since birth. Both of you are cruel and horrible, and you deserve each other."

Katy noticed Rebecca's eyes catching fire and a spread of red crossing her cheeks. Unflinching, she accepted the challenge full force.

"You're right," Rebecca said. "I was wary of you from the beginning and for good reason. You can't be trusted to understand the damage you're capable of inflicting."

"Right…" Katy said. "Because I'm an

otherworldly enchantress who pushes produce onto unsuspecting victims, when all the while trying to lure them into my bed. To what end?"

"Money," Rebecca hissed. "You seem to have a penchant for rich celebrities."

"Not fair," Katy said. "I had no idea who Jon was until I got here."

"That's true," Rebecca said. "But it didn't stop you from pursuing him once you arrived. Who's next? Zac Efron? Drake? Jake Gyllenhaal?"

"What?" If Katy ever encountered another famous person, she'd be moving to the boonies. "Of course not."

"Are you sure? They're all alike, don't you think? Easily interchangeable from one to another? I could wrangle up a few prospects," Rebecca said, going in for the kill. "Isn't that what country bumpkins like you say in the south?"

"You win," Katy said, feeling like a beach ball losing air. "I'm done playing this game, and I'd rather not be here when Jon gets back. Can you give me that much dignity at least?"

"I can do one better," Rebecca said, dialing her phone. "I'll book you an expensive hotel room by the Space Needle and schedule your transportation. And, best of all, we'll put it on Jon's tab. It's the least he can do for disrupting your plans."

****

Jon burst through the guesthouse door and searched every room. Except for a booklet on the counter and garments in the garbage, Katy's things were gone. He was too late.

"I told you," Rebecca said, standing on the porch.

"She doesn't want to see you."

"I've got to find her," he said. "She needs to know how I feel."

"It doesn't matter, Jon," Rebecca said. "I don't think she feels the same about you."

He stopped and stared. "Why do you say that?"

"I saw how she behaved at the ballgame. She's still hooked on that ballplayer," Rebecca said. "And he wants her back."

"Did she tell you that?" he said, thinking it impossible after the night he and Katy shared she would return to Greg.

"She didn't have to," she said. "Listen to this."

Rebecca pulled out her phone and played a recent podcast. Greg Daniels was the special guest, and he was talking about dating. "I can't lie," he said in his southern drawl. "I do love the ladies. But I could see myself settling down one day. And if you're listening, Katy, I'd sure like to hear from you. I'm in Seattle through Monday, so give me a shout."

Jon felt physically ill—a sudden need to vomit.

"That doesn't prove anything," he said. "She probably didn't even hear it."

"Maybe not," Rebecca said. "If you want to ask her yourself, I know where she is."

****

Katy walked through the lobby of the Hyatt House Hotel to the elevators. A bag full of necessities swung from her fingers—saltines, vegan butter, pack of Virginia Slims, book of matches, and a fifth of Patrón.

Stepping off the elevator on the fourteenth floor, she followed a long corridor to her room. As she set the bag down to retrieve her key card, she heard Jon's voice call from behind.

"Katy, wait," he said, limping toward her. "I need to talk to you."

"Go away, Jon," she said. "There's nothing more to discuss."

"It was only one night," he said.

"I get it," she said, fumbling with the key. "Harmless experiment."

"And it was before I became vegan," he said. "I didn't even know you then."

"What?" She turned and looked at him.

He was disheveled and his eyes were bloodshot and wild.

"That's what I was trying to tell you on the beach," he said.

"You hadn't been completely honest about Rebecca," she said, remembering his words. "You slept together."

"Only once," he said. "I didn't think she'd want to take things further."

"That's why she'd never leave us alone," Katy said, relieved. "I was in the way of her plans."

"I should've told you sooner," he said.

"Maybe. If I'd ever asked…" Katy said. "But we all have secrets, and some aren't worth repeating."

"That's so true." He audibly sighed.

"What are your feelings for her now?"

"She's my best friend, and I'll always care about her," Jon said, brushing a tress of Katy's hair behind her ear and resting his palm on her cheek. "But you're the one I want to have and to hold from this day forward."

Before Katy could register the gravity of his words,

the door to her hotel room swung open. Naked except for a towel draped around his waist, Greg held a bottle of champagne in one hand and an empty ice bucket in the other. "I thought I heard voices."

Jon's hand pulled away from her face as if he'd been burned.

"What...where did you..." Katy stammered to Greg.

"Say," Greg said to Jon. "You look familiar. Are you the concierge?"

Katy glanced at Jon, but his expression was unreadable.

"Could you grab us some ice?" Greg said and thrust the bucket into Jon's hands.

Jon turned with it and limped down the corridor.

With her palms against Greg's bare chest, Katy shoved him back into the room. "Put some clothes on," she hissed before closing the door and following Jon.

"Where are you going?"

"To get ice." Without turning, he lifted the bucket above his head and smashed it against the wall.

"Jon. Wait."

He stopped at the elevators, standing rigid like a tree.

"That's not what—" she started.

"Don't insult my intelligence, Katy," he said, voice low and dry. "I know exactly what *that* is."

"No, no—"

"You said you weren't over him. You told me you weren't ready," he said, pounding his finger on the elevator down button. "I should've believed you."

"But I—"

He pulled his phone from his pocket and made a

show of blocking her number. The elevator opened, and he stepped inside. He turned to look at her, light vanishing from his eyes like a cyborg. "Don't worry about sending me a refund," he said, sizing her up and down. "I got my money's worth."

"Please let me—"

"I don't *ever* want to hear from you again."

The elevator closed on his stone-cold face, leaving Katy to stare at her destroyed reflection in the stainless-steel doors.

****

Katy sat on the hotel bed next to Greg, legs dangling. He was wearing a pair of faded jeans and a T-shirt.

"That wasn't the concierge, was it?" he said.

"No," she answered.

"It was that musician…what's-his-name? John Mayer. How'd you meet him?"

She didn't feel like correcting Greg or going into details. Her anger at his interruption had faded, and now she felt tired and sad. After all, she had believed seeing Greg at the ballgame would bring closure. What was the saying? We bring things to ourselves?

"How did you know I was here?" she asked, gently.

"Some woman called my service. Said it was you and there'd be a key card at the front desk in my name if I felt like dropping by for old time's sake."

Things were starting to make sense. *Helps to have connections. Hotel room by the Space Needle. Jon will pay.* Rebecca.

Greg dropped his head like a hound dog and stared at his lap, appearing even younger than his twenty-eight years. "I need you, Katy. I really do."

"I know," she said. "But that's not enough for me now."

"I thought you loved me."

"I did…I do…" She leaned in and put her hand on his knee as if consoling a small child. "Just not in that way anymore."

He glanced at her. "If this is about that girl at the ballpark, she doesn't mean—"

"It has nothing to do with her," Katy said. "I need more than you're able to give."

"What do you mean?" he said, clearly confused. "I thought I made you happy…you know…in the bedroom."

Katy turned her face away to hide the sudden flash of heat in her cheeks. "Sex isn't everything."

"Oh…"

"I need commitment."

He sat for a moment and then nodded ever so slightly. "No one deserves it more than you, but…"

"You're nowhere near ready."

"Not now, anyway," he said. "I'm really sorry."

"Don't be. You made no promises," she said. "Besides, you're young. You should enjoy yourself as much as you can."

"You think?" he said, smiling. "But…"

"Yes?"

"It was fun while it lasted, right?"

"Tons."

They sat for a bit, nothing more to say on the subject.

Then Greg broke the silence. "Feel like going for pizza?"

She hooked her elbow around his. "If it's vegan and you're buying."

"It'll be my pleasure, darlin'."

Chapter 28

Jon sat at the kitchen table in his cabin on Bainbridge, devouring Dick's cheeseburgers in the dark. He'd been binging for a week, and even though he felt like shit, he had no intention of stopping.

How had things gone so wrong with Katy?

At first, he couldn't believe his luck, finding her on the vegan forum of all places. Their phone conversations were the highlight of his day. But when they finally met in person, dopamine flooded his system and turned his brain to pulp. He couldn't even hug her properly, because his physical reaction had been too obvious.

But that was only part of her appeal. She was everything he'd been searching for—smart, generous, funny. Her undeniable warmth drew him to her, as if he were a weary traveler glimpsing the glowing lights of home.

He would've sworn she felt the same. Otherwise, he wouldn't have poured out his heart and soul and told her things he hadn't told anyone. He'd even cried in front of her, for fuck's sake.

Why had she chosen that ballplayer over him? Jon wondered if Greg had stayed faithful. Not likely given his maturity level. She'd be heartbroken again. Her wellbeing shouldn't matter to Jon, but it did. If he'd been honest about Rebecca in the first place, Katy wouldn't have felt betrayed. And she wouldn't have called Greg.

He'd been furious when he found the ballplayer in her hotel room. Jon's first thought, after the murderous one, was to contact past lovers and work his way through the alphabet. Instead, he'd driven to Bainbridge and plucked his guitar until his fingers bled. An entire sketch pad contained doodles of demonized horses and baseball bats morphing into serpents.

He once teased Katy she needed rescuing, but in all honesty, he was the one in peril. After a week without her, the hole in his heart had expanded.

Chapter 29

Katy spent the remainder of her vacation at home in bed—curtains closed, music off, phone dead. Her sheets were crusted with saltine crumbs and vegan butter. A bottle of Patrón—almost empty—had fallen to its side on the nightstand next to an overflowing ashtray of cigarette butts. It wasn't true a person couldn't smell their own stink.

On Sunday morning, she heard a knock at the door but didn't bother getting up. She had no desire to deal with solicitors—the only people who came to the farmhouse these days. She closed her eyes and fell back asleep.

At noon, she roused herself and slogged to the bathroom. When she passed through the living room on the way to the kitchen, she was startled to find her father on the couch reading one of her *Southern Living* magazines.

"Hello, baby girl," he said.

"Oh, Dad." Katy slumped next to him, putting her head on his shoulder. "What are you doing here?"

"Lori called," he said. "She gave me quite the earful."

"It's really not—"

"Why didn't you tell me yourself?"

"Dad, I…"

"All these years…" He shook his head.

Katy watched as he struggled for words, but she didn't know what to say to help him find them, so she waited.

"All these years, you've been taking care of me instead of the other way around." His eyes began to fill, extinguishing their normal twinkle. "You must really hate me."

Seeing him like that was too much. The tears she'd been damming since her encounter with Jon suddenly burst. She felt her father's arm slip around her back, and she curled her legs underneath, snuggling into him as she had as a small child.

They remained in that position for what seemed like hours. Sniffles layered on top of each other as they recalled painful memories without saying a word.

Katy broke the somber mood with a giggling fit, which started slowly, but picked up momentum rather quickly.

"What's so funny?" he asked, shoulders already shaking with mirth.

"I'm pretty sure I stink," she said.

"You smell like a garbage scow," he said. "When was the last time you showered?"

"I don't remember. Tuesday maybe?"

She snorted loudly, which sent them into another outburst. They eventually broke apart and stared at each other, bellies jiggling as the last of the giggles left their bodies like bubbles.

"Thanks," she said. "I needed that."

"Me too," he said.

Katy rose from the couch, wiping tears on her sleeve. "Would you like some tea? I'll put the kettle on."

"Let me do that for you. I've been thinking about your project," he said, following her to the kitchen.

"Oh, yeah?" she said.

"How 'bout I help you get this place in shape?" he said. "Free labor until school starts in the fall."

She sprang toward him and wrapped her arms around his neck, smooching him multiple times on the cheek.

"Baby girl," he said, wiping off her kisses and laughing. "You really don't smell very good."

****

After taking the best shower of her life, Katy stood at the kitchen counter in a clean bathrobe, hands wrapped around a cup of Orange Blossom tea.

Her father tidied the kitchen, putting away the box of saltines and returning the vegan butter to the fridge.

"This reminds me of when you were a kid and we were living in our car in Mexico."

He rarely spoke of those times, so Katy listened intently.

"That waitress at the breakfast place on the corner used to give us saltines and butter packets. On a good day, she'd slip us a whole jar of Yucatan honey."

How had Katy forgotten? No wonder that was her go to crutch. She couldn't remember when the tequila and cigarettes were added, though.

"Are you still seeing your lady friend?" she asked. "The psychiatrist?"

"Nah. She dumped me," he said. "Accused me of using her for free advice."

"Were you?"

"Not initially," he said, eyes lighting up. "But I sure learned a lot."

"Like?"

"What a horrible father I was to you." He brushed a lock of hair behind her ear. "I'm really sorry, baby girl."

"You were young," she said.

"No excuses. I ran away from responsibility. Your mother would've been furious with me."

"Can you tell me something about her?"

"You bet," he said. "What would you like to know?"

Katy thought of the one thing she never dared ask her father but needed to know desperately, especially now. "Did she want me?"

He pulled Katy into his arms and held her tight. "Right before she died, you were fast asleep in her arms. She kissed the top of your bald little head and with the most blissful look I've ever seen on her face, she said to me, '*El amor abre todas las puertas*.'"

Katy knew exactly what that meant. *Love opens all doors.*

Chapter 30

At the cabin, Jon flipped through the instruction booklet Katy had created for him. After he'd found her with Greg, Jon had buried the booklet in the backyard in the dead of night and marked the spot with a Halloween-type RIP sign. He must've known then how valuable it was, because he'd wrapped it in protective plastic to keep out moisture. Now the booklet was his salvation.

The month following her departure, Jon ate nothing but junk. No vegetables. No fruit. No beans, nuts, or seeds. He stuffed his face with nachos and ribs and hot wings. It was as if he were living inside a tailgate party. His bike never left its rack, and he only ate out.

But then he made a pass at a cute weekender at the coffee shop, asking if she wanted him to write her a song.

"Oh, gross," he overheard her tell a friend. "That hairy fat guy tried to pick me up."

That was two months ago and now he felt fit and strong. Physically anyway.

Katy had designed the instruction booklet especially for him. She must've taken copious notes on his likes and dislikes. She included the recipes they'd made together, and many more that looked as easy and delicious. She added sample menus and grocery lists allowing him to enjoy a full day's worth of food without repeating for an entire week. Every recipe came with pictures. And she made sure the calories were sufficient for a man his height.

His favorites so far were the tofu and mushroom scramble served with hash browns and biscuits, burrito with no-fry re-fried beans, sweet coleslaw with apple and pineapple chunks, and air-fryer chickpeas. But that might change when he sampled more recipes.

She included simple dressings, sauces, and dips, such as "honey" mustard, strawberry vinaigrette, and "sour cream" made with cashews. She listed natural sweeteners, like dried figs and dates. She suggested he peel bananas and freeze them for smoothies. She mentioned dark chocolate with cocoa of 70% or more, but cautioned it might taste bitter at first. She recommended he add ground flaxseed whenever possible to promote healthy nail growth.

There was even a section for restaurant menus from local places such as Wayward Vegan Cafe, El Chupacabra, and MOD Pizza. She'd written a message on the pizza menu, noting he could take-out an 11" with red sauce, black olives, and mushrooms and then add air-fryer tofu and two cups of arugula at home. A post-it read: *If you like Indian, Ethiopian, Thai, and/or Greek, they're good sources for tasty vegan cuisine.* He ran his fingers across the pencil marks, hoping to feel her warmth in the etchings.

Biking was another story. Rocky wasn't forgiving of his neglect. Jon could only ride fifteen minutes until cramping set in, because of his month-long binge. He had to pass that damned alpaca twice everyday until he re-conquered the killer hill. His sweat smelled clean these days and not like grease pouring out of a vat.

Jon was also writing songs again. Something he hadn't been able to do since his hiatus began. And the ones coming to fruition were good and true and among the best he'd written to date. As for "Katy's Song," that was in limbo for now, although he caught himself humming it from time to time.

When Rebecca visited, they rarely spoke about Katy. But, occasionally, Rebecca commented on how fortunate it was he hadn't known Katy for long, so she'd be much easier to forget. He didn't mention he slept with Katy's discarded garments under his pillow and kept lavender in his pocket.

He called his parents on a weekly basis. At first, they were evasive, thinking his time was too precious to waste on them. Then they fell into an easy rhythm of rediscovering each other as adults, and the conversations lasted more than a few minutes.

"You loved picking wildflowers," his mother told him about a childhood he'd mostly forgotten. "I kept them in a birdhouse hung above the kitchen table so the cat wouldn't eat them."

"I remember Stubs," he said, thinking about the creature with its broken tail he'd found under the rhododendron in the guesthouse garden. "He drooled when he purred."

"That's because he was taken from his momma too soon," she said. "Your father had to feed him milk with an eye-dropper when he was a kitten."

"I remember that too," Jon said, finding comfort in reconnecting with the loving couple who cared deeply for him before and after his heart had been repeatedly broken.

Jon's sorrow wasn't nearly as dark as when

Charlotte and Emily died, because Katy was still in the world. But she wasn't in his world, and that was almost too much to bear.

Chapter 31

For three months, Katy and her dad spruced up the farmhouse and barn. When her mind wandered to thoughts of Jon, as it often did, she researched lighting fixtures and exterior paint colors. If she was tempted to turn on the radio to catch one of his songs, she hid it in the barn behind the pitchforks and shovels. While straightening the dining room, she found his CD under the table, so she attached it to a pole in her garden as a sun-catcher to scare off the crows. His doodle drawing of Godzilla Duck was pressed between the pages of a recipe book and placed out of reach.

Katy still needed money for her project, and one afternoon, she had an idea. She opened her contact list on her phone and found the number she was after.

"Ms. Young's office," Julia said on the other end.

"Hi, Julia. It's Katy. Greg's friend?"

"Oh, my gosh," Julia gushed. "Claire would love to talk with you. I'll put you through."

"Wait. I didn't call to speak with Claire."

"But she's so grateful. You wouldn't believe how much Greg's changed. It's like he matured into a man overnight. He even sold his Harley. I don't know how you did it."

"It was all him," Katy said but felt a little swell of pride anyway.

"Greg gave me his copy of your business plan. I

think it's brilliant. And Claire's going to fund your project after all. No strings attached."

There was no such thing in Katy's mind. "Actually," she said to Julia, "I called to talk to you."

"Me? What about?"

Katy touched the horse pin on the counter. "Are you still making jewelry?"

"Yes, but—"

"Have you ever thought of selling your pieces?"

"Well, no, I mean, yes, but, no…"

"Listen, Julia, I'm opening a store on my property featuring local artists," Katy said. "I'll be busy with the animals, so I'll need some outside help. Maybe you and I could come to an agreement."

There was a long pause, and Katy worried the call had been disconnected. Finally, Julia spoke.

"Are you saying I could display my jewelry?"

"More than that," Katy said. "I'm building an artist's studio in the back of the store, and there'll be a designated space for you to create. But you'll need to run the store when it's open."

"I could do that," Julia said.

"My hope is you'll invest in the project," Katy said. "But I'll pay you an hourly rate if you'd rather not."

"You bet I'll invest," Julia said. "I've wanted an opportunity like this for years."

"Great," Katy said. She'd been right. She knew another dreamer when she saw one. "We'll meet soon to go over details."

After hanging up the phone, she dug through the junk drawer, looking for a scratch pad. Her fingers snagged a stapled piece of paper, and she pulled it out for closer examination. It was Jon's address in Seattle with a vegan recipe attached. She must've thrown it in the drawer when she'd returned home.

From talking to Elliott, Katy knew Jon had been meeting women at the Bending Bough on a weekly basis. To Elliott, the news seemed harmless, because Katy had never told him about her feelings for Jon.

On the one hand, she was happy for Elliott, because he and Jon were becoming good friends. On the other hand, it rankled, because her feelings for Jon hadn't diminished one iota. She didn't want to hear about his active love life.

And why was Jon taking his dates to the Bending Bough anyway? There were tons of restaurants in Seattle. Why Elliott's? Was he trying to punish her for what he believed she'd done?

That's when Katy decided to write Jon a letter to set the record straight.

Dear Jon. I hope this letter finds you well…

She crumpled the piece of paper and tossed it in the recycle. Too formal.

Yo! Jon! How's it hangin'?

That one sailed into the bin next to the last one. Too silly.

What to say? What to say?

Jon. It's been a few months since we saw each other, and I'm the last person you expected or wanted to hear from, but I feel it's only fair for you to know my side of the story. I did NOT invite Greg to my hotel room that night. In fact, I was as shocked as you were to see him standing there. We were not then, nor are we now, together. If you haven't already talked to Rebecca about this, please do. I'm certain she can shine some light on the whole situation. If nothing else, I think you owe me the courtesy of reassessing your opinion of my character and to remember our time together fondly, as I know I will. Take care. Katy.

She addressed the envelope, stamped it, and dropped it in the mailbox before she had time to rethink her decision to send it. What he did with the information was his business.

Chapter 32

On a drizzly Friday evening at the Bending Bough, Jon studied the woman sitting across from him—his sixth blind date in as many weeks. She was candy-box pretty with flaxen hair, beacon-white teeth, and cloying center. Transplanted from Venice Beach, she'd moved to Seattle to test outdoor gear for an online sports magazine. Her yoga clothes carried a sour scent of dried sweat.

The woman wasn't anything like he'd expected. Rebecca described her as inquisitive, lively, and quirky. More accurately, she was nosy, hyper, and disturbing. And her darting eyes and machine gun laughter made him anxious.

But, then again, none of the women fit Jon's tastes, especially intellectually.

"That's not the point," Rebecca said. "Pick one. You need to get back on the bike."

The woman at the table disrupted his trance by saying his name.

"I'm sorry," he said, touching his ear. "I didn't hear you?"

"You're vegan," she said. "Right?"

"Yes," he said, thinking she might be self-conscious about eating meat in front of him, as some of the others had been.

"Then why are you eating the bread?" she asked.

"What's not vegan about soda bread?"

"It's made with wheat. I didn't think vegans ate gluten."

"Where'd you hear that?" he said. "If I didn't eat wheat, I'd starve."

"Oh, well," she said. "I thought vegans were more disciplined, I guess."

It wasn't worth it to him to explain further.

She ordered the most expensive items on the menu, food enough for four people. He was toying with the idea of sending her an invoice if she wasted a single crumb.

"I was surprised you sent Lyft for me," she said.

"I thought you'd be more comfortable meeting in a public place," he said. "What with us being strangers and all."

"That part was smart," she said. "I've been through my share of bad hook-ups."

Finally, they were discussing real life and not her extensive skin care routine. Maybe they could talk about the trials and tribulations of modern-day dating. After all, she was in the trenches too. Perhaps he'd judged her too harshly. She'd been nervous at first and was now settling down.

"It's that, well…"

"Yes?"

"Considering who you are, I figured you'd send a limo."

His previous opinions were restored.

"I bet you're super-rich," she said.

Here we go, he thought, glancing down at his veggie potpie and losing his appetite. Unfortunately, this line of dialogue was common—although most people were more subtle in their probing.

"Is that your Hummer out front?" she said. "God, it's gorgeous."

"It belongs to someone else. My car's *way* smaller," he said, side-smiling at his lame joke about overcompensation. The comment zinged past her without registering.

"Oh," she said, clearly disappointed her date hadn't arrived in a vehicle that guzzled gas and was originally designed for war.

"Maybe we could figure out whose it is," he said, "and they'll take you for a ride."

"Nah, that's okay," she said, not catching his second and final joke of the evening.

He flipped the conversation on her and asked, "What kind of car do *you* drive."

"Nothing fancy," she said, taken aback by his question. "Does it matter?"

"Not to me."

"Oh good," she said. "Say, Magnolia's close by, right? What about the Highlands?"

And like that, she'd moved from autos to houses, naming two of the most expensive neighborhoods in Seattle. Was she a home decorator or real estate agent on the side? A guy could hope.

"They're not within walking distance," he said. "If that's what you're asking."

"I'm trying to imagine where someone like you might live."

Did she see him as an exotic animal that required a special habitat?

"Someone like me?" he asked.

"Yeah," she said. "Famous."

"Ah." He took a swig of Manny's.

"I'm guessing you live in a gated community. Somewhere exclusive and posh."

"I live in my great-grandpa's fishing shack," he said, deliberately omitting details and allowing her to jump to conclusions.

"Seriously?" she said, wrinkling her nose in disgust. "Doesn't it smell?"

Was she now wondering if she'd been set up with a Noe Burke look-alike? Wouldn't that be a wicked thread to pull.

"With all your…" she said. "Why wouldn't you own…"

He could almost see the mechanisms in her brain chugging and sputtering. It brought a doodle to mind, but he was without a pen.

"What's the use of having money," she said, "if you don't spend it on things you want?"

"I *do* spend it on things I want."

She tilted her head and stared like a mantis, puzzling with a question he hadn't asked. Then she clapped her hands and laughed in delight, squirming in her seat.

"I've got it," she declared. "You own a plane."

He felt like a condemned prisoner, eating his last meal before execution. Only they'd nixed his request for ambrosia and brought liver and onions instead. He fought the compulsion to escape through the kitchen, throwing a wad of cash at Elliott on the way out. But interaction with other people, no matter how mundane, kept his darker thoughts from devouring him. This woman, however, made it difficult to remember why he even bothered.

"What makes you think I own a plane?" he said.

"Because," she said, too loudly. "You're a rock star."

An Irish band performed in the corner, so only the couple at the next table turned their heads to look. They were polite and glanced away the second they recognized him.

"Is it a Learjet?" she said. "Can it take us to Paris?"

"I hate to disrupt your travel plans, but I don't own a plane."

"Private island?" she said, still hopeful.

"Nope."

"A yacht?" she said, grasping for straws. "There are tons of marinas around here."

"Sorry."

"Then I give up," she said, slumping in her chair and folding her arms under her augmented breasts. "What *do* you spend your money on?"

Ignoring the compulsion to mention how inappropriate it was for her to ask, he said, "On non-profits, start-ups, family, and friends. *Things* like that."

Her lips formed the words, as if she were following along in her early reader.

He clarified further. "I don't spend my money on *stuff*," he said. "I give most of it away."

She looked utterly perplexed by his statement.

One day, when this woman was much older, she might look back on her twenties as carefree yet foolish. She'd be in a loving and chaotic relationship and have kids or pets or both. She'd donate to the local food bank or animal shelter. She'd be interested in world issues. Jon certainly hoped so, because it saddened him to think anyone could go through their entire life caring only about money and the shit it can buy.

Before walking to Elliott's restaurant, Jon had made a decision. Either he'd be seducing tonight's date for a much-needed romp. Or he'd be buying a bottle of whiskey on the way home. One thing was certain. He wouldn't be pressing his lips to any part of this woman's body.

****

Jon stepped onto his deck, holding a fifth of Jameson. No need for a highball glass, because he intended to drink straight from the bottle. He hadn't had a drop of whiskey in a year and a half, so it shouldn't take long to numb the pain.

Why could he not stop thinking about Katy? It didn't help he haunted the places reminding him of her. He signed onto the vegan forum and read her old posts. He drove to Green Lake and sat in his car, listening to Tim McGraw songs. And he played music with Elliott during slow afternoons at the Bending Bough. "Galway Girl" was always in the mix.

Then Rebecca talked him into dating some of her single friends—her watered-down suggestion after he rejected hiring a matchmaker for millionaires. And why the hell not? Katy wasn't coming back, and he sure-as-shit wasn't going to chase after her. Elliott said she'd gone into business with the ballplayer's sister, so clearly Greg was still in her life.

Jon thought maybe if he met his dates at the Bending Bough, Elliott would relay to Katy Jon was unaffected by her absence and had quickly moved on. Who was being immature now? Besides, both he and Elliott knew the truth. Jon could date a thousand women and they'd all have one thing in common. They were not Katy.

He twirled the Jameson bottle in his hand like a gunfighter. The golden liquid was as beguiling and dangerous as midnight lightning. He twisted the cap slightly but didn't break the seal. He knew the ramifications of freeing the poisonous genie. But loneliness weighed heavy, and he was exhausted from its constant companionship.

He spun the bottle on the table, as if looking for a new lover. It stopped at Katy's empty seat. He pressed the unopened whiskey to his lips, tipping it back. So easy, he thought. So easy to forget, at least for a little while, the hope Katy shattered by rejecting him. But then he grabbed the bottle by its neck and hurled it into the Sound. It splashed and popped up, bobbing like a buoy.

Jon strolled into the living room and sorted through the mail—bills, solicitations, postcards listing homes for sale. His heart thumped when he found an envelope with the return address of Fort Worth. What could Katy possibly tell him he didn't already know? He didn't want to restart the grieving process by poking the slow-healing wound.

Jon struck a match and held it to the corner. When it lit, he threw the envelope into the fireplace. But then he stomped out the fire, ripped open the envelope, and read the letter inside.

Chapter 33

Katy and Lori sat on the deck of Bird Café in Sundance Square, waiting for their dates. The night was warm, and the light breeze felt good on her face. She was to meet Sara's colleague, a heart specialist named Robert. Lori and Sara offered to double date to make the situation less awkward.

"He's really nice," Lori said. "Some of the nurses would love to date him, and that's a good sign."

"It's too soon," Katy said. "I'm not ready."

"Think of it as practice then," Lori said. "Nothing more."

When Sara and Robert arrived, the four shared a bottle of Chardonnay. The meals were exemplary. The conversation flowed.

"I hear you're building an animal sanctuary," Robert said. "I have three mutts myself."

Robert was forty-three, divorced, and a father of teenage twin boys. He was born on the Big Island of Hawaii, and after high school, he spent a few years teaching surf lessons. His only ambition had been to open a shop of his own. But when he was twenty, he found his father dead from a heart attack in the bathroom. So Robert became a surgeon. He had transferred to Fort Worth fifteen years ago and lived on an acre of land not far from Katy.

He was an elegant man and distinguished dresser

who indulged in expensive tastes. When he hugged Katy hello, his smooth cheek brushed against hers and she felt a spark of hope. Maybe she wasn't completely dead inside.

After dinner, Robert drove Katy home. His black Mercedes was a newer model at the higher end of the price range. He'd had it professionally cleaned and detailed earlier in the day.

"Beautiful things should be treated with the utmost respect," he said. "Don't you think?"

She couldn't recognize beauty these days, but she didn't contradict him.

"Nightcap?" she asked. A stiff drink might be the thing she needed to invite him into her lonely bed.

"I have surgery in the morning, so I should go," he said. "But I'd like to see you again."

She gave him her number, and they kissed goodnight. His lips were full and strong.

The next day, Robert sent flowers with a thank-you note, underlining his desire to get to know her better. On their second date, he took her to an outdoor movie and packed a vegan picnic. They held hands. The goodnight kiss lasted longer than the first.

He shared her interest in country music, and they made plans to see Tim McGraw in Dallas. He texted her every night and wished her sweet dreams. He stopped eating meat, even though she hadn't asked.

When Katy was with Robert, she only thought of Jon. But one day that would change. So she continued dating Robert. And he was patient. But it was only a matter of time before he'd expect her to share his bed. She knew it would be pleasant. And, eventually, it might be enough.

Chapter 34

Pounding on Rebecca's front door, Jon felt like a madman. She answered, wearing purple silk pajamas and a confused expression.

"I thought you were on a date," she said.

"That was no date. It was a job interview."

"Come again?" Rebecca said. "She wanted you to hire her?"

"Not for a position I'm trying to fill."

"Still not getting your—"

"She wouldn't have been satisfied with the perks anyway," he said. "What with me not owning a McMansion or a jet or a private island."

"I think you're exaggerating a—"

"I didn't come here to talk about tonight's date."

He shoved Katy's letter into Rebecca's hand and waited while she read it.

Rebecca raised her eyes to his and flicked the paper. "This…it's not…"

Jon glared at her, waiting for a plausible explanation that didn't involve deceit.

"I did it for you," she said, pouting.

"For me?" he growled, not falling for her overused tactic. "Why?"

Rebecca shrugged. "She wasn't right for you."

"How could you possibly know that?" he said, snatching the letter from her. "You only just met her."

"I could say the same to you," she said, becoming defensive as she always did when in the wrong. "Katy was still involved with that ballplayer. You saw yourself."

"Because *you* set it up to look that way."

The neighbor's dog howled, and Rebecca tried to coax Jon inside, but he refused to budge.

"You let Katy believe I was in love with you," he said, finger pointing back and forth between the two of them. "Didn't you?"

"She assumed, and—"

"How dumb was I?" he said, pacing. "Thinking you were doing me a favor by keeping her company."

"I was trying to understand what you—"

"But the whole time you were scheming and plotting. Weren't you?"

"It wasn't premeditated, if that's what you're—"

"She probably got that ridiculous *favored fan* idea from you."

Rebecca pulled her eyes away for a moment, indicating guilt.

"Damn you to hell!" he said. "You knew I was celibate."

"I thought maybe you started up again."

"Bullshit," he said. "That's a lie."

"Okay, okay," she said, stalling for time. "It's because Katy was a bit of a—"

"What?"

"Flake," she said. "She got over that ballplayer pretty quickly, don't you think? Soon after meeting you?"

Jon raked a hand through his hair. He glanced at the moon for a moment, as if life's answers could be found there. Before Katy's letter arrived, he considered maybe she returned to Greg to give the relationship a fighting chance. After all, their breakup happened mere weeks before her visit to Seattle. She was honest about not looking for a replacement, but Jon pursued her anyway. He returned his eyes to Rebecca's. "We're pathetic, you and I."

"I'm not sure I agree with—"

"She deserved better treatment from both of us," he said. "I should've taken her to San Francisco, and you had no right to persecute her."

"*Persecute* is kind of harsh."

"You unhinged your jaw and went for the jugular."

"She appeared out of nowhere," Rebecca said, voice escalating in volume and pitch. "What was I to do?"

"Not a damn thing." He was on the verge of tears, feeling as if he were liquefying from the inside out. "It was none of your fucking business."

"You wait one minute," she said. "We've gone through too much for you to say that to me."

He was silent for a moment in the eye of the storm.

"You're right, Becks. I'm sorry," he said, feeling like shit for belittling her rescue mission after the accident. "But couldn't you see how happy I was with her?"

"Yes, but it would've been temporary," she said. "She had a lot of baggage."

"Who doesn't have baggage after a certain age?" he said, temper flaring again.

They glowered at each other, steaming like boxers in the ring. Neither blinked, as if locked in the staring contest they'd played as children. Jon's victory was hollow, though, when Rebecca pulled her gaze away before her retinas exploded.

"Oh, Jon." Her shoulders drooped and tears ran down her cheeks. "I did it for *us*."

Not that again. He stepped back. "We talked about this, Rebecca. Remember?"

"I don't understand why we can't be together."

"Let me ask you this," he said, trying to wrap his head around her insistence they were meant for each other. "How would you rate the sex?"

"What?"

"Scale of one to ten. Ten being the best," he said. "What would our number be?"

"Hard to say, because we only did it one night."

"Which usually means it's the most uninhibited. Wouldn't you agree?"

"Well…yes…"

"What was our passion level?"

"I don't know. Maybe an eight?"

"An *eight*?" Eyes widening, he couldn't help but laugh. "Let me get this straight," he said, breaking it down for her. "You think knocking heads and knees, not to mention dissatisfaction on both our parts, rates an *eight*? We didn't even get completely undressed or go a second round."

"Okay. It wasn't good. In fact it was bloody awful," she said. "But we can do better."

"Can we? What if you're wrong? Do you want to live the rest of your days with mediocre sex? Because I sure don't," he said and then drove his point home. "Are you even remotely attracted to me physically?"

Rebecca dropped her eyes. "Not really, but I was hoping I could be."

"But…why?"

She slumped onto the porch stoop, resting her head against a pillar. "You disappear when you're in love, Jon," she said quietly. "I couldn't go through that again."

Chapter 35

Saturday morning, Katy drove with the windows rolled down to Horse Haven Physical Therapy Center in Fort Worth. Tucked between summer's swelter and winter's chill, autumn was Katy's second favorite season. One of the first to arrive at the center, she parked in her usual spot under a pecan tree.

Her dad had returned to teaching in Atlanta and promised to visit between semesters to help with repairs on the house. Not much was left to do, they both knew, but it gave them an excuse to see each other on a more regular basis. He'd called last night to wish her good luck for this morning's meeting.

Katy was early for an appointment with the center's new director, Ben Abernathy, to negotiate Bandit's sale. Vic, an instructor and dear friend, had agreed to attend and to attest to how Bandit's value was a result of Katy's efforts, and how she shouldn't be charged extra as a result.

"I'll be with you in a minute," Ben said, poking his head outside his office door. "I need to make one phone call."

Katy remained standing—too anxious and fidgety to sit. Today marked a milestone for her dreams. She needed to keep her emotions in check.

Unlike the last director, Ben had praised her for her expertise and seemed open to discussion. He'd only been at the center a month, though, so it was too soon to tell for sure.

"Hey," Vic said to Katy as he barreled through the lobby door. "Are you ready?"

"As I'll ever be." She hugged him, avoiding the temptation to pat his expansive belly.

With his beard and his gut and the gap between his two front teeth, Vic looked like a human-sized teddy bear. It was hard not to want to cling to him, especially in times like these.

Ben reappeared and ushered them into his office. "Come in. Come in."

Katy and Vic sat in the metal chairs across from the messy desk. Vic's chair groaned from his massive weight.

"I'm still untangling all this," Ben said, embarrassed by the chaos. He was an attractive man with graying sideburns and a five o'clock shadow that started first thing in the morning. A photo of his lovely wife and three young children was on his desk next to the phone. "So you want to buy Bandit?"

"Yes. Yes I do," Katy said and handed Ben a printout. "I think this is a fair price."

He examined the offer and then looked at Katy. "Seems a bit low," he said. "Considering Bandit's value to the—"

"I know what you're going to say," Katy said. "And I'm willing to make you a deal if you accept my price."

"Oh?" Ben said and sat back in his chair, tapping his fingers and thumbs together, palms apart. "I think it's only fair to tell you I received a call from an interested buyer this morning."

"What?" The breath was knocked out of her. No one had shown interest in Bandit for almost two years. Why today? "Do you know who?"

"Some guy," Ben said. "Asked a lot of questions."

Katy looked at Vic and he shrugged.

"First I've heard of it," he said.

"Has this guy been around in person?" she asked.

"I don't think so," Ben said. "Seemed serious, though."

"Did he make an offer?"

"Not yet," Ben said. "He's calling later today."

Katy shifted in her seat. Who could possibly be interested in Bandit? Had the previous owner changed his mind about the donation? Seemed too late for that.

"Are you still open to negotiations with me?" Katy said, feeling less confident of her offer.

"Give it your best shot," Ben said. "But I owe it to the center to make the best deal possible."

"Fair enough," Katy said, hiding the panic threatening to present itself as tears.

"There's a horse at the center named Ringo," she said, voice shakier than she would've liked. "We both know he needs extensive training."

"Yes," Ben said. "The Shetland."

"I'm willing to work with him for three months at my place to get him in tip-top shape. I won't charge the center for my time."

"Hmm." His eyes lit up. "What about feed and transportation?"

"The center will pay for transportation, including Bandit's. It will also cover all expenses for Ringo while he's in my care."

Ben looked at Vic. "Why are you here? She seems

to have this handled."

Vic shrugged. "Beats me."

Ben was quiet for a moment and then leaned forward. "We could use some help with another horse's manners too. Penelope's been mouthy lately."

"Send her along," Katy said. "Same conditions."

"You've got yourself a deal."

Katy jumped from her seat and shook Ben's hand. She would've agreed to train twenty horses to get Bandit.

"Does next weekend work for you?" Ben asked.

"Everything's ready," Katy said with a smile that could've rivaled the brightest star. "But what about the other buyer?"

"He didn't seem to know much about horses," Ben said. "I'll show him one that better suits his needs."

****

"I got him, Lori," Katy said on the phone, standing outside the horse stalls. "Bandit's officially mine."

"I'm so happy for you," Lori said, groggy.

"I'm sorry, did I wake you?"

"No, no. Sara had a patient emergency last night, and I couldn't get back to sleep. I'm a bit out of it," she said. "Let's celebrate your good news. Why don't you swing by after your session with Luna and I'll treat you to lunch?"

"Sounds great," Katy said. "Oh, I forgot to tell you."

"Yes?"

"Luna and her parents are flying to Mexico City next month to see the ruins of Tenochtitlan," Katy said.

"I thought they couldn't afford it."

"Luna found a way," Katy said.

"Oh, yeah?"

"She's been teaching Spanish to neighbors for a small fee."

"Smart girl," Lori said.

"She said I inspired her."

"I'm proud of you both."

"Me too," Katy said, smiling to herself. "See you soon."

Chapter 36

Jon worked all night and finished "Katy's Song." He called his band mates, and the ones who were available helped him record the single. He invited Elliott to join as well.

During breaks, they enjoyed a smorgasbord prepared by Jon—celery stuffed with vegan cream cheese, nut bread with vegan butter, tabouli salad, and more. A few members even requested recipes.

When the song was ready, Jon contacted 99.5 The Wolf in Dallas. They agreed to keep his song secret if he granted an exclusive interview. The date was set for Saturday. He booked his flight and transportation.

There was a problem, though. Elliott told Jon Katy was dating a surgeon, and the guy was pushing for the next level. For all Elliott knew, it hadn't happened yet, and Jon felt an urgency to call Katy. But that would ruin his grand gesture of declaring his commitment. How else would she believe his sincerity?

"You need to be sure Katy's listening," Rebecca said, making an effort to support his decision.

"I'm working on that," he said, stuffing his bag with jeans and tees.

"I could call her," Rebecca said. "Explain everything."

"You're not exactly her favorite person," he said. "Elliott can do it."

"Please let me try?"

Jon wanted to trust Rebecca, but this was too important. "I don't think that's a good idea," he said. "Besides, the conversation would be pretty damned awkward, I imagine."

"I can handle that."

He glanced up from packing, and the expression on Rebecca's face gave him pause. It was a look he hadn't seen in ages. She'd worn it after loosing her father. It was as if the world stopped making sense to her and never would again. When she spoke now, her voice was childlike, heartbreaking in its soft pleading.

"I need to make amends to you and Katy," she said. "I promise to do what it takes to make this right."

He reached toward Rebecca and wrapped her inside a bear hug, knowing she would be true to her word. And, also, because if all went well, he wouldn't be seeing her for a while.

****

The flight to DFW was the longest of his life. When the plane touched down, the minute he hit the ramp, he sprinted to the radio station's van, dodging others as if he were running for a touchdown. Traffic was a mess, and he worried they wouldn't make it in time. He felt exhilarated and terrified, wishing he could slow his heartbeat. If his plan worked, he'd be in Katy's arms by nightfall.

Chapter 37

At four-thirty, Katy's phone vibrated in her pocket. She was mending a fence and almost let it go to voicemail. But she was expecting a call from Robert and didn't want him thinking she was avoiding him. Which, of course, she was.

When she saw the number, she panicked. The only reason Rebecca would be calling was if something terrible had happened to Jon. Or maybe she wanted to invite Katy to their wedding. But that would be too cruel, even for Rebecca.

"Please tell me he's okay," Katy answered.

"What?" Rebecca stuttered. "Oh, ha, yeah. Jon's okay."

"Then I guess there's nothing more to say."

"Don't hang up," Rebecca said. "Please."

"You've got five minutes."

Rebecca told Katy everything. How she'd convinced Katy Jon was only interested in a fling. How she'd manipulated Jon into thinking Katy was still in love with Greg. How she was afraid of losing Jon as a friend as she had when he fell in love with Charlotte.

"He misses you," Rebecca said.

The declaration made Katy's heart pound faster. But so what? The last thing she needed was to be caught in that web again. And what about Jon's profession? He'd be touring soon. Beautiful women would be coming on to him, and Katy would be home alone. It was time to face facts. Robert was more her pace.

"Why didn't Jon call me himself?" Katy asked.

"Because you blocked his number."

"What if I'd blocked yours?"

"Elliott was our backup," she said. "I'm really sorry for what I did, Katy, and I hope we can be friends one day."

"I appreciate the sentiment," Katy said. "But we probably won't cross paths."

"Jon wants to see you."

"I can't fly to Seattle right now," Katy said. "Besides, I'm dating someone."

"Yes. We know," she said. "Elliott told us it wasn't serious."

Katy was beginning to think Elliott was a double agent. Feeding both sides enough information to keep them interested. Was he playing matchmaker?

"Listen, Rebecca," she said. "I'm busy and I don't feel like rehashing the past, so—"

"Do one thing," Rebecca said before hanging up. "Tune to 99.5 The Wolf at 5:00. You'll be glad you did."

"We'll see," Katy said, and then something dawned on her. "Did Jon try to buy Bandit?"

"Did he try to buy whozit?"

"The horse I told him about?" Katy said. "The one I wanted to own. Did he try to buy Bandit for me?"

"I doubt it," Rebecca said. "It doesn't sound like him."

"Why not?"

"For one thing," Rebecca said, "horses are

expensive to buy and to upkeep, and Jon doesn't throw his money around without extensive research. Secondly, if it's *your* dream or ambition, he wouldn't interfere without asking. That would deprive you of the thrill of accomplishing something on your own. And thirdly—"

"Yes?"

"Jon doesn't give animals as gifts," Rebecca said. "He thinks people should choose their own pets."

****

Katy's mind oscillated between following Rebecca's instructions or accepting Robert's invitation for dinner and then breakfast at his place. But by 5:00, she was sitting on her porch listening to 99.5 The Wolf.

"Every Mile a Memory" by Dierks Bentley was finishing when a DJ named Crystal made an announcement.

"You folks aren't gonna believe who dropped by the station this evening," she said. "*The* Noe Burke."

What the...?

Katy almost fell off her porch in the scramble to find her phone.

"We'll be interviewin' him right after these commercials. Stay tuned."

Katy called Lori, fingers fumbling with the numbers.

"Turn on the country station. 99.5 The Wolf."

"Well, hello to you too," Lori said. "You know I don't listen to that crap."

"Please. You have to hear this."

"Okay, okay. Give me a second."

Katy cranked up the volume. The commercials seemed to last forever, but Crystal finally returned.

"I guess y'all are wonderin' why Grammy-winnin' megastar Noe Burke would bother stoppin' by our little ol' station. Turns out he's got a new single. And it's *country*."

"Holy hell," Lori said on the other end of Katy's phone.

"Shush, please" Katy said. "I don't want to miss anything."

"What inspired you to write this song, Noe?" Crystal asked.

"An amazing woman," he said.

Katy's heart sped faster at the sound of his distinctive voice.

"She must be real pretty."

"Well, sure…I mean…that's only part of—"

"Why country?"

"It's her favorite music."

"How sweet. And this mystery woman? Is she your girlfriend?"

"We were headed in that direction if I hadn't been so stupid."

"Well, there are plenty of other fillies in the field," Crystal said.

"Is she flirting with him?" Lori asked.

"And what's with the accent?" Katy could almost hear Crystal's lashes batting. "She's from Iowa."

"*I'm* free tonight," Crystal said.

"Thanks." Jon chuckled. "But I hope to have other plans."

"Oh, well, let me know if things don't work out."

"I wouldn't be good company if that were to happen."

"What I have in mind would cheer you right up."

Through her phone, Katy heard Lori yell at the radio. "God, lady, give it a rest. The man told you *NO*."

"He's polite that way," Katy said.

"I'd like to say a few words to her if I could," he said.

"Let's hope she's listening," Crystal said, sounding less enamored.

"Hi, uh, Katy. It's me. Oh, uh, of course you know that."

Her eyes misted and she smiled wider.

"Well, uh, you probably think this gesture is over the top, but I wanted to 'publicly show our association' and—"

"Over the top?" Crystal interrupted. "What woman wouldn't welcome this kind of attention?"

Jon ignored the question. "And, well, uh, I wanted you to know…" He cleared his throat. "Listen, uh, God, I can't believe how nervous I feel right now."

"Why don't you take a sip of water, Noe," Crystal suggested.

"Oh, yeah, thanks." There was a quick pause. "Katy, I got your letter, and…uh…um…everything I wrote back sounded lame, and I didn't want to show up on your doorstep if you didn't want me, so I thought…um…maybe if I came on the radio—"

"My goodness. His hands are shakin', ladies," Crystal said. "The man's fallin' apart before my eyes. It must be serious."

"It is to me," Jon said and took a deep breath and let it out through the microphone. "Katy? Will you give me another chance?"

"Okay, Katy," Crystal said. "If you're listenin', please call the station and answer three simple questions. Whoa. Whoa. Whoa! The phones lit up. Come on people, you can't all be Katy."

"Oh, no," Katy said to Lori. "How am I going to get through the phone system?"

"Wait. Crystal's talking again," Lori said.

"We're going to make this easy, folks," Crystal said. "If you don't know the answers to the followin' questions, please don't tie up the lines. These are for Katy. He'll repeat each one twice for clarity. Noe?"

"Ok. Here goes. What was your username on the vegan forum?"

"Easy. KatyPatata," Katy said to Lori.

"What dessert did you add black beans to?"

"Ooh, I know this one too."

"You should," Lori said and laughed into the phone. "The questions are for you."

"Brownies," Katy said. "I substituted black beans for eggs and milk."

"That's gross," Lori said.

"You can't taste 'em," Katy said. "And they add necessary protein."

Jon continued talking through the radio. "When we walked the lake," he said. "Who was the last person you spoke with before we left?"

"The last person I…" Katy imagined Green Lake. If it was at the end of their walk, then it was after lunch. "A man teaching Spanish lessons."

"I was getting a little worried," Lori said. "You didn't tell me about that one."

"I have an idea," Katy said.

"Lay it on me."

"You call the station, and I'll drive over there? If you get through, tell Jon I'm on my way."

"Will do," Lori said. "Be careful. I can only imagine how distracted you must be."

Katy looked up the address on her phone. Dallas. Crap. She invariably found herself going the wrong way on one-way streets in that city. Commercials played as she whipped through traffic. Miss Peabody had never been pushed so hard in her life.

"All the calls have been bogus," Crystal said. "Ladies. Noe Burke isn't looking for a baby-momma. Nor does he want your panties."

Jon chuckled. "They wouldn't fit me, I'm afraid."

"I think it's time we listened to Noe's new single," Crystal said. "Of course it's called 'Katy's Song' and we're the first to hear it. What a treat!"

The song Jon wrote for Katy began to play. Memories of him flooded her senses. Beautiful eyes. Lips tasting of rosemary and pomegranate. Large hands and callused fingers that knew exactly where to touch. Midnight whispers and morning kisses.

"We have a winner," Crystal said during the last of the harmony. "Katy, you're on the air."

"Way to go, Lori," Katy said aloud, stuck at a red light.

"Actually, I'm Katy's friend, Lori."

"Hi Lori," Jon said. "I've heard of you. No offense, but I was hoping you were Katy."

"She's on her way to the radio station," Lori said.

"I'm afraid she won't get anywhere near here," Crystal said. "Noe Burke has lots of fans."

"Well, she's listening," Lori said. "So she knows that now."

"Does that mean she wants to see me?" Jon asked.

"Do you have her address with you?"

"Yes," he said. "I do."

"Meet her there," Lori said. "And you'll find out how much."

Chapter 38

Jon flung off his headphones at the radio station.

"What's the fastest route to Fort Worth," he asked Crystal.

"Well," she said. "The station has a helicopter."

"Is it available?"

"Maybe." She smiled and rested her palm on his lower arm. Red nails sharpened, her fingers curved into a grip. "For the right price."

"Um…" He stared at his limb as if a pterodactyl had landed. "I…"

"Kiddin' darlin'," she said in her fake southern accent. "The station will want a follow-up interview before you leave town."

"You got it," he said, knowing damned well the follow-up interview was her second choice.

They whisked him to the rooftop, and in no time, they were flying over Katy's property. Jon could see why she loved it so much. A creek meandered through a small patch of woods, and there was a horse trail leading to her cozy farmhouse. He wondered how long it would be before he and Katy were skinny-dipping in the creek.

Katy wasn't home when they dropped him. He paced along her front porch, waiting for her to arrive. A black Mercedes pulled into the drive and parked by the barn. Not the kind of car he predicted Katy would drive.

A man emerged and strolled toward the house. He was handsome in an obvious sort of way. Trim, well dressed, old-moneyed. He looked to be Jon's age.

"You must be the doctor," Jon said, extending his hand. "Robert, is it?"

"I had no idea Katy knew you," Robert said. "Until I heard Lori on the radio."

Robert's grip lasted longer than expected, but Jon met the challenge by squeezing harder. Robert reacted in kind. When they pulled away, their knuckles were white. A foolhardy act for two men who required nimble fingers to perform their jobs.

"Katy's full of surprises." Jon rubbed his hand to bring back circulation. "Did you know she speaks Spanish?"

"Not until now," Robert said, eyes piercing. "But I do know one thing."

Just one?

"Someone broke that sweet woman's heart," he said. "And I think it might've been you."

"I assure you—"

"What?" Robert said. "Things are different now?"

"Well…" Jon felt as if he were promising his date's father he'd bring her home by midnight. "Yeah."

"You people think you can take and take and—"

"My *people?*"

"Celebrities." Robert said.

"Ah," Jon said, bracing himself for the usual lecture from the uninformed.

"Because you're famous, you think you can grab any woman you fancy, and then disregard her whenever—"

"Hold on, fella," Jon said, temper flaring at the

289

accusation. "I've *never* grabbed any woman. Not without her permission anyway."

"Of course you'd say that," he said. "You all do."

How many more generalizations was this guy going to pull out of his ass?

"You should go home, Robert," Jon said, voice low and dry. "I was the one invited here, not you."

"You're the one who should go home," Robert said, plucking Jon's bag from the porch. "I'll give you a ride to the airport."

Right then, Katy pulled into her drive.

****

Katy barely avoided the corral fence, because she was distracted by Jon and Robert sparring on the front porch. Why was Robert there, and how had Jon arrived from Dallas so quickly? She'd hoped to freshen up before seeing either.

Getting out of her car, she felt like prey when they both turned their eyes on her and started speed-walking in her direction.

"Katy," Robert said, arriving first. "Could you please tell this guy we have a date tonight, and he's not welcome?"

"Katy," Jon said, seconds later. "Could you please tell this guy I flew seventeen hundred miles and I'm not leaving until I talk to you alone?"

Why did things have to be so complicated? When she drove to the house, all Katy was thinking about was Jon's lips on hers. Now she had to deal with Robert. Kind-hearted and understanding Robert who didn't deserve to be in the middle of this mess.

"Robert?" she said. "Could I please speak with you?"

"Of course, dear," Robert said, grinning at Jon as if she were a prize at the carnival he'd snatched from under Jon's nose.

She handed Jon the keys to the house. "Make yourself at home."

Jon stepped inside, but he left the door slightly ajar. Was he planning to eavesdrop on their conversation?

Katy steered Robert toward his Mercedes.

"Oh, I get it," Robert said.

"Get what?"

"You're choosing him over me."

"It's not that simple," Katy said. "He and I need to talk. There's history between us."

"Of course there is," he said. "You women are all alike."

"Excuse me?"

"Always going for the bad boys."

"I wouldn't call him a *boy*," she said. "He's older than I am."

It's as if Robert hadn't heard her.

"You complain about how he treats you. How lost you are when he leaves you. How you'll learn to live without him."

What started this? She hadn't discussed Jon with Robert at all. And Lori and Sara wouldn't have told him. So he couldn't be talking about Katy. She stopped to look at him, hand moving to her hip. He'd carefully hidden this ugly side of himself to move their relationship forward. And to think she planned to sleep with him had Jon not surprised her.

"But when a nice guy like me comes along," he said. "You go back to him."

"I've got news for you, Robert," she said. "You're

not exactly being nice."

But the conversation had become one-sided, and he was no longer tracking her words.

"I even tried to buy that mangy horse for you," he said. "But they sold it out from under me."

She stepped back. "That's an expensive gift, Robert," she said. "And we're nowhere near that point in our relationship."

"Can't you see, Katy," he said, holding his palms open as if they were full of gold. "I could give you everything you needed."

"Why would you even want me?" she said. "I'm in love with another man."

****

Unable to see or hear Katy and Robert from inside the house, Jon explored. Her home had a lived-in feel reminding him of his own. There were traces of what he thought of as "ancestral essence"—comforting scents that were impossible to eliminate even with thorough cleaning. He immediately felt welcome.

The kitchen was exactly as he expected—updated, tidy, and clean. But in the dining room, there were pencil marks down a corner wall. On closer inspection, he saw they signified Katy's annual height, starting at the age of six and ending at adulthood. He flattened his hand against his head and compared his height to hers. The gap was wider than he thought.

Without opening any doors, Jon popped his head into her office and bathroom. He peeked into her bedroom, but the curtains were closed, and it was too dark to see. Turning on the light seemed like a violation, but he could smell lavender. He longed to stretch on her bed and bury his nose in her pillows.

With no more rooms to snoop, he went into the living area. Plopping on the couch, he picked up *Southern Living* and flipped through the pages without focusing. When he accidentally ripped the back cover, he tossed the magazine back onto the pile. And then hid it at the bottom of the stack.

What could Katy possibly be discussing with that jerk? Routine checkups?

Jon could maybe understand how she'd be drawn to Robert. The guy's appearance was above average if you were into the primping type. And there was prestige to being a surgeon's wife. And there was the flashy car. And the extensive education. And the altruistic job.

Oh, who was Jon kidding? He was jealous as hell.

Five minutes later, Katy blew through the front door, stirring a warm breeze. Jon jumped to his feet and stepped toward her, intending to pull her into his arms. But she put her hand out to stop him.

"You sit over there," she said, pointing to the couch. "And I'll sit here."

Jon did as he was told, watching her every movement.

"I don't see how this can ever work between us," she said.

"Katy—"

She held up her hand as before. "Please let me finish."

He nodded his agreement.

"I have been living with misery ever since you stepped onto that elevator three months ago."

He wanted to say something, go to her, but he remained on the couch, as was her wish.

"And we're miles apart in every aspect," she said. "Your fame alone allows others to interfere in your daily life. Look how that Crystal woman treated you."

Never before had Jon felt the trappings of celebrity as intensely as he did in that moment.

"But you handled the situation expertly," she said. "And I realize you're not responsible for other people's actions."

Thank God for that.

"If we're going to do this."

We're going to do this.

"Then I need a promise from you."

Anything and everything.

"From now on," she said. "You listen to my side of a story before jumping to conclusions."

"You have my word," he said.

They sat for a moment, breathing each other's air from across the room. Both afraid, perhaps, to disturb the magic that had brought them back together.

"I have something for you," Jon said, digging into his bag.

"Oh?" She stood.

His legs wouldn't move fast enough, as he bounded from the couch to meet her halfway. She took the bundle and opened it carefully. Inside was an instruction booklet—much like the one she'd made for him.

"What is it?" she said as she flipped through the pages.

"It's a mock-up," he said. "I hired a designer in case you wanted to follow through with your vegan consulting. If not, then consider it a memento."

Running her palm across the beautiful cover photo

of her quinoa salad, she met Jon's eyes. "You did this for me?"

"I…well…" he said. "I did it for myself really."

"Yourself?"

"So I'd have an excuse to see you again," he said. "Even if you only wanted to be friends."

"Oh, Jon," she said, dropping the book in the chair and moving closer to him. "I could never only be friends with you."

When they embraced, his heartbeat found hers and he knew he was finally home.

****

That evening, Katy stood at the butcher block in her kitchen, slicing apples for a vegan pie. "Are you almost finished with the dough?" she asked Jon.

"Yep," he said, sliding the bowl toward her.

He was wearing her grandmother's pink apron—gingham with frilly-laced shoulders. Was it kinky Katy found him sexy in that getup?

She'd been keeping him at bay all night, and they'd been flirting as if they'd just met and hadn't already seen each other naked in Seattle three months ago. She couldn't believe three months before had started the whole thing, when he found her on the vegan forum. So, technically, they were celebrating six months of knowing each other.

Mixing the apples with sugar, cinnamon, and a little bit of flour, she pinched a few slices between her fingers and fed them to Jon.

"Delicious," he said, eyes on hers. He slipped behind her, wrapped his arms around her waist, and nibbled her neck. "You're tasty too."

Katy giggled and twirled to face him, her backside

pinned against the counter.

"We're never going to get this pie in the oven, are we?"

"Not if I can help it," he said, beaming like the cat that had found the cream. "Did you know we're coming up on our six-month anniversary?"

"Oh?" she said.

Of course it had crossed her mind. His first post had been in the spring, but she didn't think it'd be noteworthy to him. Those kinds of milestones seemed more important to women.

"I haven't slept with *anyone* else since then," he said.

She was ecstatic but also surprised. Jon's reaction at finding Greg in her hotel room led Katy to believe he'd seek comfort in another woman's bed. She wouldn't have blamed him. She knew how it must've looked, and Lord knows what she would've done if the situation had been reversed.

"What about your weekly dates at the Bending Bough?" she teased.

"Elliott told you?" he said, eyes widening.

The Bending Bough belonged to Katy, so to speak, because she'd found it first—an unwritten rule of breakup etiquette. Jon had no business being there with other women unless he had ulterior motives.

"Wasn't that your intention?" she asked.

"Well, um…I wanted to prove I'd moved on, so you wouldn't worry about me."

"Hmm," she said. "Sounds nobler than it actually was, don't you think?"

"Absolutely." He grinned.

"By the way," Katy said, knowing the answer

already. "How'd your last date go?"

"The worst I've ever had," he said. "When it was time to leave, she boxed everything, including the salt and pepper shakers. I recovered the shakers when she went to the bathroom."

Katy suppressed a giggle, imagining Jon frantically unknotting the bag and digging through the containers before his date returned to the table.

"Then she suggested we go to the Metropolitan Grill for dessert," he said.

"Did you?"

"Hell, no," he said. "She already had two servings of Irish apple cake in her goody bag."

At that, they laughed, as if they'd known each other for years and were adding to their precious collection of inside jokes. But then his palm brushed against Katy's ribcage, and she inhaled from the sudden tingling.

Noticing immediately, he sobered. "What's wrong?"

"Nothing…it's…" she said.

"Yes?"

"It's been three months since we've done this," she said. "I might've forgotten how everything works."

"It's not that complicated," he said. "Only a few moving parts."

"You're making fun, I know," she said. "But…"

"But what?"

"Are you absolutely sure about this? About us?"

He leaned in and whispered into her ear. His whiskey voice pulsated down her spine, and she closed her eyes, relishing the sweet sensation.

"I love you, Katy," he said. "I'm as certain as the

sun and moon and stars, and if they were all to fall, I'd want us to be together until the end of the world."

"I…I'm…" Apprehensive, she grappled with her irrational fear. If she declared her love aloud, he'd pack his bags and leave.

"Please tell me how you feel," he nudged. "I need to hear the words as much as you do."

Lightheaded from his proximity, she exhaled slowly. Gazing into his smoky-gray eyes, her doubt was replaced with euphoria.

"I love you too, Jon," she said. "So much so if the sun and moon and stars were to fall tomorrow, I wouldn't even notice."

"There you go. Feel free to say so anytime," he said, smiling. "One more thing."

"Yes?"

"*Por favor*," he said. "*Déjame estar contigo siempre y crea buenos recuerdos.*"

Although his Spanish wasn't perfect, his words certainly were.

"Please. Let me be with you always and make good memories."

Katy rested her forehead against Jon's chest and sighed. He smelled of cinnamon and apples. The beat of his heart was rapid and strong, and heat emanated from every pore of his body. She'd never wanted anyone so badly in her entire life.

Cupping his cheek, she gently touched her lips to his. Then she kissed the base of his neck, pleased to hear his intake of breath.

"*Nuestro tiempo juntos acaba de comenzar.*" Reaching for his warm, dry hand, Katy led Jon toward the bedroom. "Our time together has just begun."

Vegan Appetizer Recipe—Deconstructed Crostini

Part 1: Garlic Toast

Ingredients:

French Baguette (1)
Olive Oil (2 tbs.)
Pressed Garlic Clove (1 large)
Sea Salt (to taste)

Directions:

1. Preheat oven to 375 degrees
2. Cut bread at an angle into ½ inch slices
3. Whisk together olive oil, garlic, and sea salt
4. Brush mixture onto both sides of bread (create more olive oil mixture if needed)
5. Place bread on non-stick cookie sheet
6. Set timer for 3-5 minutes, checking often until golden-brown
7. Let cool, then transfer to serving plate or bowl

..

Part 2: Eggless Salad

Ingredients:

Garbanzo Beans/Chickpeas (15 oz. can)
Vegan Mayo (2 tbs.) or Avocado (1 pitted and scooped)
Vegan Mustard (1 tbs.)
Pressed Garlic Clove (1 large)
Sea Salt (to taste)
Green Onion/Chives (1/8 cup/thinly sliced)
Dill Pickles (2 medium/diced)
Celery (2 stalks/diced)

Directions:

1. Drain and rinse chickpeas and toss them into a bowl

2. Stir in mayo (or avocado), mustard, garlic, and sea salt

3. Mash to desired consistency

4. Fold in chives, pickles, and celery

5. Transfer to serving bowl

..

Part 3: Tomato, Basil, and Vegan Mozzarella

Ingredients:

Olive Oil (2 tbs.)

Lemon Juice (1/2 tbs.)

Pressed Garlic Clove (1 large)

Pepper and Sea Salt (to taste)

Fresh Basil (1/8 cup/minced)

Cherry/Grape Tomatoes (1 cup/diced)

Red Onion (1/8 cup/diced)

Vegan Mozzarella (1 cup/diced)

Directions:

1. In a mixing bowl, whisk together olive oil, lemon juice, and garlic

2. Add pepper and salt to taste

3. Stir in basil

4. Fold in remaining ingredients until well coated

5. Transfer to serving bowl

Top toast with egg salad or tomato mixture and enjoy.

A word about the author...

Alison Reese graduated from Central Washington University with a BS in Business, but despite her practical background in accounting, she considers herself a hopeful romantic.

Having lived in many places—such as Utah, Alaska, Nevada, Texas, and Washington—she's gathered rich material over the years. In 2015, she became vegan and found the learning process quite fascinating.